W9-ALL-685

DeMarínis

Sky Full of Sand

Also by Rick DeMarinis

Novels
A Lovely Monster (1975)
Scimitar (1977)
Cinder (1978)
The Burning Women of Far Cry (1986)
The Year of the Zinc Penny (1989)
The Mortician's Apprentice (1994)
A Clod of Wayward Marl (2001)

Short Stories
Jack & Jill (1979)
Under the Wheat (1986)
The Coming Triumph of the Free World (1988)
The Voice of America (1991)
Borrowed Hearts (1999)
Apocalypse Then (forthcoming, 2004)

Non-Fiction
The Art and Craft of the Short Story (2000)

SKY FULL — OF — SAND

A Novel

Rick DeMarinis

INTRODUCTION *by* JAMES CRUMLEY

20 03

Dennis McMillan Publications

FIRST EDITION
Published September 2003

This first edition of *Sky Full of Sand* consists of
1,000 cloth-bound copies, and 104
quarter-morocco bound copies.

Dustjacket design and interior artwork
by Michael Kellner.

ISBN 0-939767-47-3 (cloth)
ISBN 0-939767-48-1 (quarter-morocco)

Dennis McMillan Publications
4460 N. Hacienda del Sol (Guest House)
Tucson, AZ 85718 Telephone: (520)-529-6636
Website: http://dennismcmillan.com

INTRODUCTION

AN HOMAGE TO RICK DEMARINIS:
OR, HOW I LEARNED TO EAT BUTTERFLY
SHIT AND KEEP LAUGHING

No one knows how it might have happened—an early satellite, a rock of cocaine in my eye, a late bomber on the Sofia run—but something streaked across the corner of the sky. An ember from the campfire, a flashlight glittering off a charm bracelet. Something. Nothing exactly explains my confession to Rick one full moon night up Fish Creek. I was running down my career, the naval scholarship to Georgia Tech, the disenchantment upon discovering that some imbalance in my 20-10 vision was going to keep me out of flight school. It helped me lose my way into the Army, then into fiction. But the irony of it all—drum roll now—was that even if everything worked out perfectly I was fifteen or twenty years too young to even hope to be the first man on the moon. "Too young?" Rick said. "Too fat!" Fireflies gathered around Rick's grin, sexual foolishness on their minds.

If it is true that we choose our friends, then we surely must choose how they behave. I can tell you what Rick will say upon seeing the word 'homage' in the title. *Homage. Ain't that one of those Frog cheeses that smells like the butt floss on a Hamburg whore's thong a week past ripe.* Then he'll chuckle, like a genial giant elf.

I am going to assume, Dear Reader, that you're familiar with Rick's work, a reader of warmth, a reader of some intelligence. If you ain't, it ain't my fault. New York seems to have done everything in the world to keep him a secret. He's had almost as much bad luck as I've had. Editors abducted by boring aliens, agents moving from bad checks to embezzlement, reviewers dumber than recycled horsetacks. So we've spent most of our adult lives as academic saddle tramps. A thankless task, I assure you. But Rick has always hung in there, nailing the heart of American humor to the gall bladder of American foolishness.

There has never been a monster as lovely as Rick's, created with the soft and gentle touch of cell glue, burdened with the apparatus of a Shetland pony named Luigi, and cursed with the heart of a man. A wino falls asleep in one of Rick's books, knocks over the genie jar, and can think of nothing as sweet as flying, so the genie takes him up in the air as a condor, perhaps the last of his kind. But don't mistake all this peace as passivity. A hopeless, helpless photographer blows a hangover crap all over a well-tended lawn, then wipes his ass with the rich man's white, yappy dog—one of those dogs that you can't tell where the dog turd ends and dog begins.

Rick DeMarinis is an amazing writer, and they don't make many like him anymore.

With love and butt floss,

Jim Crumley
July 28, 2003
Missoula, Montana

PS: Butterflies are best on Harleys with *foie gras*.

Sky Full of Sand

ONE

Anest of huffers squatting in 7-A ruined my afternoon. They'd cracked open the door with a pry bar and set up shop, keeping a low profile for over a week. An asthmatic in 9-A bitched about the acrid smell seeping through the walls. I checked my records: 7-A had been vacant since February 14 when the couple occupying it had a spat. He came home with chocolates but he stank of rut. She broke his jaw with a cast-iron skillet. Valentine's Day, a bad day for lovers.

The apartment reeked of industrial solvents, spray paint, and body wastes. I went in with pepper spray and a six-battery flashlight. Huffers are too brain-damaged to put up a fight, but a hairy giant in bib overalls got indignant. He called me names. "Pimp for the landlords," was one that was fairly accurate. His head was as big as a basketball. His eyes traveled, looking for focus. He babbled something about human rights and came at me with a piece of galvanized pipe. I hit him with the spray from six feet but he only sneezed.

"Human rights in your case is an oxymoron," I said. He tried to process this. His massive head was knobbed with bone, the ridges above his eyes thick as battery cables. His wild black hair looked tarred. "You callin' me a moron?" he said, his indignation rising.

He came at me again. I sidestepped his charge and clubbed him across the bridge of his already flattened nose with the

1

flashlight. He didn't seem to understand that he'd been hurt. His nose bubbled snot and blood. It didn't faze him much but it distracted him. He held the galvanized pipe out in front of him like a wand, as if he expected it to turn me into a pumpkin and was puzzled because it didn't. I kicked his knee and he went down howling, his kneecap detached. He patted his thigh, looking for it. I clubbed him again, wrecking my flashlight. The lens popped off, the batteries flew out. The big huffer's eyes rolled back and an odd apparitional smile cracked his lips, which were silver with spray paint. The silver smile transfixed his face. He looked like he'd kissed an angel.

The others stayed oblivious to the big man's problems. They kept their faces in their plastic bags, sucking in the fumes. I could smell the toluene, an industrial solvent that stripped the cerebral cortex of brain cells with the same efficiency it stripped paint and varnish from wood.

They were four men and three women but at their level of huffing sex differences were academic. I herded them out to the parking lot and used my cellphone to call the cops. I let the huffers keep their plastic bags so they wouldn't get nervous. The bags inflated and collapsed like oxygen masks as the huffers breathed the transporting gases. The cops were pissed. They didn't like dealing with bottom-level humanity. Busting huffers lacked prestige. And the huffers were going to stink up the squad cars.

I didn't sympathize. 7-A was a mess and the clean-up job was all mine. I'm manager, maintenance man, security guard, and counselor to the terminally confused. It took me two hours to clean the place up. One of the huffers had taken a dump in the bathtub. I felt contaminated and took a long hot shower, imagined the water and soap washing away fleas, crabs, lice, and fungus as well as the fecal and chemical stenches. I figured I'd earned a margarita, maybe two.

2

I took a handful of vitamins, dressed, then crossed Mesa Street to the DMZ. The bar was empty except for an expensive-looking couple. They were adventurers from the upper world, trolling the polluted waters of my neighborhood. The woman looked hard as chilled wax. The porky guy on the barstool next to her looked like wax in an early stage of meltdown. She was compact and petite, a concentration of color and form that grained your eye like desert sand. The big boy she was with was wearing dark blue double-breasted pinstripes—a banker's suit—but he wasn't a banker. The red Mohawk that divided his white skull and ended in a foot-long ponytail ruined the effect. But he had money. He'd fanned it out on the bar in front of him, tens and twenties. He sipped single malt whiskey through a straw. The soft damp flesh of his neck spilled out of his shirt collar. He had a pinky ring that held a diamond big as a peanut. He wheezed softly, the wheeze of large men who have large appetites and the resources to satisfy them and no reason not to. Without any self-consciousness, he reached into his crotch and scratched his groin.

The woman looked at me, then looked away. "You like to play, hon?" she said. But she hadn't looked away, she'd just changed perspectives: She spoke to my reflection in the bar mirror. She was drinking something mint green three stools away. Tendrils of her fragrance—the electric smell of money and musk—coiled around me.

The bar, a dark, unapologetic seedy place, is owned by a defrocked English professor. It's a relatively uneventful little cantina, but "DMZ" doesn't stand for demilitarized zone. It stands for the "Dangling Modifier Zoo." My wife and I used to spend our afternoons here, even when we lived two miles away. Now it's just me. One look at the late night clientele and you understand the "Zoo" reference, but what the Dangling Modifier part signifies no one knows. Alcohol modifies your thinking and those who spend their time here are dangling men, dangling at the ends of their ropes. I guess that comes close to an explanation. Cryptic signs hang throughout the bar. This one, on the mirror behind the gin bottles:

> When dipped in butter
> you can taste the lobster's
> delicious flavor.

The owner, Güero Odonaju, smirks a lot. The sign is some kind of in-joke, the kind that makes you smirk. I didn't get it. No one did.

I loved this old bar, a private little cave in the walls of the city. It was always humid with human heat, even in winter. The ancient plank floors sagged. The plaster walls, brown with the oily smoke of a million cigarettes, were pocked with historic bullet holes. John Wesley Hardin, the myth goes, killed a man in here. The turning blades of the overhead fans moved so slowly that fat bluebottle flies slept on them undisturbed.

I'd had my two margaritas and was getting ready to head across the street to watch Jeopardy. I would have ignored her except that she was hot-looking and I was lonely and bored and the margaritas weren't enough. I needed an uplifting experience.

"Play what?" I said.

"Just play. You know. Mess around. Some people don't have any playfulness, others live for it. Where do you stand?"

"Outside the playground," I said. She gave me a long inquisitive look. "I'm going through a divorce," I explained.

4

She twisted toward me on her stool, her sharp breasts testing the lime green weave of her blouse. She was about forty and knew she cut a lasting image in the brains of men. She had ripe, collagen-enhanced lips fixed in a show-me pout. Her sea-green eyes were big and arresting, and her heavy, un-plucked eyebrows were permanently arched with doubt, as if she saw the nasty truth under every bright surface. My neck hair prickled. I swiveled back to the bar and raised my empty margarita to my lips, borrowing time.

My apartment building is called The Baron Arms. It's also called The Barren Arms (not much love-making goes on here), The Bearing Arms (most of the tenants own weapons), but it's mainly known as The Divorce Courts. Back in the forties and fifties it was the best motel on the old border highway which was bypassed in the sixties by the Interstate. Luxury motels grew in clumps around every off-ramp of I-10 like cubist fungi. The new motels siphoned travelers off the Interstate and the roadhouses along the old highway either died or lowered their prices so much they only attracted ragtag, cash-only nomads. Some went to hourly rates. The owner of The Baron Arms chose to convert the motel into furnished apartments. A good third of the tenants are middle-aged males whose wives have decamped—men on the final downslope of their lives, full of regret, self-pity, and paranoia. The rest are marginal citizens at best. Sirens and strobe lights come and go. It's part of the scenery. I watch television, read, and work out three times a week at the Y.

I moved here after Gert left. I had a good job but I walked away from it. She won thirty-three percent of my pay in the settlement and I wasn't about to work a third of every day for her and her boyfriend. She ran off with a NASCAR driver named Trey Stovekiss. No way was I going to finance their high-octane romance. I could live a while on squirreled-away money, about eight-thousand. Then I'd get some warehouse job under another name. Meanwhile, I manage The Baron Arms and do light maintenance in exchange for rent. My situation isn't all that bad. I still think of myself as a man with a future.

An assumed name appealed to me. My life under my given name had been a flop—teased now and then by streaks of good luck. Maybe a name that had the ring of success to it would change things. A name like Strobe. Strobe Champion the Third.

The woman was a mind reader. "So what's your name, hon?" she said.

"Strobe Champion the third," I said, trying it out.

She laughed. "I *like* it. I'm Mona Farnsworth. This is my husband, Jerry. Come on now, what's your real name, *Strobe?*"

"You're the mind reader," I said.

She gave me a sidelong look, squinting. She slid off her stool and sat next to me. The point of a breast scraped my arm. Sweat tickled my pits.

I gave it up. "Walkinghorse," I said. "Uriah Walkinghorse."

"No *way!*" she laughed. She had a nice laugh, an explosive little scream. I had a fleeting erotic daydream centered around that scream, me being its cause.

"Would I lie about a name like that?" I said.

She turned to her husband. "Would he, Jerry? Would *you* invent a name like. . . ." She turned back to me. "What was that again?"

"Uriah Walkinghorse."

"You look about as Indian as I do," she said.

I shrugged. "I was adopted by a minister who had a Sioux ancestor," I said. "His wife couldn't have kids. He gave us

Bible names. I've got a sister named Zipporah and brothers named Moses, Isaiah, and Zacharias. All agency orphans."

The woman laughed again. *"Uriah* for God's sake. Isn't that some Dickens loser?" she said.

Fat Jerry finally spoke. "Who gives a shit what he calls himself?" he said. "Names don't mean dick anyway. It's what you do that counts. Some Strobe Champion demento might be waxing his dolphin all day long watching soaps while his wife mops out toilets for minimum wage. A guy named Uriah might have something going for him, right Uriah?"

I nodded. The nod was a lie. "Call me Uri," I said.

"What *do* you do, Uri?" Mona Farnsworth said, touching my arm. I popped the biceps. Her hand jerked away as if she'd touched 110 volts AC.

"Crane operator," I said. "Right now, an unemployed crane operator."

I quit my job at Munk and Weismer Steel when I found out the terms of the divorce. I was making eighteen dollars an hour running the indoor overhead crane, but I'd be working almost three hours a day for Gert and her stock-car speed freak. I hated quitting that job. I was lucky to get it in the first place. They wouldn't have hired me except that their regular crane jockey had a heart attack and they needed a replacement. I'd never operated a crane before, but I'm a quick study and working an overhead crane in a warehouse isn't exactly rocket science. As long as you didn't drop a pallet of sheet steel on a hardhat, you'd be okay.

I'd been teaching bonehead math part-time at the community college for eleven hundred a month. I found out about the Munk and Weismer job from one of my students who worked there. I was sick of teaching remedial math to kids who couldn't balance a checkbook. I was sick of lousy

7

pay. I made more in ten days running the crane than I made in a month at the JC.

"Fascinating," she said. She pursed her lips as if thinking something over. Her lips looked like the bud of a wine-dark flower. They parted slightly. I stared into the deeper darkness of her mouth.

"You pump iron, Mr. Walkinghorse?" she said. "You've got some hunky steroid-fed muscle under that shirt. How old are you?" She breathed this at me. I smelled her breath—the humidity and warmth cut by the mint of her green drink.

"Thirty-five," I lied. "And I don't use steroids." Not quite a lie. I used to stack Oxandrin with Anadrol, but that was years ago.

I'd just turned forty-two. My hair was shot with gray, I had wrinkles around my eyes, my ears were sprouting hair. But I could still bench four hundred, squat with six, and run the treadmill for an hour. Blood pressure a consistent 120 over 80, thanks to oat bran and salt-free margaritas. I felt thirty-five. Hell, I felt *twenty*-five.

"You want a job?" Jerry asked.

I looked at him. His Mohawk stood up like a rooster's comb. Face pink as a baby's, jawline buried in leaflard. He scooped his money off the bar, squared the bills like playing cards, then fanned them out again.

"The easiest two-hundred you'll ever make," she said. She opened her purse, rummaged in it for a few seconds, then gave me her card. I studied it.

The Farnsworths owned an upscale address. The cheap houses there began in the mid six figures. The top-end spreads were in the sevens. The street was El Cielito, in Heaven's Gates Estates up in the Franklin mountains. I used to jog on those streets. The air is better there, the crime rate non-existent, and you can smell the liquid assets.

"What do I have to do?" I said.

"I'll explain when you get there. You won't have to do much of anything. I might even teach you something." She gave me a sly, cryptic look. She put her hand on my arm again. Her fingertips worked my biceps as if she were feeling for fatty deposits. There weren't any. I flexed again.

It's one of my vanities. A woman touches my arm, I make it jump. This time her hand didn't leap away.

"*Big* guy," she said, her amused eyes searching mine.

"Big, but is he bu-bu-bu-bu *bad?*" her husband said.

"To the bone," I said, finishing the retrorock joke.

"Six this evening," she said, suddenly all business. "Don't be late."

TWO

U.S. 80, over the past forty years or so had become The Strip—used car lots, *taquerías*, lap-dance bars, massage parlors, *casas de cambio* where you could change pesos to dollars or dollars to pesos, and the quickie in-and-out motels. No one called it U.S. 80 anymore. It had a name: Mesa Street.

Across Mesa from the DMZ The Baron Arms looked like a sand castle carved into a hillside. The architect who designed it back in the fifties had good taste. The building fit the terrain of El Paso—it looked like a natural outcropping of the terra cotta hills. The place could have been built by the Anasazi a thousand years ago. It wasn't a stretch to think of the tenants as cliff dwellers. I always thought the Anasazi were hyper-vigilant, in a paranoid sense, hiding from some real or imagined enemy in their high cliff-houses set in carved-out rock. That description could apply to many tenants of The Baron Arms. They were hiding from some real or imagined threat. In most cases the threats *were* real. Low rent lawyers, skip tracers, repo thugs, jealous exes, and mumbling psychotics stalked the hallways, balconies, and landings.

From the balcony of my fourth floor apartment, you can see forever into the desert, the horizon so distant you might think the world is flat. In that flat distance you can watch the sandstorms rising, graining the sky. The heat-corrugated air makes the distant Malpais wasteland ripple as if it were painted on thin sheets of tin. You can get thirsty just looking out at the endless miles of badlands. Sometimes the hot wind and sand coming off that wasteland makes you pray for rain.

I had six messages on my voice mail, all from Rosie Hildebrand. Each message was the same: "Hey, mister manager. Something's wrong with my goddamn tureen." *Tureen,* that's what she calls her toilet.

I figured it was plugged again. I earn my free rent just dealing with the apartment complex's seventy-five toilets alone. You pay your rent, you figure you can put anything you want into your toilet. Last Christmas a twenty-year-old woman tried to flush down a second trimester fetus. She was up-front about it. "Bring your snake, Walkinghorse," she said. "My toilet won't fucking flush. I went to pee and then I had this bad cramp. Maybe you heard me yell. 'Oh *fuck* me! OH FUCK ME!' real loud like that. Man, I was wailing. Next thing, my baby slips out. I lost my little baby. It's a tragedy I won't be able forget. I hope nobody heard me yell. The gay guys next door I think are Christian types." By the time I got there she had cleaned herself up and was wearing cut-off Levis and a Nashville Pussy tee shirt, no bra. She was pretty but already used-up at twenty. Twenty going on forty.

She looked anything but tragic. She looked as if she'd forgotten it already and was preparing to go out into the world to find her next disaster. To cover myself I called the cops, and they brought in a crew from the medical examiner's office. The Crime Scene Unit pulled the bloody lump out of the pipes. "Merry Christmas, Tiny Tim," Ted Lopez from the CSU said to the dark little mass that looked more like a road-killed rodent than something that one day might walk and talk and want its opinions taken seriously. The question was: Did she kill a living preemie, or was the fetus dead on arrival? No conclusion was drawn, no charges filed.

11

I was grateful to Ted Lopez and the CSU people. Grateful that they unplugged the toilet, not me. I knew them. We had a murder-suicide last month, a hostage situation a month before that. I was on a first-name basis with the CSU crew.

Bill and Rosie Hildebrand lived in a three room apartment—what used to be called a suite, back when this was an upscale motel. They plugged their toilet on a regular basis. Last week I pulled a water-logged paperback out of it. A few weeks before that, a pair of knit doilies. I went down to 24-D, snake, augur, plunger, red bandanna, and shit-dissolving chemicals packed in my tool box, ready for war.

The Hildebrands are dedicated winos. Rosie's in her seventies, Bill isn't sixty yet but looks older than Rosie. The two of them look alike. Gray little people, no life in their faces. They have six overfed cats—four above the limit set by the building's owner—and an aquarium. The owner of The Baron Arms lives in Austin, six hundred miles east, so enforcing the rules is up to me. And I'm flexible. I try to keep the tenants pacified.

The bloated cats were lying around the apartment like fur-bearing iguanas. I didn't say hello. Bill and Rosie were watching Jeopardy, a jug of Gallo Vin Rose between them on the dinette table. Rosie was in her housecoat and slippers. She was wearing nylon knee stockings rolled down to her ankles. Her legs looked like shrink-wrapped bones. She has a bald spot big as a silver dollar on the top of her head. "My skullcap," she calls it. Bill, as always, was wearing his bean-green wide-lapel suit circa 1974. His milk-white feet were bare, the ragged, pre-gangrenous toenails were blue. He pointed to the bathroom. The stink was catching in my throat. I've got a quick gag-reflex, a real handicap in plumbing jobs. I tied the bandanna over my nose and mouth and went in.

The water in the toilet was murky and up to the rim. I

worked my augur into the mess, but nothing came up. I pulled the bandanna off my face and went back out to the living room. "Rosie," I said. "Did you dump the kitty litter into the toilet?"

Rosie, annoyed at the interruption, turned away from Jeopardy. "Sure," she said. "I went out and bought twenty-five pounds of kitty litter and poured it into the tureen. I do things like that for laughs." Her sour face had the color and texture of oatmeal. A basal cell carcinoma wide as a dime scabbed her nose.

I dipped the water out of the bowl, then pulled the toilet off its wax seal. I bored straight into the exposed pipe with my augur. Pieces of organic material came up but the mess didn't drain. I pulled out the augur and tried the long snake. I worked it in about eight feet. When I pulled it out, a fish was impaled on it. An overgrown pirhana. When it quit dripping slime I carried it out into the living room.

"That would be Carlotta," Bill Hildebrand said, indicating the fish. He stood up and took me aside, out of Rosie's earshot. "Rosie got real pissed at Carlotta for eating all the little guys," he whispered.

We both looked at Rosie. She was riveted on Jeopardy. "What is Pavlov's *dog?*" she said, supplying the correct question to the stumped panel. "Come on, fungus-brains: *What-is-Pavlov's-dog?*"

"Rosie could make a mint if they'd get her on that show," Bill clucked proudly.

"Why did she put Carlotta in the tank in the first place?" I asked.

Bill gripped my wrist with his trembly fingers, leaned close to me. His breath smelled like dead meat rotting. "It's the little tropicals. She got fed up with them. They never showed any gratitude. 'You get in there and teach them *fan*tails and neon *tet*ras how to behave, Carlotta.' That's what she said."

"I don't think fish can show gratitude," I said.

"That's exactly what *I* told her. See, it's this temper of hers. If she feels she's getting taken for granted, she gets real testy."

"You shouldn't flush fish down the toilet, Rosie," I said. I checked out the aquarium. It was empty, but fresh air still bubbled up from the aerator. I thought about threatening her with the two-cat rule. But she always paid her rent on time.

"What-is-excelsior, hemorrhoid-brains," Rosie said, ignoring me by edging her chair closer to the game show.

I like Jeopardy's "what is the question?" approach, but it sometimes makes me feel uneducated even though I'm ten credits and a thesis short of a master's degree in math. ("In ancient times, the political rulers of this modern country were the Zipa at Bacatá and the Zaque at Tunja." What is the question? Good luck.)

"You should get that cancer taken off your nose, Rosie," I said. "It could give you grief down the road."

She looked at me with her fearless rheumy eyes. "If I want medical advice I'll call me a doctor not a plumber," she said.

I put their toilet back together, carried Carlotta the pirhana out to the dumpster, then went to my apartment and took a long hot shower to get the Hildebrand's various stinks off my skin. After that I fixed myself a yogurt shake, with the whites of three eggs and a handful of desiccated liver mixed in. I spread some tofu on a half dozen kelp and sunflower seed crackers. Supper.

I didn't compete anymore, but I liked to keep my body fat below five percent. You look better when the network of veins and muscle under the fascia aren't hidden behind a quarter inch of tallow. It's an ego thing. But what isn't? I was Mr.

Westside in 1983. I'm not proportional enough for the big national competitions. Torso and arms too long, legs and neck too short. Nothing freakish. But in the heavyweight division they want Schwartzenegger perfection.

I took my blood pressure—124 over 79—then popped some sub-lingual B-12s. Whatever the Farnsworths had in mind, I'd be ready.

I got dressed, set the timer so the lights would come on at seven to fool thieves into thinking the place was occupied. I knew better. The only way to fool thieves in this town would be to leave the apartment dark and the doors and windows wide open. That would give them pause. They'd think you were sitting in the shadows with a 12 gauge in your lap.

I took the elevator down to the parking lot, cleared my windshield of fliers from *The Healing Witch*—the storefront down the street that sold herbs, vitamins, and *bruja* fetishes that guaranteed a thriving libido, and headed for Heaven's Gates Estates and my easy two hundred along with whatever it was Mona Farnsworth thought she had to teach me.

THREE

It looked like the Farnsworths didn't have any secrets. Their mountainside house was made of glass. The house faced west and the low tangerine sun was repeated a dozen times in its floor-to-ceiling windows. The winding road was steep, about a nine percent grade, and I kept my '88 Ford Escort in low gear all the way up. By the time I reached the top, the temp gauge had red-lined.

I drove into the circular driveway and parked behind a new Lexus. I got out, stretched, inhaled the particulate-free air of Heaven's Gates Estates. I walked up the wide flagstone steps to the front door and looked for a doorbell. I couldn't find one. A huge woman in a formal evening gown opened the door. My doorbell-punching finger was still poised.

"Sensors," she said. "You were announced electronically." She looked at her bracelet watch. "You're twenty minutes late." Her alto voice fit her size.

"Late for what?" I said.

She waved her hand at me, as if clearing the air of smoke. "Come in, Strobe. We've got to get you dressed."

"Uri," I said. "Not Strobe."

"For this evening, you're Strobe."

I began to recognize her. "Jerry?" I said.

His gold lamé gown shimmered in the late afternoon light.

16

His wig was a Jackie Kennedy bouffant, his make-up was slutty. He wore long, artificial nails painted transparent pearl. His brassiere held enough conical foam rubber to launch a pair of operatic Brunhilda breasts that suited a woman of his height and girth. His patent leather pumps were big enough to accommodate bricks. He hid his neck under a paisley scarf. With surprising grace, Jerry Farnsworth spun full circle, putting all his weight on the ball of his right foot. His brocaded gown swirled around him, chipping rainbows out of the afternoon sun.

"You like?" he said.

I cleared my throat. "You big fox," I said.

He grinned.

The room behind Jerry was huge—big enough to hold four of my apartments with a few walk-in closets thrown in. The furnishings were quality but not remarkable—severe Danish modern stuff. The walls were white, the carpet was white, the furniture was high-gloss ebony. The carpet stopped at a wide, tiled hallway that led to the back of the house. There were paintings on the walls. Imitation Miró. Primary colors in basic forms. How did I know that? Jeopardy. ("This Spanish artist's work is characterized by bright colors and simple forms.") Trivia sticks to my brain like electrostatic dust.

I heard high heels clicking against tile. Mona Farnsworth came down the hallway. She was wearing a tweed suit and tortoise shell glasses. Her hair was set in hard windproof waves. Her skin looked tight and poreless. "You're late," she scolded. June Cleaver on the rag.

"Sorry," I said.

"Come with me, we've got to get you dressed."

"I'm not putting on any women's clothes," I said, looking at Jerry again.

Two children came in. A chubby little boy, maybe five years

old, and a big-eyed "goth" in her early teens. "Who's the muscle muffin?" the girl said. She had short black hair with crisp bangs, black blouse and skirt, dull black lipstick and shiny black nails, twin eyebrow rings, a nose stud. Her hard white face reflected light as if it had been coated with clear lacquer. She appraised me with heavily shadowed eyes that gave her a tubercular look. She stood, one hip cocked, her arms folded under her perky tea-cup breasts. Her nostrils flared as she studied me—an albino vampire sensing warm blood. She was simultaneously cute and sinister, innocent and rotten with knowledge. If she had a soul, it was older than dirt.

"Strobe Champion," Jerry said. "Meet our kids, Harry and Babs. Babs, honey, would you get Mr. Champion a cola? You want a cola, Strobe?"

"No," I said.

"You look so excellent, father," the girl said.

"Thanks, princess," Jerry said. He twirled again and batted his eyes. "Have you done your homework, sweetie?"

"Ages ago. I'm doing a book report for my Contemporary Society class. I've decided to use Mother's Krafft-Ebing. I've read it twice. I love the chapter on body-defect fetishism. And the 1895 Cantarano study of toe-sucking is like so *now*, father dear." Her affectations were delivered dead-pan.

Jerry beamed proudly. "She wants to participate—in a hands on way—in the business. But I want her to get a degree in business law. I'd like her to manage the money."

"No time for chit-chat," Mona said, taking me by the hand. "We've got a customer waiting downstairs. No one's asking you to wear women's clothes, Strobe."

"Uri," I said. "My name's Uri."

"Not tonight. Tonight you are Strobe."

She led me to a room at the end of the hallway. "This is our dressing room," she said. "What size waist are you?"

"Thirty-one," I said.

She felt my abs. "We'll want those on display."

She rummaged through a dresser drawer and pulled out a pair of black tights and a black silk jock. "Take off your clothes and put on these," she said. "And hurry up." She stepped outside while I changed.

I stripped and put on the jock and tights. I put my shoes back on. Mona came back in and appraised me. "Yummy," she said, but it was a lust-free, purely analytical comment. "The shoes are wrong," she said. "You'll have to go barefoot. Do you mind if I put some baby oil on you?" My curiosity was peaking, but the thought of June Cleaver rubbing me down with baby oil put my questions on a back burner.

"Feel free," I said.

Her hands were warm and her fingers were expert. She worked the oil into my shoulders and back, concentrating on the lats, traps, and deltoids. When she came around to my pecks and abs, I embarrassed myself. The silk jock was no help.

"Busted," I apologized.

"Tell your pocket rocket to chill, Strobe. I'm not your girlfriend. This is strictly business." There was ice in her voice. It cooled me off.

She worked the oil into my arms and forearms, all business. She stepped back and looked at me, finger in her cheek, judging her work.

"Why is it you don't have any tattoos?" she asked. "I thought big bad boys like you always wore some kind of macho skin art."

"I used to compete," I said.

She looked at me, not comprehending.

I nailed a pose for her, a Schwartzenegger special—the front double biceps—and then moved fluidly into a kneeling three-quarter back shot. From there I went into a front lat spread, spun around and did a rear lat spread, then the side triceps. I still had good definition thanks to my low body fat. I can still make an impression: Twenty-inch arms, fifty-inch chest. Thighs like sculpted limestone, thick as nail kegs. I relaxed and made my pecs jump like cats in a bag. I heard her catch her breath. "You don't mess up a body like this with bad art," I said.

"*Very* nice," she said. "But next time—if there is a next time—I'll fix you up with some prison tattoos. We'll use henna so you can scrub them off. You'll look like you've done hard time at Huntsville."

"Why?" I said, getting back to my curiosity.

"It makes you seem more intimidating."

"Who am I supposed to intimidate?"

"You'll find out in a couple of minutes."

She rummaged in the dresser again, pulled out something made of leather. "Put this on. It's the final touch."

It looked like a leather ski mask, the kind of thing worn by ax-hefting executioners in the days when beheading was in vogue. I pulled it on. She cinched and buckled a strap at the back of the mask, pulling the leather tight against my face.

"There," she said. "You look very nasty, a real heart-stopper." Her eyes behind the fake lenses of her glasses were intense. She was working herself up for something.

"Thanks," I said. "What's next?"

"What's next is next," she said. "I think you might enjoy it. If you don't, just remember it's all an act. You won't have to do anything nasty. In fact, you probably won't have to do anything at all."

She took me by the hand and led me away.

FOUR

The big naked man stood at attention. June Cleaver—the dark side of June Cleaver—slapped his face hard. He had a strong noble face, the kind of face that could wear self-importance well, but he started blubbering after the third slap. June Cleaver reached under her skirt and pulled down her panties and stepped out of them. It was a delicious maneuver. It got me a little excited. I took a deep breath and forced myself to think of other things.

She pinched the man's nose shut. With her other hand she stuffed her panties into his air-sucking mouth. Then she put a dog collar around his neck. She attached a leash to the collar and said, "Heel!" The man dropped to all fours and, dog-like, tried to nuzzle her feet. She kicked him away. He whined like a whipped mutt. She pulled up her skirt and straddled him, pulling back on the leash. She reached back and slapped his pale buttocks. "Giddyup!" she said, and the man, on his hands and knees, carried her around the room, the pink panties dangling from his jaws. He was gray-haired, about fifty, and he shimmered with yellow fat. I imagined his heart-tripping excitement as he felt the moist warmth of her panty-less bottom riding his spine.

Somewhere, children were playing in a green park throwing frisbees to excited puppies under an innocent blue sky while their normal moms and dads looked on. Something in me wanted to believe this. Something in me knew better. Like the old joke goes, "normal" is a setting on your washing machine. And "innocent" is a technical term, useful in court.

The basement room had been decorated to look like a dungeon. Instruments of torture lined the walls—iron maidens, chairs with thumbscrews on the arms; stocks and chains and cages. Like me, most of these things were props—designed to create an atmosphere of intimidation. A heavy, crescent-edged beheading ax leaned on the wall next to me.

On the way down to this dungeon, Mona explained the nature of *Mind Me!*—the name of her business. She was a professional dominatrix, and had over a hundred wealthy clients who paid five-hundred to a thousand dollars a session to be abused by her. *Mind Me!* was fully licensed; she paid a business tax to the city. When she started *Mind Me!* five years ago, she talked to the city attorney about its legality. He told her she could sell any service she wanted to. If there were men out there who'd pay money to be abused, then the city wouldn't object. There was one stipulation: No penetration of any kind. Penetration would re-define the nature of the business, and the city could not sanction a bordello.

She had a website, a 900 call-in line, and ran ads in the local papers. The ads in the daily papers were discreet, written in a kind of code only the experienced could decipher. In the independent tabloids, though, the ads were explicit and titillating:

> Bad boys! You need some real discipline now! You *know* who you are, don't you? You *know* what you've done. You need corrective punishment *now*. You *crave* it! Your unpunished life is a fraud! Stop pretending innocence! Come to me, dears, Mama has ways to make you *squeal!*

My job, she told me, was to stand at one end of the dungeon

with the beheading ax held loosely in my hands. If she pointed at me, I was to raise the ax and take one step toward her client. "Try to stay pumped," she said. "I want those muscles to look like instruments of torture." I did fifty push-ups and some isometrics to get the effect she wanted. I think I looked pretty good. Hell, maybe I could still cut it in some senior bodybuilder's meet. Maybe I could be Mr. Somebody again.

After about ten minutes of Mona's routine, I began to get bored. The first ten minutes were interesting, but her scenario after a while became repetitive. I daydreamed and missed one of her signals. She had to get my attention. "Strobe!" she yelled, snapping me alert. "Strobe, raise your ax! Show him we mean business!"

I raised the ax and stepped toward the client. He cried out, "Oh Jesus, please, no!" I waved the ax over my head and he cringed. Mona gave him a menacing look. I snarled. He blubbered. We were all acting out a perverted little farce. It disgusted me.

I went a little crazy. I'd never have the kind of money this idiot had, and yet here he was using his wealth to get his rocks off in a phony torture chamber. "You fat-ass son of a bitch," I said, and came at him with the ax. I swung it past his head and hit the wall behind him, missing his skull by inches, shattering the plaster. "Die, motherfucker!" I yelled. He scrambled away from me on all fours, cringing with authentic terror. Mona looked at me, her eyes wide with a perfect imitation of real fright. "Strobe!" she said. "For God's sakes, control yourself!"

The client, realizing that she was not acting, tried to stand up. Mona slapped him hard and ordered him to get back down to all fours, maybe for his own safety. "And you," she whispered to me, "get yourself under control or you're gone, mister!" She stuffed her client's mouth with her panties again,

23

and I went back to my place at the far end of the dungeon, my heart pounding. I took the moment to take inventory: Jesus, I'd *wanted* to behead the rich wimp. Is this what she meant about me learning something?

The game went on: she rode him, beat him, made him lick the floor. She made him dance a jig and sing "Love Is A Many Splendored Thing" while she lashed his legs and buttocks with his own belt. Now and then she cast a nervous glance at me, to make sure I wasn't taking all this to heart. I didn't give her the satisfaction of a wink or a shrug. I hefted the ax with something more than indifference.

The sad-ass client was red in the face from his exertions. He was panting with fatigue and excitement. He looked bad. I could see his heartbeat ticking in his florid neck. "Mistress, may I worship your divine waters?" he begged. An emotion surfaced from its deep underground hiding place. It twisted his face with two competing expressions: the unjustly punished child, and the grown man anticipating paradise.

He was on his knees before her. Mona put a spiked heel into his shoulder and shoved him over onto his back. She pulled up her skirt and squatted low over his face. "Say please, you undeserving pig," she said. He did. She released the golden shower. He came.

The game was over. The man, stumbling with fatigue, went into the dungeon's small bathroom to clean up and dress. Mona and I went upstairs. I felt a little played out myself. I pulled off my executioner's mask. It was unvented and my hair was soaked with sweat. It looked like I'd held it under a tap. Mona showed me into the bathroom next to the dressing room. My clothes were already hanging on the door. I showered, dressed, then found the Farnsworth family in their kitchen where Jerry, still in drag, was serving snacks to Harry

24

and Babs. Bacon-wrapped hotdogs and fries. Mona was
sipping iced tea.

"What the hell got into you down there?" she asked.

I shrugged. "Just playing my part."

"Like hell. You scared the liver out of the client. You had
me wondering if I'd made the mistake of my career. I thought
you really wanted to kill him."

I laughed. "I guess I'm a pretty good actor if I fooled the
pro."

"You weren't acting."

"We're all acting, twenty-four seven. Don't you think?"

She looked at me for a long moment, then changed the
subject. "You want something to eat, killer?"

"Not that junk," I said.

I sat down with them. Jerry brought me a tall glass of iced
tea. "Sugar?" he said.

"Sweet 'n' Low, if you've got it."

"We've got it."

I had to ask: "Jerry, how come you're in drag? Is that part
of the business?"

"He just likes to cross," Mona said. "It's his hobby. Everybody should have a hobby."

"No connection to the business," Jerry said. "It's just, you
know, my *thing*." I glanced at little Harry. Jerry picked up on
it. "The kids are fine with it, Uri. Hey, you're not some kind
of demento prude, are you?"

"Can I have another hot dog?" Harry said. He was a chip
off the old block, a pudgy, guilt-free optimist. Babs looked
like Mona. She had Mona's seen-it-all eyes. When she filled
out, she was going to be desirable and frightening.

Jerry served Harry another bacon-wrapped dog smothered
in Velveeta. These people obviously never heard of nitrates
and saturated fats, or didn't care. Didn't they know what they

were doing to their kids' health, feeding them crap like that? I started to remind them that hotdogs are made with the trash that's swept off the slaughterhouse floor and that Velveeta isn't real cheese, then thought better of it. What corruptions of food they fed their kids was their business.

Mona looked at her watch. She was still in her June Cleaver costume. "Mr. Renseller's taking his time," she said. "Maybe we'd better go check on him."

Clive Renseller, Mona had explained, was a prominent banker in the city. He'd been one of her first top-dollar clients and was now a regular. He paid a thousand dollars for each weekly session. He was a highly visible citizen, a leader in the community. He was friends with the governor and had golfed with the president. Feature articles had been written about him in national magazines. "Clive Renseller on the Future of Optimism," was the title of an interview published in *Money Magazine.*

Renseller liked the six o'clock sessions, the last of Mona's working day–if he came up with a new twist on an old scenario, then the session could last another half hour or so and not interfere with another appointment. Mona didn't mind since the added session–ten minutes or a full hour– brought in another thousand. She worked roughly an eight hour day. I did the math. If they were all thousand dollar clients, then, given a five day week, she was making a minimum of a hundred sixty thousand a month. Throw in a few five-hundred dollar sessions and her monthly income would still gross out to six figures. And that wasn't counting the 900 line and whatever services they sold on their website.

Mona went down to the dungeon. She came back a minute later. "We've got a problem," she said.

FIVE

Clive Renseller was sitting on the floor of the shower stall, staring at something across the universe. The water coming out of the showerhead had turned cold. His skin, not so pink now, had begun to pucker. Under the driving water, his hair hung straight down from a centerpoint at the top of his skull like radii. He looked deep in thought. He might have been a twelfth century monk working out a tough metaphysical puzzle.

"Can you do CPR?" Mona said, hoping for the best.

I turned off the shower and felt his neck for the pulse I knew wasn't there. It might have been a new obedience scenario he dreamed up: *Slave fakes fainting spell in the shower, Mistress whips his ass until he wakes up and begs for more divine waters.* But it wasn't. Clive Renseller, banker, pillar of the community, was dead.

"Christ," Mona said. "This is all I fucking needed."

"Call 911," I said. "Looks like Clive had a coronary."

"No. First I'll call his wife. We've got a very sticky situation here."

We went back upstairs. Mona made her phone call. "Jillian Renseller is close by," she said. "I got her cellphone—she'd been out to dinner. The poor woman begged us not to call anyone right away. I'm going to honor that."

"That's something you can't honor," I said. "The law—"

"Listen to me," Mona said. "There's a lot at stake here. The publicity will ruin my business. Most of my clientele are highly placed citizens. They don't want their private lives put under a microscope. You *can* understand that, can't you? We'll have people from the tabloids camped on our lawn for weeks if this gets out. My clients will have to stay away. I can't afford that. Jillian has a lot to lose, too. In fact, the whole community has a lot to lose. Please, Uri, don't give me static about this."

Compassion was not among Mona's more visible qualities. But not reporting Renseller's death was a no-no, and she was asking me to cooperate. A while back, a top administrator from our local university collapsed and died in his girlfriend's apartment at The Baron Arms. I called 911, and the scandal broke in the dailies the following day. The local tabloids feasted on the story for weeks. The man's family was devastated. But it's the kind of fallout that can't be avoided. If a man won't protect his family and reputation by not misbehaving why should anyone else be expected to?

"Count me out," I said. I headed for the door.

"Wait, Uri," Mona said, catching my arm. I didn't flex. "You could be implicated in some pretty nasty publicity, too. I know you haven't got a lot to lose, but think about this: there'll be photos of you in the papers, pictures of you wearing black tights swinging an ax at Mr. Renseller. The mask won't shield you. Your name will come out. Could you cope with that?"

"What pictures?" I said. But I felt the sinking sensation you get when you remember what you always knew: the deck is always stacked.

"Everything we do is videotaped. Four cameras are hidden in the walls of the dungeon and two in the ceiling. We have to do it to protect ourselves. We need to have proof that what we do is a consensual activity. If a client, for whatever reason, should decide to claim he was abused against his will, the tapes will prove otherwise."

"You're blackmailing me into cooperating with you."

"No I'm not. But if the police investigate Renseller's death, they'll probably find out about the tapes. I wouldn't be able to stop them."

"The law will eventually find out that Renseller is dead."

"Yes. But what they find can be . . . *adjusted.*"

I heard tires screech in the Farnsworth driveway.

"That will be Jillian," Mona said.

Mona let her in and brought her back to the kitchen. She was small woman in her late thirties. She had short-cropped black hair with blond streaks. Her fine-boned face looked Mediterranean—beaky nose, olive skin, dark liquid eyes. Her lips were thin and held in a grim line. She was wearing faded jeans, sweatshirt, and tennis shoes. "Where is the goddamned fool?" she said, her voice shaky.

"Downstairs, in the shower," I said. "The goddamned fool had a heart attack." It looked like Clive Renseller's death wasn't going to throw many people into bottomless despair.

"Who are *you?*" Jillian Renseller said, noticing me for the first time.

"I'm Strobe, the living prop," I said. "I helped scare the life out of him."

She looked at me for a long moment, then turned to Mona. "Okay, so he's dead," she said. "But he can't stay here. I've got to get him home."

Mona turned to me. "We're going to need your help."

"Sure," I said. "I love risking jail sentences for no particular reason. It's my hobby. Like you said, Mona, everyone should have a hobby."

"He died a natural death," Mona said, softening her approach. She touched my arm again. "Where's the problem if we just take his body home?"

"Natural?" I said. "He's got bruises all over his legs and

whip marks on his ass. His lips were bleeding. He's got a mouse under one eye. There's probably some of your divine waters in his sinuses. I don't think the coroner is going to buy Clive's death as purely natural."

Jillian Renseller covered her eyes with her hand and staggered sideways. Jerry Farnsworth caught her and led her to a chair.

"Oh my God," Jillian said. "Everything we've worked for is in ruins!" She started sobbing, hysterical little hiccups. Mona gave her a handful of Kleenex tissues. Jillian blew her nose. Her loud honks seemed unlikely coming from a small woman with such delicate features.

She got control of herself and looked around the Farnsworth's kitchen, as if for the first time realizing where she was. Jerry handed her a glass of water. Jillian looked up at him, grateful for his attentions. "Oh I'm sorry, Jerry," she said. "That's a *lovely* dress. Where did you find it? I want one exactly like it."

"I bought it in San Francisco ten years ago," he said.

"Don't ask him how much he paid," Mona said, rolling her eyes a bit. This gesture to normality would have been touching if it weren't also a bit insane. I started to say something but Little Harry came into the kitchen.

"I'm still hungry, Da," he said. He was in bunny pajamas, ready for bed. The Irish "Da" was cute. This family had style.

"Hey guys, I'm going to order pizza for the grown-ups," Jerry said. "We're all going to relax, have a bite to eat, then think about what should be done. Once we've all calmed down and have gotten something substantial in our stomachs, we'll be able to sort things out. My motto is, Never make major decisions on an empty stomach." He'd taken off his bouffant. His red mohawk lay flat on his head like a pelt.

"You were a participant," Mona said to me. She was playing

June Cleaver's dark side again. Behind her glasses her green eyes were tending toward gray. The invulnerable gray of steel vaults. It occurred to me suddenly that she *enjoyed* her work. I smiled—at myself. What an idiot. I'd been around the block a few times, but here I'd been surprised by what would have been obvious to a cloistered nun. Mona Farnsworth took great pleasure in beating the crap out of men. Getting paid big bucks for it was a sweet bonus. Live and learn. Another cliché that carried weight.

"You'll be implicated if there's any question about Clive's death," she said. She gripped my arm hard. I kept the muscle slack. "Think of yourself, Uri. You should be *eager* to help us fix this mess."

Her nails dug into my biceps. I was seated and she was standing. She bent down so that her face was close to mine. Her mouth was slightly open. I thought she was going to bite me.

SIX

I didn't want my picture in the paper, masked or not. And I didn't want to be implicated in Clive Renseller's "natural" death. Mona and Jillian convinced me there would be no fallout if I helped take Clive home. Jillian would call their family physician in the morning. She would tell him that when she went into Clive's bedroom she found him dead. Clive had been taking three meds—a beta blocker for his high blood pressure, digoxin to stabilize his heart rhythms, nitroglycerin for his angina. The sudden death of a man his age and physical condition wasn't going to take anyone by surprise.

As for Clive's contusions, welts, and broken lip, Jillian would take the blame. She'd confess, tearfully, to the doctor, that Clive needed kinky sex in order to achieve erections and to ejaculate, and that she was willing to accommodate him. Sometimes, Jillian would say, she'd have to work Clive up by getting a little wild, and last night they were a little wilder than usual. But violent sex was too much for his battered heart. The doctor was an old friend, a companion on the links, and would understand the need for discretion. He'd be more than pleased to sign the death certificate without mentioning Clive's love lumps. Jillian was sure of this.

The plan seemed reasonable. It seemed more reasonable when she offered me five hundred to go along with it. The hard part was getting Clive Renseller out of the shower stall. He wasn't stiff yet, wouldn't be for another hour or so, and

32

picking him up was like picking up a rubber bag filled with forty gallons of water. I can lift a lot of weight—iron disks balanced at the ends of a steel bar—but Clive was weight without a fixed center of gravity. I pulled him out by his arms, then got him into a sitting position. Jerry helped me raise him upright. When we had him more or less vertical, I put my shoulder into his belly and picked him up. He weighed two-seventy, maybe two-eighty.

I felt a twinge in my lower back. It was a reminder: I'd had a lumbar disc rupture a few years ago while trying to clean-and-jerk over four hundred pounds in a showdown at the Y with my lifting partner, Ray Fuentes. I got the bar halfway to my chest when I heard the disc pop. It sounded like firewood cracking. A vise of white hot pain cramped my lower back. I dropped the bar. It dented the tile floor of the weight room. I fell down roaring. Fuentes grinned down at me. "You owe me ten bucks, chump," he said. We're good friends.

By the time I got Clive into the back seat of the Mercedes my back had started to seize up. I lowered myself gingerly into the passenger's side of the front seat. I sucked in air and held it, jaws clenched. I might have made a small noise. Getting Clive out of the car and into his house was not going to be fun. Five hundred didn't seem half enough.

"What's wrong with you?" Jillian said as she backed the big car out of the driveway.

"Bad back," I said.

"You? A muscle-man like you has a bad back?"

"We dropped out of the trees before our bodies were ready. The back hasn't had enough time to adapt. Same goes for knees. We became *Homo erectus* without a decent break-in period. We should still be eating bananas and picking nits out of each other's fur, standing upright only for pissing contests."

"You're a funny guy," she said, forcing a smile. Forced or not it was nice. It lit up her face.

The Renseller's lived in an area that could have been the jacket illustration for a book of fairy tales. It didn't belong in the desert. It was a twenty-acre shelf carved out of a barren sandstone hill that rose out of the surrounding desert. The shelf had been layered with rich topsoil and held a mini-forest of northwest pines and hardwoods. Vast lawns and shrubbery made it lush as a wetland.

We entered her property through a tall wrought-iron gate which she'd opened by pushing a button on the Mercedes' dashboard. The drive to the house took another couple of minutes. Her place made the Farnsworth's house look like an equipment shed. It was a replica of a Victorian mansion, a three-story brick, many-gabled structure. I counted four chimneys. Leafy shade trees—elms and oaks—surrounded the house. The Rensellers must have had their own pipeline to the Colorado River to keep the place green. It didn't fit in with the southwest desert environment at all. In fact, the Renseller property seemed designed to disavow any connection to the bleak reality that surrounded it. I wondered how they dealt with scorpions, rattlesnakes, and the occasional sand-blasting by the desert wind.

"Nice place," I said.

"I know what you're thinking," she said. "You're thinking we were arrogant and deluded to build a place like this in the desert."

I didn't say anything.

She interpreted my silence correctly. "Well, you're right," she said. "When we left Oregon to come here five years ago, I hated it. So we created our own little piece of suburban Portland. Clive called it Oak Grove on the Rio Grande. I'm a little ashamed of it now. We probably use more water every day than half of Juárez."

"The aquifer's running dry," I said.

"Thanks to people like us." I glanced in the back seat to check on the other half of "us." Clive looked serenely indifferent to desert ecology.

Jillian started to cry, but I didn't think her tears were for the depleted aquifer. They were for herself.

"Bad things happen to good people," I said. She shot me a quick glance to see if I was being a smart-ass. I was and I wasn't. All the clichés are true at least half the time. I didn't dislike her, not on ecological grounds, anyway.

She brought the car to a stop under the porte-cochere next to the mansion. The illusion of 19th century north-country opulence was convincing. When I got out of the car I half expected to step into cool damp northwest air. But the parching desert wind was gusty enough to rattle the thirsty elms next to the house. I could almost smell a sandstorm brewing.

I opened the back door. Clive Renseller looked like he'd been on a long, dull drive and had dozed off. The seat belt and shoulder strap held him on the seat. Jerry and I had started to put his pants and shirt on but decided it was pointless. No one was going to see him, and when Jillian and I got him home we were going to put him into his pajamas. Jillian had driven the Mercedes into the Farnsworth's garage. I'd carried Clive into the garage through the kitchen door and strapped him in the back seat of his car. And now, under the porte-cochere, we had complete privacy again. We would have had complete privacy if I had carried him all the way to the house from the front gate. But in the porte-cochere we were only steps away from an entrance to the house.

Jillian stood beside me. We both looked down at Clive. His

serenity was impressive. He looked better dead than alive. Less florid, less troubled, all the sexual kinks untangled. Blood pressure a serene zero over zero, no arrhythmias, no fear. We stood above him, unable or unwilling to speak. Silence seemed fitting.

"Poor bastard," I finally said.

Jillian touched my arm. "Thank you," she said. "Those are probably the only honest words that are going to be spoken over him." There wasn't much emotion in her voice. I decided the marriage had been loveless for quite some time. I could identify with that.

I unbuckled Clive's seat belt/shoulder strap combo and knelt before the open door. I tugged his arm. He leaned toward me. I turned his legs so that they were out of the car. I pulled him into my shoulder, planted my feet, and lifted him, using my legs, keeping my back straight as a board.

Jillian led the way into the house. "We're going up to his bedroom," she said. "It's on the third floor. But don't worry, we have an elevator."

I didn't see much of the house. I kept my eyes on the floor, directly in front of my feet. If I tripped I'd never get him back on my shoulder. I saw Persian carpeting, a lot of it, and then the elevator floor. Upstairs, I followed more Persian carpeting to Clive's bedroom.

After I dropped him on his four-poster I felt weightless. I felt as if I might float to the ceiling, like a kid's balloon. I grabbed Jillian's shoulder to steady myself. She didn't expect the weight. Her knees buckled and she staggered away from me.

"Sorry," I said. "My gyros wobbled for a second."

She smiled again. This time it wasn't forced. "I'll get you a drink," she said. "But first, let's get Clive into his pajamas and put him to bed."

We did that, then went downstairs. She led me to a paneled room with leather furniture in it. The carpeting was deep enough to sleep on without waking up stiff. There was a fireplace in one wall that looked as if it had never been used. A portrait of an elderly man hung over the mantle. He looked important and rich and capable of anything. She opened a teak liquor cabinet. The cabinet had a built-in bar sink. "What do you drink?" she said.

"Tequila."

"Ugh. Turpentine. Clive liked it, though. We have a few bottles. What do you back it with, paint thinner?"

"I just want a couple of shots, neat."

I thought of tequila as medicine. Especially for the back. It had muscle relaxant properties other booze didn't. When I was recovering from back surgery, Ray Fuentes brought me a liter of Herradura, a good tequila made from the blue agave. "For back pain," he said, "there's nothing better. Not even Demerol. But you've got to drink a lot of it. You've got to come close to blackout. When you wake up to no pain you will want to go to church and light a candle to our Lady of the Blue Agave." Ray was right. Even the hangover was relatively mild.

"You're wondering why Clive and I had separate bedrooms," Jillian said. I wasn't wondering. The rich are different, someone once said. Yes, they have more money, was the famous response. But money probably forces you to be different. It gives you options. The rich have choices the poor can't dream of. Poor couples, happy or unhappy, must sleep together; the rich, like cats, sleep where they want.

She had given me a shot glass and a nearly full bottle of tequila. I didn't know the brand. I checked the label to see if it was made from *agave azul*. It was. I poured myself a shot, downed it, then poured another.

"We haven't had relations for several years," she said.

She made herself a whiskey sour and sat down next to me. We sat in twin wingback chairs, a small leather-top tea table between us.

"Clive was no good in bed," she continued. "He couldn't get it up unless I tied and gagged him and threatened him with physical pain. It's hard to love someone that fucked up. You can pity him but not love him."

I knocked back a shot, then another. The medicinal heat of the tequila radiated out from my stomach to my extremities.

"The SM games turned him on but they turned me off. So I let him go to Mona. It kept him happy."

I had to ask: "What keeps you happy?"

She looked at me for a long moment, judging my motives. "Nothing much," she said. "Happiness is overrated."

I thought, *Maybe that's it. Maybe that's how the rich are different. The poor have to believe in happiness. Work hard, save, accumulate, happiness will come. The rich don't have that advantage.*

She launched into a history of Clive's childhood. He wasn't born rich. His mother, Lenore, was a psychotic and his father was a drunk. His mother looked for evil in every dark corner of her life. She found it in abundance in young Clive. She beat him with a belt, beat him with a stick, beat him with her fists. She beat him until he bled and once put him in the hospital with a cracked suborbital bone under his eye. Child Protective Services didn't exist in those days or at least didn't have the kind of power they have today, and so nothing was done to stop the abuse.

But Lenore Renseller was sane enough to be capable of remorse. She would console little Clive after beating him. She would hold him in her lap and cuddle him for hours, weeping, asking for forgiveness, and promising him the world. Clive came to associate the beatings with affection. Severe

38

physical abuse became the prerequisite for love. His adult sex life could not possibly have been normal.

"He was a great success, but all he wanted was to be happy," she said. "Happiness for the Rainmaker was Mona Farnsworth squatting on his face."

"Rainmaker?" I said.

"That's what they call him at his savings and loan. The Rainmaker. All Clive had to do was wave his arms, do his song and dance, and depositors and prime investment opportunities fell from the skies like Mona's divine waters—yes, I know what she made him call it. Clive brought in the Helmstrom Enterprises people." I looked blank. "The people who are putting in the new Upper Valley theme park. It's going to be the biggest playland east of Phoenix and west of Houston. Clive went to them, made his pitch, and had them eating out of his hand. Cibola Savings and Loan—his company—is going to carry half the paper and farm out the other half to a Mexican bank for a very handsome finder's fee. I don't really understand this stuff, but then I don't have to."

She saw me looking at the portrait of the old man. He looked like a nineteenth century robber baron. The black eyes burned with greed and ruthlessness. "It's a phony," she said. "Clive wanted a pedigree that went back to the days of unregulated kick-ass capitalism. He told our guests that the man over the mantle was his great uncle Clayton Renseller, owner of an Astoria shipping company. I think it's a portrait of Teddy Roosevelt's gunsmith."

I raised my glass to Teddy Roosevelt's gunsmith then knocked back my third tequila. "I'd better get going," I said.

She stood up. "I'll drive you back to Mona's. I'm not going to spend the night here, with Clive up in his bedroom."

"I don't blame you."

39

"It's not what you think," she said. "I'm the least superstitious person you'll ever meet. I don't believe in ghosts but I believe in god. Not the Christian god. My god is more like an Aztec god, or the god of the Masai, in Africa. The old pissed-off Hebrew god comes close. This is a god that likes to fuck with people. He doesn't believe in happiness either. He believes in irony, he believes in rocking boats. He makes sure that injustice rules. He makes us comfortable in hell, then repossesses the furniture and forecloses on the house. Right now he's mocking me. See, if I sleep here tonight, it will be just like every other night for the past five years. Clive in his bed, oblivious of me. It's the business-as-usual aspect of it that irritates me. No, I'm going to spend the night at the Farnsworth's. They're good solid people. Salt of the earth."

She started to write me a check but after she thumbed through the register she closed the checkbook. "Damn, that account's overdrawn. I'd better give you cash." She rummaged through her purse, came up with everything but money. "Fuck, I'm out of cash," she said. "I'll have to send you the five hundred. You don't mind waiting a few days, do you?"

I shrugged. "I guess there's no choice." I gave her my address. "Your god has the corner on irony," I said.

She looked at me again, that long analytical look, then decided it was okay to laugh. I laughed, too, but I was thinking about that pointlessly re-emphasized bit of old news: *Clive in his bed, oblivious of me.* Was this a message meant for me? Was she in need? I looked into her eyes, trolling for clues, but the steel shutter behind them had already slammed shut.

We left the house by a back door. "I wanted to show you this," she explained. She flipped a wall switch, and beyond a hedgerow maze, a swimming pool big as a small a lake was flooded with light. It had an irregular shape and held more

40

water than two Olympic-size pools. It was surrounded by beargrass and baneberry shrubs and had the look of a mountain tarn. The surface was dimpled with fish rising to take evening bugs. A fairy tale lake.

"His trout pond," she said. "He converted the pool to a fishery. I think it was the only thing in his life he really loved. He'd come out here every morning and fly-fish for his beloved cutthroat trout. It made him think he was back in the northwest, living in simpler times." We both stared at the expanse of clear water as if looking into the Rainmaker's defenseless soul. "I'm going to have the scummy thing drained and the fish removed," she said.

SEVEN

The following day the paper carried a front-page obit:

COMMUNITY LEADER DEAD AT 51

It was two columns of praise for Clive Renseller, a man who had made major contributions to the city's recent spurt of economic growth. It extolled his virtues as businessman and citizen, listing the many charities he sponsored, his school board membership, his strong church affiliation. His photograph was set into the twin columns, a flattering portrait of a younger Renseller with dark hair and a tight, jowl-less jawline. He looked willful and determined, a man who could be counted on, but the almost imperceptible wry smile that dimpled the corners of his mouth tended to undermine the effect. Maybe I was reading too much into it, having seen a less heroic side of the man. The picture in my mind was of a much older man—the Rainmaker—lying on his back on a cold dungeon floor, helpless and thrilled, as Mona Farnsworth squatted over him.

There was a statement by the Renseller's family physician certifying that Clive had died of natural causes. There was no mention of his "love lumps," no mention of an autopsy, no mention of Mona Farnsworth, no mention of police interest.

A spokesperson for Cibola Savings and Loan assured customers and stockholders alike that the institution was healthy and, though it would close its doors for one day of mourning, business would be conducted as usual thereafter. "We have a strong and enduring commitment to our stockholders and to our community," the spokesperson said, "and our assets continue to grow at a pace exceeding that of our nearest competitors. The future, though momentarily darkened by the passing of our president, Clive Renseller, is, I assure you, very very bright."

The governor expressed his condolences to the Renseller family (consisting only of Jillian as far as I knew), and to the community for its "grievous loss of such an outstanding role model for our youth. Clive Renseller," the governor rhapsodized, "was the ideal example of how hard work, dedication, and solid family values invariably produce a winner. Clive Renseller was the kind of man who made America what it is today."

Arrangements were to be handled by the Stockbridge, Wilts, and Morena funeral home, and the public was asked to contribute any memorial donations to the Children of Abusive Homes fund. This last request had to be Jillian's covert acknowledgment of the childhood abuse and subsequent perversion that in the end were responsible for Clive's early death. I liked her for that.

I set the paper aside and groped under my bed for my dumbbells. I always try to get in a set of biceps curls and deltoid raises before breakfast. I loaded the dumbbell bars with seventy-five pounds each and worked out for ten minutes. Then I rolled out my Thomas Inch dumbells–replicas of a design by the great English strongman of the early 20th century, Thomas Inch. These monsters weighed 135 pounds each and consisted of two solid spheres of black cast iron connected by a bar that was over two inches in diameter, almost impossible to grip. I picked them up, did a few triceps presses, then made myself breakfast: six scrambled eggs—whites only—whole wheat toast, and a bowl of oat bran. I topped that off with low-fat cottage cheese mixed with flax seed oil.

I got dressed and went out onto the balcony. The sky was painted red with a broad brush—one of those spectacular desert sunrises that makes even atheists look up with second thoughts. Fine herringbone clouds corrugated the sky all the way to the horizon which seemed a thousand miles away. The canopy of light covered the city and surrounding desert like the vault of a rosy cathedral. Even the traffic on Mesa Street moved slower than usual, as if the drivers had decided, collectively, that speed and impatience were forms of blasphemy.

I went down to check out the grounds. Now and then a tagger would spraypaint his gang symbols on the lower level walls. And sometimes vandals would chip away at the old motel with rocks and pellets and, on at least two occasions, bullets. Sometimes the vandals were the tenants themselves. It was an ongoing headache, but I had long since given up any kind of visceral response to it. Vandalism came with the territory. You lived with it, or you moved to upper Maine and contemplated your potato fields.

The laundry room had been broken into again, the money boxes on the machines uprooted and gutted by someone with a crow bar, someone who went through a lot of work for the ten or twenty dollars he ran off with. I unclipped the cellphone from my belt and made the perfunctory call to the police. The cop who took my call yawned his way through the standard questions. Crimes against property were so common that the police almost didn't consider them crimes any more. They were part of the landscape. On the upside, violent crimes against persons were fairly infrequent for a city of this size. A remarkable statistic some credited to the aquifer that supplied El Paso with drinking water. The Hueco Bolson was rich in a naturally-occurring lithium salt, credited with keeping the bi-polar extremes of manic behavior in check. Nobody got too high; nobody got too low. Of course there were exceptions. The exceptions tended to accumulate in places like The Baron Arms. Such low-rent apartment complexes were holding areas for stability-challenged refugees from ordinary life.

I called the concessionaire who handled the laundry machines and gave him the bad news, then went back to my room on the fourth floor. The sky had changed. The sun was high enough now that the atmospheric lens no longer bled it of its coppery red. The thin clouds had moved out and wind from the west had grained the sky with sand. The traffic on Mesa had shifted back into its normal state of adrenalized horn-blowing hysteria.

A scorpion big as a mouse sat on my kitchenette table. When it saw me its tail arced up into stinging position. I slammed it with the latest issue of *Men's Health*. Brown juice thick as syrup foamed on the Formica. I cleaned up the mess and spent the rest of the morning looking for the second scorpion. Where there's one, there's always another.

EIGHT

Jillian's check came on Friday, three days later. Then, a week after that, a second check came for the same amount. A third check came the following week. When the fourth check arrived, I was expecting it. All the checks were for five-hundred and they all came on Fridays, like clockwork.

At first I thought there had to be a glitch—that they were bank-issued checks and some mindless computer loop no one had bothered to fix was kicking them out like a suicidally-loose slot machine kicks out quarters. But no, all the checks were signed by Jillian Renseller herself and they were on her personal account. There was no phone number on the checks, and the Rensellers weren't listed in the phone book. I could have called the Farnsworths for Jillian's number but I didn't want to stay on familiar terms with them. Besides, they hadn't asked me to work another dungeon routine so I figured my performance had been unsatisfactory. Everybody's got an ego, even masked executioners.

I hadn't cashed the first check by the time the second arrived. The second check made me hesitate. And by the time the fourth check came, I figured I'd better talk to Jillian before I cashed any of them. Money is nice, but I wasn't desperate for it. My situation at The Baron Arms was comfortable and my needs were minimal. The old motel was my fortress against a world that was getting crazier and more error-prone by the year. The lower-case craziness of some of my tenants was nothing compared to the spectacular everyday lunacy the world was beginning to accept as normal.

It was a painfully beautiful southwestern Friday in early May. Cool winds were gusting out of the west but so far had not kicked up any desert sand. The weather channel said it was stormy and unseasonably cold everywhere north of Albuquerque and east of Reno. This made me feel smug.

The smugly brilliant afternoon made up for the previous night, which did not make me feel smug. I got a two A.M. telephone call from an irate man on the third floor. Someone had been pounding on the door of his neighbor's apartment since midnight. He needed his sleep. He wanted something done about it. I got dressed, clipped a cellphone to my belt, armed myself with my new six-battery flashlight, and went down to the third-level balcony. Our balconies are communal, all doors on a given level open out to the same long ribbon of concrete. An iron railing prevents you from walking out into a ten- to thirty-foot drop to the parking lot, depending on your floor. The brochure describing The Baron Arms calls this ribbon of concrete a balcony. But "balcony" suggests an architectural refinement, a feature an upscale apartment might have. Here it's nothing more than an outdoor hallway. We have indoor hallways and we have outdoor hallways.

A man in a topcoat and Astros cap had propped himself against the door of 36C. He was leaning his forehead on his left arm and pounding the door with the heel of his right fist. He looked arm-weary.

"Cut it out," I said. "People are trying to sleep."

"She's in there," he said. "Don't tell me she's not."

"I don't care who's in there. If they don't want to answer the door, that's up to them. Now beat it."

"She's with that son of a bitch Caldwell. I know for a fact he lives here. You expect me to do nothing while that son of a bitch Caldwell is in there having a field day with my wife?"

"I expect you to quit disturbing my tenants," I said.

"I don't care about your tenants. This is a personal matter."

"It's personal for my tenants, too. They need their sleep. Caldwell probably has to get up early for work." I unclipped the cellphone from my belt. "I'm going to call the gendarmes, bud. You've got five seconds to split or spend a couple of nights in the drunk tank."

"Look, what if it was *your* wife in there with Caldwell? You wouldn't pound on the door?"

"I'm not his goddamned *wife!*" a woman screamed from the other side of the door. "I divorced the creep a year ago! Call the cops! He's in violation of the restraining order!"

"Fuck you, Verna!" the man screamed back. "Fuck you dead! I mean it, Verna! Fuck you and that bastard Caldwell dead."

"We're working on it!" Caldwell yelled cheerfully.

The man took off his hat, threw it on the balcony floor, then kicked it through the bars of the railing. It helicoptered into the parking lot. He was imagining it was Verna, or maybe Caldwell. He was about forty and his eyes were sick with misery and hate. I took him by the arm and made him walk to the landing by the elevator. "Go home," I said. "She's gone, man. Get used to it."

He took a swing at me. The nearest target syndrome. I caught his fist and squeezed until the bones of his hand touched.

"What home?" he said, crying in pain now. "It's me and Verna's mother! You call that home? The old lady's in a fucking wheel chair! I'm supposed to change her diapers and feed her mush while Verna is in there banging Lonnie Caldwell? You think that's a reasonable thing for a man like me to do?"

"Bad things happen to good people," I said, thinking of Jillian Renseller's god who made sure injustice prevailed.

He jerked away from me and headed back toward 36C. I

caught him and wrapped his head under my arm. I squeezed until his feet got wobbly. I dragged him to the elevator and held him in the headlock until the old creaky elevator made it up to the third floor landing. I released him, pushed him inside. "Go home," I said. "I see you around here again, I'm going to work you over with this." I waved my flashlight at him in the way I'd waved the beheading ax at Clive Renseller. The man, who was about half my size, wasn't impressed. Sometimes mild threats work. Most of the time, when there are life and death issues at stake, they don't. Verna banging Lonnie Caldwell was definitely a life-and-death issue for this guy. I expected to see him again.

I crossed the street—Margarita time. The owner of the DMZ, Güero Odonaju, was there. He sometimes comes to the bar on Fridays to make sure the sad drunks it caters to haven't burned the place down. Güero is a Mexican of Irish descent. His great-great grandfather, an Irish dock worker from Boston, fought on the Mexican side in the war of 1846. He didn't protest the war on the political grounds Thoreau did—America's shoddy venture into imperialism. For him, the war was just another instance of Protestants robbing, raping, and pillaging Catholics. He left Boston and fought for Mexico in the *los patricios* battalion. *Patricio,* after the Irish saint, was a term of honor given to the Irish soldiers who joined Mexico's cause. He was wounded twice, once at Vera Cruz and again at the battle of Reseca de la Palma. After the war he settled in Monterrey and changed the spelling of his name from O'Donahue to the Spanish-compatible Odonaju. Güero's family lived for generations in Monterrey until his father and mother emigrated to Texas, after Güero was born. He grew up in San Antonio and went to college in Austin, where he eventually earned a Ph.D. in English literature at the

49

University of Texas. He taught at our local university for five years before getting fired for knocking out one of his colleagues in a committee meeting. The colleague said things that were unacceptable to someone with a Mexican sense of honor. The man felt he could safely insult his colleagues because the expectation of physical retaliation in a university setting is as likely as the expectation of being served lemonade in hell. Güero knocked the man out with one punch. Güero was an assistant professor without tenure. The man he hit was a full-professor in line for a deanship. No contest. No one backed Güero, even though, privately, the other professors who were present in the meeting applauded Güero's action. The bastard had it coming, they agreed, but when the university carried out its investigation of the incident, Güero's supporters were silent. A lawsuit against Güero was pending.

"Qué tal, viejo," he said. Spanish was Güero's first language, but English was his love. He could quote from memory all of the soliloquies from the plays of Shakespeare.

"Viejo yourself," I said. He was younger than me, but not by much.

I joined him at his table. He was going over the books, making sure his bartenders hadn't stolen too much from him. He signaled the man on duty and a minute later I had my salt-free margarita in front of me. Güero was drinking a Peregrino with a twist of lime.

"Salud," he said.

I raised my drink. *"Salud."*

"You look like a warmed-over turd," he said. "What've you been doing, staying up reading books for Chrissakes? Reality TV getting too intellectual for you?"

"I was up late, entertaining an unexpected guest."

"A woman? Jesus, Uri, you finally getting laid? Here I

thought you were carrying the torch for what's her name, the Nazi."

"Gert. And no, no woman."

"Gertrude with the hiking boots, as I remember. Gertrude with the blond ponytail and the legs that went up to here." He stroked his adam's apple. "Poster girl for Hitler's Aryan breeding stock. Is she still around? I'd like to pay my respects." He winked at me.

Güero had the body of a middleweight boxer turned heavyweight by age. His kinked hair was the rusty red of iodine. He had intense blue eyes that didn't just look at you, they drilled you. He would have made a first string interrogator for the Spanish Inquisition.

"She's long gone," I said, lifting my glass.

"You sound like a grieving man. Go get her, if you want her," he said.

"I don't want her. We weren't exactly on good terms."

He stared at me, then shrugged. "Hey, here's the latest," he said. He pulled a sheet of paper out from under his books. "'After reviewing the play,'" he read, 'the ball was placed on the forty yard line.' That's a good one, right? And it came from the lips of a professional announcer. *Que la chingada,* nobody can use the goddamned English language anymore. Here's another one, this time from PBS, about the guy who died on Mount Everest: 'Suffering from hypothermia, the mountain got the better of him.' Choice, huh?" He gave me his well-known smirk.

I shrugged. I couldn't get excited about grammar mistakes, especially when I wasn't sure what the mistakes were.

Güero regarded me with those searching eyes. "You're a sad man, Uri," he said. "It's your name. The name you get stuck with always has a history behind it. You get infected by that history. You know the historical baggage your name carries?"

I shook my head no. It was a lie. My father, Sam Walkinghorse, read from the Bible every night when we were kids. I often dozed off listening to his heavy drone, but when he said my name, Uriah, I perked up and paid attention to the whole damned story of David, Uriah, and Bathsheba. I kept this bit of knowledge to myself. I don't know why. Maybe I was afraid of Uriah's fate becoming my fate, which, in a minor league way, with variations, it did. But more than likely my dumb-show was just spite—all those years of Bible stories instead of TV made me claim ignorance of the Book. I was ignorant of my own culture, knowledgeable about the ancient tribes of Israel. I make up for it now. I've got a 32-inch Sony along with a four-head VCR and DVD player. My cable hook-up has 105 channels provided free of charge by The Baron Arms. I watch Nick at Nite to catch up on the sitcoms I missed when I was a kid. I Love Lucy, Leave it to Beaver, Ozzie and Harriet—that early world of baffled husbands and baffling wives.

"Uriah was one of King David's top warriors," Güero continued. He was in his professor mode. I didn't stop him. "He was married to Bathsheba. King David sent him off to war, setting him up to be slaughtered. Uriah, the loyal soldier, was fucked over by his own king because the king wanted to squeeze Bathsheba's *chichis* under the sheets. Bathsheba had already been screwing David, in fact she was already carrying one of David's babies, but she didn't know he set up Uriah to eat an Ammonite spear. The *puta* was grateful to the king for picking up Uriah's domestic burden. A very sad story, maybe the saddest of all."

"I'm not sad," I said.

"Your sadness is inherited. Your folks intuited this when they named you. We always get the right names, the names we deserve, whether the people naming us know it or not. That's why blacks have all these invented names. It's a way of escaping history."

"My brother's name is Moses, and he's an unretrievable junky."

"He might prove out yet. *Mantenga la fe,* man. Don't give up on Moses. He may lead some spike riders out of the wilderness."

I wondered what kind of history the name Clive had behind it. Had to be a bitch of a story.

A party of six burst into the DMZ out of the windblown street. The regulars at the bar squinted into the bright doorway and at the three glittering couples crowding through it. They found a table and shouted orders to the barkeep. They were Mexicans, rich Mexicans. The women were wearing leather jackets soft as baby skin and trimmed with silver fox and ermine. The men wore Armani suits under camel hair topcoats. They plunked down their cellphones before they shed their thousand-dollar coats. As soon as they sat down their cellphones began to chime. They swiveled away from each other and spoke Spanish softly into their guarded hands. I looked at Güero.

"Slumming," he said. "They're from Campestre, the city within a city, across the Rio."

"How can you tell?"

"That's where the money is. A lot of it."

"No offense, but what are they doing in this dump?"

Güero shrugged. "Like I said, slumming."

The women were sexually dynamic in their leathers and stilleto heels. The fur-trimmed jackets were ostentatious but justified since it was technically still spring and the weather still brisk. They looked around the bar with the disdain of royalty. The regulars at the bar hunched down over their drinks as if shielding their sadsack lives from the superior glare of the women. There was something unreal about the Mexicans—as if their finery and attitudes had been scripted. I caught the eye of one of the women. She didn't look away but her lips curled down and her nostrils flared a bit, as if she smelled something rank. She nudged the man she was with and he looked at me too.

I didn't cut my eyes deferentially away. It pissed me off to be looked at as if I were a stain on their patio. I raised my drink. *"Salud,* fuckheads," I mouthed.

"Watch yourself, cowboy," Güero said. "I know you're sitting on a powder keg, but you don't want to get cheeky with the ruling class."

I looked at him. "What's that supposed to mean?"

"What's *what* supposed to mean?"

"That crack about a powder keg."

"That's where you're sitting, *compa.* You don't think so? That makes you all the more dangerous. To yourself, I mean. These people are connected, if you understand me."

"You mean they're *narcotraficantes.*"

"Or *familia.* Family most likely. They look a little too spoiled to be the heavies."

The woman and her boyfriend were staring at me again. The boyfriend got up and came over. "Is there something about us that interests you, *señor?*" His words were civil, but his manner was insulting. He had a silky black beard, trimmed by a barber.

I looked at Güero. He shook his head slightly. I took the hint. "Nope," I said. "I'm just a *turista.* Everything interests me, you know?" My voice was mild, but my eyes were saying, *I could break you in half, you prick.* He went back to his table. He said something to the others.

They all had a good laugh.

54

NINE

Let me run something by you," I said, feeling the need to unburden. "I met some people here a few weeks ago, a hot looking babe and a fat guy with a red Mohawk. The Mohawk flashed a bankroll."

"Oh shit, don't tell me you got involved with those creeps," Güero said.

"You know them?"

"They've been here a few times. Looking for geeks and goons or whatever else looks interesting. They recruited you, *verdad?*" The notion made him laugh. "And you went along?" He slapped the table and roared. "Too much, man! Never underestimate the power of loneliness. What did you do for them—strangle some loser so he could have an apnea orgasm while the bitch kicked a spike heel up his ass?"

I was sorry I'd said anything. Blame the second margarita. I liked Güero, but he enjoyed the mistakes of others a little too much.

"Geeks and goons," I said, feeling melancholy.

"You would be the goon type. They pay you well?"

"Two hundred."

"Not adequate for that kind of work, *ése*. Make them give you five next time. Minimum wage for goons these days." He laughed again.

I needed to back out of this conversation before I said too much. "Thanks," I said. "That's what I wanted to know."

He gave me his long, quizzical look. "That's what you wanted to run by me? You wanted to know the going rate for goons?"

"Right." Güero knew I was lying. He didn't press it.

I crossed Mesa Street to my apartment. There were two messages on my answering machine. One was from Jillian: "Why haven't you cashed your checks, Mr. Walkinghorse? Is my money tainted or something? Call me. I may need you again." Her voice was honey-sweet, inviting. The way she said "need" triggered a brief fantasy. My libido was grabbing at straws.

The second message was from my sister Zipporah: "Mom needs us. Daddy's acting dicier than ever. We know what's wrong now—and it's bad—but he won't do anything about it. Call me."

Need seemed to be the watchword for the day. I hoped Jillian's need was strictly carnal. But I called Zipporah first.

"Meet me at the house around five, will you?" she said. "Dad's freaking out Mother."

"The house" meant the house where we all grew up, Sam and Maggie Walkinghorse's house on the east side of town—a house of additions, emendations, and afterthoughts—built over a fifty-year span by Sam Walkinghorse. Sam was one-eighth Indian and proud of it. He hated his father, a brutal drunk, and took the name of his paternal great grandfather, a Miniconjou Sioux warrior and eventual shaman who was killed at Wounded Knee when he was an old man.

The original one-bedroom shotgun house, out of which all the other wings and shed-like additions grew, was narrow and long. It had been built in an empty half-acre of desert by Sam and two friends after they came home from the Pacific war in 1945. As the number of Walkinghorses grew, Sam tacked on the additions giving more thought to necessity than to style. From the air, the house must have looked like a train derailment—long boxes abutting one another at right, and not-so-right, angles. Sam had only one priority, and that was to keep a roof over his expanding family, not to be the showplace of the county. Maggie, in an attempt to pretty-up the place, painted each addition a different color, the brighter the better, until the orange, green, purple, and yellow boxes blazed—a wood and stucco rainbow that had crashed to earth. The house now sat like a nervous breakdown among the sane and reasonable cottages that over the decades had filled up the desert around it as the streets and roads changed from caliche to gravel to asphalt. The neighbors referred to the Walkinghorse house as The Nightmare on East San Pablo Street.

"I'll be there, Zip," I said.

"It's only you and me, Uri. Isaiah can't shed his UPS truck till six. He might come out later. And Zack's in Brussels, making deals." She didn't mention Moses, who was living in a junkie hovel downtown. He wouldn't come out to the house, and Sam wouldn't welcome him if he did.

Zipporah is black, as is Isaiah. Zacharias is Korean. Moses and I are ethnically challenged. When I look in the mirror I think: Italian? Sephardic Jew? Black Irish? Slav? But settle on nothing. Moses thinks he's Irish, but he looks French fur-trapper Indian to me, except for his pale eyes which are German intense. None of this matters of course. We're all Walkinghorses, all the children of Sam and Maggie, and that one indelible fact makes race and ethnicity an irrelevance.

I called Jillian next. A man answered the phone. I double-checked the number I'd written down. "Is Jillian Renseller there?" I asked.

"Why do you want to know?" the man said.

"I'm returning her call, " I said.

"I see. And to whom am I speaking?"

He was a "to whom" type. A professor or butler, or just an asshole.

"Walkinghorse," I said, not wanting to waste more breath on this guy.

He muffled the phone with his hand and said something. The background noise—faint music, strings and flutes—came back as he passed the phone to Jillian. "Uri?" she said.

"I've got two thousand dollars of your money," I said.

"Cash the checks, sweetie," she said. "The money is yours."

"We agreed on five hundred."

"No, we agreed on five hundred a week."

"Forever? I don't think so."

She covered the phone with her hand and said something to the "to whom" guy. Then, "Why don't you come over. We'll discuss the arrangement in detail. I think you misunderstood me."

"What's this about needing me again?" I said. "You've got another dead husband to move?"

"Don't joke, Uri. I'm a grieving widow." She sounded like Imelda Marcos grieving over a pair of misplaced pumps. "Can you drive over here now? Please say you can. We need to talk."

The honeyed lure of her voice spoke to my own need. "No," I said. "I've got to go to see my folks. Maybe later tonight, though."

"I'll come to your place, then. It's that old motel on lower Mesa, isn't it?"

"The Baron Arms. Number 41A, take the elevator. I should be home by ten."

I parked in front of the old house. Zipporah came out to meet me. "It's loony tunes in there, Uri," she said. "Mom's

58

got her hands full. Daddy's rappin' with Jesus in the kitchen."

Zipporah is tall and lean and very dark. She was wearing jeans and sandals, and a T-shirt that showed her long, stringy arm muscles. Her tightly kinked close-cropped hair had a jagged streak of white that passed over the top of her skull, from forehead to nape. I hadn't seen her in months. We hugged, then she stepped back, holding me at arm's length. "My little brother looks down. Wife trouble again?"

"Gert left me, Zip. Ran off with a race car driver. But that's not it. I mean, we hadn't been getting along for months."

"Oh honey, that's too bad. Tell you the truth, though, I never liked her much anyway. She always acted kind of uppity, you know what I'm saying? Wore those fuck-me boots on those skinny white legs and acted like she *never* had to clean the funk out of her moneymaker." She squeezed my biceps. "Still getting ready for the jailhouse, I see."

I got a kick out of Zipporah talking street. None of us grew up talking any kind of jive, but Zip was the principal of a tough middle-school on the gang-thick east side and felt she needed to stay even with the kids, which was probably a losing effort.

We went inside. Maggie was standing in the middle of the front room, holding a pair of slippers. She gave me a quick, distracted hug. She looked her age–seventy-five–which was unusual since she always had looked ten years younger than she was. She was plump but her face was drawn and her white hair was lank, as if she'd been sick in bed for weeks. "These are for Jesus," she said, holding up the slippers. "He's in the kitchen. Daddy said it's too cold on our linoleum for wounded feet. He's in his shroud and He's cold from the damp tomb." I looked at Zipporah. She rolled her eyes a bit, but not so that Maggie noticed.

"He's going to die inside a month unless we get him into a hospital," Zipporah said to me.

"Will you try to talk to him?" Maggie said. "He acts like he doesn't even hear me. I don't know what I'm going to do." She quaked a bit and tears spilled from her faded blue eyes.

"We'll take care of it, Mama," Zipporah said.

"Will you, honey? Oh, thank God. I just can't deal with it any more."

"What's wrong with him, Mom?" I said. I'd been out of touch with Sam and Maggie for some time. Whenever I came home, Sam got on my case about my life-style—aimless, pointless, and Godless. Sam didn't hide his disappointment in what I'd become. My Mr. Westside of 1983 trophy, my only accomplishment, didn't impress him. Whenever I showed up he preached hellfire at me. So I tended to steer clear of the old Walkinghorse homestead.

Isaiah and Zipporah were Sam's favorites. They had their own families, led normal lives, and went to church. Maggie hadn't called me about Sam, which meant that she had probably given up on me, too. I had become, by default, an outsider.

"Brain tumor," Zipporah said. "A big malignancy in the right cerebral hemisphere. They think gamma radiation might get it. But they need him in the hospital now, not a month from now."

I took the slippers from Maggie and led the way. The windowless kitchen was illuminated by a grease-coated globe mounted in the ceiling. The globe surrendered enough light to keep you from sticking a fork in your eye, but if you wanted to read the newspaper you needed to strap on a miner's lamp.

The long Formica-and-chrome table where we took our meals—all seven of us—was bare, except for a liter of red wine. Sam had a glass and another glass sat on the opposite side of the table from him. Both were full. Neither Sam nor Jesus were drinking. The glasses were crystal, Maggie's best–the wine was ceremonial.

"Hi, Daddy," Zipporah said. "Watchya up to?"

Sam Walkinghorse looked formidable enough to have been a Biblical character himself, or a Sioux holy man. He glowered at Zipporah but said nothing. He was tall and gaunt, and though he was sick, his stern glare still had the power to shrivel opposition.

He'd lost a lot of weight. Knobs of bone poked against his ratty old bathrobe. His white hair hadn't been cut for weeks, and his untrimmed eyebrows looked like tangles of wild grass hanging from the bony crags above his sunken eyes.

"My children," he said, explaining us to the hallucination across the table. "They are of different races."

In spite of myself, I looked for a reaction from the dim air opposite Sam. "Here's the slippers, Pop," I said.

"Set them down under that chair," he said, pointing across the table. "The Son of God's feet are cold and still bleeding."

"We're going to take you to Providence Memorial," Zipporah said.

"I'm with Providence now, Zipporah," he said. "I have no need to go anywhere."

"I mean Providence Memorial hospital. You've got a brain tumor the size of a walnut, Daddy."

"I know what I have. I'm not a fool."

"It will kill you, if you don't let them operate," Zipporah said.

"We all owe God a death," he said. "I've been living on borrowed time since Iwo Jima. I'm eighty-one years old. How much time does a man need?"

I tried another tactic: "You're being damned selfish, Pop. Think of us. Think of Mother."

He looked at me as if I was not his son but a hostile intruder. "Doors are open to me," he said. "They have been swung wide. I can see Him, and beyond Him I can see the lawns of Heaven itself. You can call it a tumor if you want to, but it is a gift not a disease. If you could only see what I see."

"Daddy, you're going to the hospital one way or another," Zipporah said. She was pretty formidable herself.

The old man shook his head sadly. "You see?" he said to the vacant chair. "You take in unwanted babies, you save them from desperate circumstances, and now they would close the door on You. They would cast You out as if You were a symptom. But never mind them. You were going to tell me, sir, before we were interrupted, why Your wounds have not healed in two-thousand years."

Zipporah and I both looked across the table at the empty chair almost expectantly.

"I'm taking a break," I whispered to Zipporah.

I went back to the front room. Maggie was sitting on the couch. The TV set was on but she wasn't watching it. I sat next to her. It was time for Jeopardy. I picked up the remote and clicked my way to channel 4.

"Did you give Jesus the slippers, son?" Maggie said.

"There isn't any Jesus in there, Mom," I said. I put my arm around her. Outsider or not, I still loved her. She was the kindest person I knew.

She looked bewildered. "I know that," she said. "Of course I know Jesus is not sitting in our kitchen."

"You don't sound too convinced."

"No, no. I know it's because of the tumor in his brain. That's why he goes on and on about Jesus and the lawns of heaven. I know that." It was clear she was struggling against Sam's power to convince.

The TV picture was crossed with wavy lines. "What's wrong with the TV, Mom?"

"It just started doing that," she said. She glanced at the kitchen door. I knew what she was thinking: Could a mere tumor-caused hallucination have the power to scramble a TV picture with zebra stripes?

"Sunspots," I said, giving her a rational explanation she could hold on to. "The weather guy warned about it. Happens every ten years or so. Plays hell with satellites."

I surfed through the channels. They were all cross-hatched with patterns of black lines. Maybe this tumor-Jesus hated TV and had influence over the sun. I watched Jeopardy through the wavy lines anyway.

When I got up to leave, she put her hand on mine. "Uriah, go see Moses. I'm so worried about him."

"Mose is long gone, Mom."

Her eyes filled with tears and I was sorry I'd said it. "I won't believe that," she said. "You go talk to him. Tell him to come home. I'll take care of him until he's better." She thought of heroin addiction as something you caught, like the flu.

I promised to see him anyway.

TEN

I was sitting out on the steps of the front porch when Isaiah drove into the yard. He hoisted himself out of his car. Isaiah weighed at least two-eighty and was all of six-feet-five. He could have been a retired NFL lineman. In fact, he'd played offensive tackle for the local University until he blew a knee. Yet he drove a VW bug, an old one. He was too big for his clothes, too. His UPS uniform was stressed at the seams. His pants looked like they were stuffed with barrels.

Isaiah and I shared a room growing up, but we were always somewhat formal with each other. He squeezed the blood out of my hand in his cigar-thick fingers. "What's up with the old man, Uriah?" he said.

"Sam won't go to the hospital. He's got Jesus in there backing him up."

Isaiah narrowed his eyes, studying me. He was a religious man and didn't find snide remarks from agnostics humorous.

"It's the tumor," I said. "It's giving him hallucinations. Zipporah says he'll be dead in a month if he doesn't get it taken out."

"So what're we supposed to do? Carry him off to the hospital against his will? Nobody's gonna make Sam Walkinghorse do anything he won't do on his own." He took off his cap, mopped his ebony forehead with his thick forearm, let out a huge sigh.

Isaiah's birth-mother was a twenty-dollar working girl who

lived on the streets. She died in an emergency room, eight months pregnant. Her pimp hit her with a ball bat for skimming, fracturing her skull. Shock, crack cocaine, and the vein-dilating *mota,* had lowered her blood pressure to single-digits over single-digits. The ER people barely had time to pull Isaiah out of her belly via C-section before her morbidity affected him. Isaiah did this family research himself. He wanted to know exactly what his handicaps were before he started the game of getting along in life. I never wanted to know my own handicaps. When I was a kid I made up romantic tales that explained my parents' need to abandon me. My mythical parents were always noble sorts who, for justifiable reasons, were forced to give me up to the adoption agency. I knew the truth—if I ever found it—would not be inspirational. And who needs that? Isaiah did. He wanted to know what he started from so that he could build his life on whatever ashes he found.

It touched me, whenever I thought about it, how this morally upright and good-hearted giant had come out of that grim beginning. Isaiah was a deacon in his church, a community volunteer, a good husband, a patient father of six. It had to be genetics. Somewhere in his biological history, there had to be African nobility, a tribal chieftain or high-ranking warrior. On the DNA roulette wheel, that powerful gene turned up in his architecture, a gratuity of nature. Isaiah was two years my junior, but I always felt like a little brother, even when we were kids, and not just because of his size.

"It's Maggie who needs our help," I said. "She can't deal with the situation."

"I'll talk to him, but if he wants to die at home, I won't oppose him."

Isaiah went inside. A minute later Zipporah came out. She lit a cigarette. "Risking hellfire, sis," I said. If Sam saw her

65

lighting up, he'd have a stroke. Even though we were middle-aged, we became guilty teenagers—Isaiah excluded—in the vicinity of Sam. Maggie had that effect on us, too, but for different reasons. She was too soft-hearted and vulnerable to cross. We looked out for her by behaving ourselves. But now she was too distracted to notice Zipporah sneaking a quick smoke.

"Can't quit these damn things," Zipporah said. "Especially dealing with shit like this. The coffin nails help."

But she only took about half a dozen drags then crushed it out. Isaiah, after visiting with Sam for ten minutes or so, came out. "He's talking about you and Mose," he said. "He's trying to convince Jesus to let you off easy, putting the blame for your fouled-up lives on himself."

"Nice," I said. "He lumps me in with Moses, our beloved junky."

"He's praying for you, Uriah," Isaiah said, planting his heavy hand on my shoulder. "The old man means well."

"Let's hope Jesus is taking notes," I said.

"Go easy, brother," Isaiah said. "It may be the tumor causing it, but you never know. There's enough mystery left in the world to stump the experts."

"Oh for Chrissakes," I said. "Both you and Maggie are acting like kids in a haunted house. How about you, Zip? You buying into the metaphysics of Sam's brain tumor?"

She dodged the argument by lighting up another cigarette. "You act like you got the world by the tail, Uriah," Isaiah said. "But when it comes down to it, what do you believe in? Anything? A man's got to have some notion of his purpose."

"I believe in surfaces," I said, "not purposes."

Isaiah took his hand off my shoulder. "That kind of easy sass gets you nowhere."

"There's nowhere to go," I said.

66

He shook his big head, allowed himself a little grin. "If I believed that crap I'd put a .44 to my head."

"Surfaces are pretty interesting, Isaiah," I said.

"But they don't last."

"And that's bad?"

We looked away from each other, both of us unwilling to carry out a meaningless discussion of our belief systems. Isaiah had a fixed system, mine was flexible and not backed by conviction, but we could manage to irritate each other just the same when we got on the subject.

"So, Zack's in Brussels," I said in an effort to change the subject.

"Money humpeth money and begat more money," Zipporah said. "That's from Genesis, I believe."

We all laughed. Zack was a high-powered corporate lawyer. He worked with multi-national conglomerates and spent half his life in airplanes. Sam had a hard time approving of Zack's mammon-oriented life but he never sent back the checks that arrived each month from Zack's San Francisco bank. Sam and Maggie had no income other than their social security checks. Zack's monthly contributions kept them afloat.

ELEVEN

On the way home I had dinner at the H&H Carwash on Yandell Street. The carwash had a small café built into it. The 1950s style carwash had no automated machines, just men with high-pressure hoses, sponges and rags. The café served the best huevos rancheros on the planet. Even Julia Child raved about them on her only visit to El Paso. And for ten dollars more you got your car cleaned inside and out while you ate. I usually steer clear of high-caloric, high-fat Mexican food, but the huevos rancheros here were light as air. The paper-thin tortillas melted on your tongue. The dish was served without the typical lava of melted cheddar and heavily-larded refried beans. The potatoes were delicately fried in light oil and the salsa was an edible form of napalm. I ate here now and then when I figured I'd earned myself a treat or needed a good sweat. The afternoon at Sam and Maggie's house qualified on both counts.

I stopped at the DMZ hoping to find Güero—I wanted his take on Sam's lunacy and Isaiah's willingness to let it play itself out—but he wasn't there and the bar was almost deserted. I had a margarita anyway—another earned treat—then went across the street to The Baron Arms.

Jillian Renseller's Mercedes was parked in my slot. I parked next to her and got out. Both front doors of the Mercedes opened. Jillian got out on the passenger side. A no-neck lump of muscle in a wrinkled Walmart suit climbed out from behind the wheel.

Jillian was wearing black leggings, slingback sandals with four-inch heels, and a red cashmere cardigan unbuttoned past her cleavage. "You're late," she said. "Let's go up to your apartment. We need to work this out." She was dressed hot, but she was all business.

Her driver was over six feet and wide as a refrigerator. He had a tall square head spotted with warts. His friends, if he had any, probably called him Mr. Potato Head behind his back. He was leaning against the hood of the Mercedes, pumping himself up isometrically, making his cheap suit inflate like a cloth balloon. He'd sized me up as a fellow muscle guy and was now trying to make an impression. I wasn't impressed. He had too much gut—too much bacon fat in his diet, too much stupidity in his eyes. What hair he had was salon-cut: burr on top, the sides long and slicked back, no sideburns. It was thickest at the back of his head. A wedge of it, bleached white and stiff with spray, hung down past his collar like a dropped tailgate. His stylist had a sense of humor. Jillian didn't introduce me to him, so I figured he was a lackey of some kind.

"What's his role?" I said.

Mr. Potato Head tried to burn holes through my skull with his flat, close-set eyes. He was heavier and taller than me but looked badly out of shape. I could almost see the steak-grease caking his carotid arteries. He was breathing hard as if anticipating physical effort. I looked at his hands. They were big, but their bigness was exaggerated by walnut-sized knuckles, which looked as if they'd been broken more than once.

"Forbes is my driver," she said. "I don't like to drive into this part of town alone, especially on weekends. The Mercedes attracts too much attention."

Forbes? Even her hired help had Fortune Five Hundred names. I nodded to Forbes. He didn't nod back but his jaw muscles lumped.

We took the elevator up to my floor. I unlocked my door and let her in.

She looked around at my four walls, the mini-range and mini-fridge, the big TV set that dwarfed the chest of drawers it sat on. She studied the motel art on the wall behind the bed: seagulls gliding above the foaming green breakers, circa 1950–a good year for cornball impressionism. No one had bothered to take it down. Then she saw my poster of Schwartzenegger–a shot of young Arnold jogging on Muscle Beach, a naked blond straddling his neck, his big hands gripping her thighs. Jillian smiled. "Cute place," she said.

"I like it," I said.

"No need to be defensive," she said.

"Someone calls your place cute, you get defensive."

"But it *is* cute. The little kitchenette, the plastic furniture, those wonderfully cheesy pictures. It's all of a piece. Sometimes I wish I could live this simply, without any ostentation at all."

"That's easy," I said. "Give all your money away to charity. Living without ostentation is one of the perks of poverty."

She put her hand on my arm. I flexed. "It's not as easy as you might think," she said.

"What? Living simply or giving your money away?" Her nails dug into my arm just enough to tickle.

"Money is a leash. The more you have the shorter it gets. Large fortunes tend to control their owners. You wouldn't know about that."

All this was preliminary to something. I wasn't in any hurry to press the issue. She crossed her arms under her breasts and toured my three-hundred-square-foot palace. She opened my tiny fridge and studied my stock of canola, olive, and flax seed oils. She examined my tofu, my meatless hamburger patties, my free-range eggs.

"What's this stuff?" she said, holding up a bottle of morinda citrifolia.

"It's from Hawaii. A remedy."

"Remedy? Are you ailing, hon?"

"It's a preventative. Keeps you in the pink."

"You definitely look in the pink," she said.

She examined the canned food on my shelves, looked into my door-less closet, tested the bed with the flat of her hand. "Oh, this bed is *terrible*," she said. "Your back must ache constantly."

"If I could afford it, I'd get a Posturepedic."

"You *can* afford it, dear," she said. "You have two thousand dollars, and more is coming."

"That's what we need to talk about, isn't it?"

"No, we don't. All you have to do is cash the checks. The money is yours, as we agreed."

"That wasn't the agreement."

"I'm sure we agreed to five hundred a week."

"I'm sure we didn't."

She sat on the bed. "Okay, let's say we didn't. Why do you have a problem with getting unearned money?"

"It's never unearned," I said.

"I'm not asking you to do anything for it. As far as I'm concerned, our business is finished."

She took my hand and pulled me down next to her. I didn't wait for another invitation. I kissed her. It was a hungry kiss. "Undress me," she said.

I did. With trembling hands.

"Are you normal–sexually, I mean?" she said unzipping my pants and reaching in.

"What's normal?" I said.

Afterward, in the shower, she said, "I feel so tiny next to you."

My shower stall is bigger than my kitchen. A tourist-attracting feature of this old motel was its spacious showers with built-in seats. At one time they were advertised, on a no longer existing marquee, as "Roman Baths." The showers were big enough for merry travelers to play short-court handball.

I felt like a merry traveler. I picked her up and set her on my shoulders, like the girl in the Arnold poster. "Whee!" she said, her head grazing the ceiling.

We fucked again, Comanche style–like horses–under the driving water. There's no tenderness or romance in Comanche style fucking, no face-to-face communion of souls. It's stone-age fucking, two anonymous, hormone-driven bodies caught in a mandate of flesh. She came hard.

I felt her cervix throb. She screamed, the scream dying to gasping sobs, and when we finally collapsed on the hard tiles the water had turned cold and our knees were chafed enough to bleed.

"You're brutal," she said.

"Sorry. I didn't mean to be."

"No–I mean I got into it. You surprised me."

"I surprised myself," I said, remembering her ragged sobs, how they covered my own strangled-back vocalizations. I'd been too long without.

"You're a passionate man, Walkinghorse," she said.

I shrugged. Other people define us. We're a bundle of opinions by the time we're lowered into the grave. The real truth gets buried with us.

I made a pot of coffee and we sat at my little table next to the apartment's only window. I could see Mr. Potato Head down in the parking lot, pacing back and forth in front of the Mercedes. It was a chilly night and he was blowing into his cupped hands and glaring up at my window every now and then, thinking how he'd like to be up here pulping my head against the floor.

I waved at him. It was a kindly wave. I felt peaceful, even benevolent, having been given the only effective antidote to testosterone poisoning.

"So, you'll cash the checks, honey?" Jillian said.

The "honey" got to me—that echo of domestic affection. "I don't know why it's important to you," I said, "but, yeah, okay, I'll cash them." I would have taken a suitcase full of money from her at that point.

I felt bought.

In my present condition, it wasn't an altogether bad feeling.

She put her hand in mine. "Wonderful," she said, and her eyes were wonderful with promises I hoped she would keep.

TWELVE

Mose lived in The Regency, a half-abandoned apartment building owned by a slumlord who lived in a commune of millionaires in the red-rock landscapes of Sedona, Arizona. The building was located on the north bank of the Rio Grande in the oldest section of the city often referred to as Junktown because of its embedded population of addicts. The Regency had seen better days. In the long ago past it had been a fine Edwardian single-family mansion but had been converted in the 1940s into a working-class apartment complex. Its current state of unsalvageable degeneration began in the 60s. Twenty one-room apartments honeycombed the old structure. Marginally functional people lived in the occupied ones— junkies, crackheads, huffers: the zombie citizens of our fair city. The unoccupied apartments had been stripped of appliances, window shades, and fixtures. The bare plaster walls were webbed with graffiti and cratered by random fits of spastic zombie rage. Only the occupied apartments had actual doors. The building had been condemned years ago, but the owner had won an indefinite stay of execution from the city fathers by making vague promises to rehabilitate it as a historical landmark.

I knocked on Mose's door, then kept knocking.

After a few minutes a cranky voice I recognized said, "Fuck off! *Vete a la chingada!*"

"Mose? It's me, Uri."

Another long silence followed as he sorted out the reasons why I would be at his door.

I heard bolts slide in their casings, chains rattle. Finally the door creaked open. Mose was in his underwear. His pale legs and arms were thin as dowels. His greasy gray hair, streaked yellow by the sun, hung stiffly past his shoulders. He held a sawed-off Louisville Slugger in his hand, two-feet of white ash, the handle wrapped in electrician's tape for grip. Mose was a few years older than me, close to fifty by now, but he looked seventy.

"I thought you were that khat-chewing raghead from downstairs. I was going to brain the fanatic with this." He leaned the weapon against the door jamb. "Who talked you into coming here? The old man?"

"Sam's probably dying," I said. "Maggie asked me to drop by."

"Sam's going to his reward, is he? He's worked hard for it. They'll give him an upscale crib upstairs."

"You're breaking Maggie's heart, you moron."

"Nice seeing you again, *mi hermano.*"

He stepped back, I stepped in. The decor was junkie-spartan: a table, two chairs, a hot plate on the counter next to a rusty sink, some paraphernalia on the counter—surgical tubing, spoons, a small butane blowtorch. The apartment's single window was covered with a gray army blanket. A swayback iron bed hugged a wall. There was a woman in it. She was unconscious.

"Who's your girlfriend?" I said.

"Maria. She's my partner."

"She looks pretty bad."

This made him smile. The smile made him cough. "Shit, we all look *bad*. That's the trade-off. Feel good, look bad."

"You don't exactly look like you feel good. You look like cat puke."

"Your perception, my brother. Most of the time I'm knocking on heaven's door, like the man says."

There was a laptop computer on the table. It was turned on. I sat down in front of it. "What's all this, Mose? They got a junkie chat room now?"

"You think you're joking, bro."

The page on the screen said, *Best Confections Now.* Below this title was a menu of candy selections: Rock Candy. Taffy. Cordials. Orange Sticks. Almond Roca. Mint Creams.

"It's a web site for hypes," Mose said. "In code, of course. Best *Connections* would've been flaunting."

"They can do that? Sell dope on-line?"

"They can sell anything on-line, bro, from babies to senators. Don't you read the newspapers?"

I guess my sigh was audible.

"When did you get so uptight, man? Don't you remember how we used to party when we were kids? We smoked *grifa,* even dropped windowpane if my memory serves. Six hundred mike tabs, wasn't it?"

"I dropped acid *once,* Mose. The worst fucking day of my life. I thought my brain was in terminal meltdown."

"I loved the shit. I toured the unfallen world, man. I was in Eden."

I got up and walked over to the iron bed. Maria was on her back. An army blanket, like the one on the window, was pulled up to her neck. Her eyes were sightless black behind the slitted lids. Her breathing didn't make the blanket move. I touched her face. It was cold.

"Jesus, Mose. This girl is *dead.*"

"We're all dead, man. *Life* is the shadow play. We're dead before we're born, dead after we die, suckered by the grand illusion in between. Dead is the rule and Thanantos is king."

"Fuck that, Mose. Maria is *dead.*"

I pulled the blanket off the body. She was wearing a message-bearing tee shirt, nothing else. The tee shirt said:

> Wine me
> Dine me
> 69 me

A fun-lover's slogan. This girl didn't look like she'd ever had fun. Her thin, shapeless legs were ice. The bed was damp below her waist. The smell made my stomach lurch.

"No way," Mose said weakly.

"Way, brother. She's gone."

He stood up too quickly, dropped to his haunches, then rolled over onto his back. He made small noises. I couldn't tell if he was grieving or laughing. Laughing, I decided.

He pushed himself up to a sitting position. "She pulls this *shit* on me," he said. "Like I am supposed to *deal* with it. News flash, Maria Guadalupe–I *can't* fucking deal with it, you bookin' out on me like this."

The junky world is simple. Me and my needle. All the rest is interference or help. He looked up at me, his eyes asking for help. He'd worked himself up, and now he'd worked himself back down, quick as a yo-yo. "Put her in one of the empty places, Uri," he said calmly. "Can you do that for me? I can't lift my dick these days. I'm kinda out of shape."

Moving the dead seemed to be my new role in life. I almost smiled. "Okay, Mose."

"The cops don't care squat about dead junkies. No one's going to come ripping down doors asking questions."

"I said okay. I'll move her."

I picked her up out of the bed. She couldn't have weighed

more than ninety pounds. Up close she wasn't so girlish. She looked more like a weathered forty-year-old. Maybe older. Her long silky black hair was deceptive. The crisp skin around her eyes and lips was cracked and flecked with sores. She made me think of mummies—all parchment and dust.

I carried her to an empty apartment down the hall and laid her down gently. The dead deserve some respect, regardless how useless their lives had been.

The empty apartment had been one of The Regency's best. A bay window gave a fine view of Juárez across the Rio Grande. An occupant in 1911 would have been able to watch Pancho Villa's muzzle-loading McGinty cannons shell the barricaded government forces. These old buildings facing south had been pocked with stray rifle and machine gun fire during that revolution—so viewing the war from the neutral side of the border was not entirely free of risk. Which made the spectacle all the more thrilling.

I went back to Mose's room. He was seated at the table, working the laptop as if nothing unusual had happened.

"I'm going to have to find another partner," he said. His loss was practical, not emotional. "I can't raise enough bread on my own. Maria Guadalupe was *good*. Her real name is Rusty Odegaard, farm girl from Idaho. Her folks wouldn't give her permission to get an abortion, so she came here to get one where the abortion laws are less primitive. She subsequently fell among unsavory characters." He chuckled a bit at this. "I got her to dye her hair black so she could pass for a Mexican." He rummaged through a stack of cardboard under the table and came up with a painted sign:

My Niños Need Food
Please Won't You Help?
May Jesus Give You
A Place In Heaven

"She brought in two, three hundred a day working the freeway exits," Mose said. "The out-of-towners think they're in the third world, so they get to feel righteous by forking over a fist full of dollars."

He pulled another cardboard sign from the stack. "This one's mine."

Homeless Vet
Crippled By War
Will Work For Food
God Bless You

"It's getting a little stale," he admitted. "There must be a couple of hundred guys my age out there doing the fucked-up homeless vet gig. Sometimes I'm Nam, other times Desert Storm. I did Panama once. Depends on how old I feel. I use a cane, sometimes a crutch. I borrowed a wheelchair once and scored big time, all slumped in like a quad."

Mose wasn't a veteran of anything. He hadn't even been a Boy Scout.

"I'm going to get you cleaned up, Mose. Even if it kills you."

"Don't do me any favors, brother. I like my lifestyle."

"I won't be doing it for you, asshole. I'll be doing it for Maggie."

He turned from his computer screen and regarded me for a long moment. "And that makes sense to you, right?"

"Yeah, it makes sense to me."

The door swung open. Maria Guadalupe a.k.a. Rusty Odegaard wobbled in. "What the fuck you trying to do," the pissed-off ghost said, "get rid of me? Who put me in that fucking empty crib?"

She made her way to the kitchen sink. She tied a tourniquet around her upper arm using surgical tubing, lit the butane blowtorch, dug into a heroin-packed baggie with a soup spoon, added a few drops of bottled spring water, applied blue flame to the underside of the spoon, sucked up the liquefied black tar into a syringe, then injected the shit into what was left of the median cubital vein threading the inside of her elbow. She managed this in less than a minute, efficient as an executive secretary. Rusty Odegaard: Idaho farm girl zombie resurrected to another day in hell. Shock, then embarrassment, moved me. "Jesus Christ," I said.

Mose took all this in stride. "Don't freak, Uri," he said. "She looks half dead most of the time. You made an honest mistake. Maria Guadalupe forgives all when fixed."

Fixed, she came back to us, serene and almost healthy looking. "What's up on the home page, Mose?" she said.

"We got to be in the parking lot on the north side of the Santa Fe bridge at six o'clock tomorrow. A joker who calls himself *subcomandante* Sam Houston will be there with a quarter. *Mierda primera.*"

Mose shut down the laptop and stood up. "Get dressed Rusty," he said. "We got to go to work. You feeling up to doing the Mesa Street exit off I-10? I'll take a bus over to the eastside and work the Cielo mall."

"I don't get it," I said.

"He doesn't get it," Rusty Odegaard said. She smiled and the smile gave life to her face. If you didn't notice the scabs and wear-marks she was almost beautiful, this woman who could step in and out of death's shadow and smile about it.

"What don't you get, my brother?" Mose said.

"If you make your connections on the internet, then the drug enforcement people also have access to it, don't they?

They're not so incompetent they can't see through that dumbass coding system you people use."

"Oh, man," Mose groaned. "He *really* doesn't get it."

Maria Guadalupe, still smiling, said, *"Ai chingao, que estúpido."*

"It's Big Business, Uri," Mose said. "Blue suits sitting around mahogany tables talking profit margins and distribution contracts. The kingpin who died after plastic surgery—if you can believe *that* shit—grossed more in one year than General Motors. He told the Mexican president, get off my back or I'll move out of Mexico. His point—the Mexican economy would collapse without the drug trade. You can look it up in *Time,* for Chrissakes. When that kind of money's involved folks get bought. Watchdogs on both sides of the Rio fight each other to get on the payroll. The DEA people *need* the traffickers. The heavier the traffic, the more bucks they can suck into the bureaucracy. Bureaucracies exist for themselves, not for whatever fucking excuse they were created for. Didn't you *know* that? You think just *Mexico* is corrupt?"

I shrugged, ignoring his superior smile. I hated to claim innocence. Güero would probably laugh at me.

"It's not just junk and coke and *mota,* you know. The big pharmaceutical companies send truckloads of uppers, downers and tranks to little Mexican villages on the border. Do they ask *why* a little retailer in a town of two or three thousand wants twenty million caps of schedule two thrusters? Fuck no, they don't. They *know* why. The stuff comes right back home, at street prices. Uri, for Chrissakes, the *Bayer* company invented heroin a hundred years ago. Why do you think the feds bust homegrown crank labs?—because the big pharmaceutical guys won't put up with amateur competition. You getting the picture? Grow up, my brother. It's all medicine, and medicine is big business, and big business rules. Get used to it."

An addict's justification. If the world is that rotten, then why not stay loaded? "Let's hear it for the junky's Ralph Nader," I said, but he was getting ready for the street and didn't respond.

I tried another angle. "Why don't you write all this down and send it to Maggie? Make her believe that wrecking your life is really the act of an anti-establishment hero?"

He laughed, then coughed. "How *you* doin' my brother? You still mainlining steroids? Made your first million yet? Got a good job with benefits and a retirement plan?"

"Fuck you, Mose."

"Love ya too, *carnalito.*"

They got dressed—Rusty put on a peasant blouse, a long Mexican skirt and beat-up huaraches for her feet. She wrapped a doll in a blanket and held it close to her flat dry chest, as if suckling it—and became Maria Guadalupe, mother of starving children.

Mose pulled on a pair of camouflage pants and a sweatshirt. He laced up a pair of jump boots. He looked like a vet who had seen too much of war to survive peace. His ravaged face fit the part.

He stopped at the door and looked back. "When you see Maggie again, and I know that might be a while since you're not exactly her fair-haired boy either—tell her I'm happy as a clam in warm mud. Tell her none of this has anything to do with her or Sam. I was just cut out for the fucked life. Okay?"

I nodded.

"Take care of your own ass, *carnalito*," he said. "And make sure the door is locked when you leave."

THIRTEEN

I didn't cash the checks, or the one that came on the following Friday, thinking Jillian might come back to twist my arm again. Her brand of arm-twisting could be addictive.

Saturday morning, I met my work-out partner, Ray Fuentes, at the Y. "You're getting *obese,* man," Ray said when he saw me in my Spandex workout trunks.

"Two pounds. That's not obese."

In fact, I'd gained ten pounds in the last couple of months. I was up to 235, an all time high. But I couldn't see where I was carrying it.

Ray caught me checking myself out in a wall mirror. "It's in your ass," he said. "You got the *nalgas* of a Russian power-lifter. You been stacking 'roids again?"

"Fuck you, Ray," I said. I picked up a free weight, a barbell loaded with 220 pounds and did ten curls, cheating a bit on form.

I'd used anabolic steroids years ago, when I competed. My upper arms were stuck at eighteen inches. A few months of steroids blew them up to twenty. With twenty-inch biceps I was a contender. I used the drugs until Lyle Alzedo, the football player, came down with what was probably steroid-induced brain cancer. One red flag like that is enough.

"You going for bulk, Uri?" Ray said. "What's up with the grunt work?"

Fuentes is a former Mr. West Texas. At five-eight and 198, he could have been cut from marble by an ancient Greek. I doubt he had three-percent body fat. He could bench press twice his body weight. I once spotted for him when he did 405 pounds, ten reps. Didn't even grit his teeth.

I did a hundred sit-ups on the slant-board, then spent an hour on the Universal Gym. When I finished my routine I was hungry for huevos rancheros at the H&H, but I skipped lunch. I needed to drop that ten pounds. Vanity rules.

When I got home, Jillian's Mercedes was parked in my slot. I took the stairs three at a time, but it wasn't Jillian waiting for me outside my door. It was Mr. Potato Head and a friend. They were sitting in canvas folding chairs they'd dragged up from the edge of the defunct swimming pool. The pool hasn't had water in it since 1973, but the tenants still take the sun on the concrete apron that surrounds it. When Forbes and his friend saw me they stood up. I got my key out and opened the door. I invited them in.

"You're basically stupid," Forbes said.

"For letting you in?" I said.

"That, too." He was wearing the same Walmart suit. It had more wrinkles now, plus a mustard stain on the sleeve. His gut wouldn't let him close the coat. I could smell his landfill breath from three feet away: last night's bourbon, today's onion and pastrami sandwich. His voice surprised me; it was high, a sandy forceless alto: His thick stumpy neck didn't leave much space for vocal cords. They produced a high dry squeak when he talked.

His friend was pint-sized but harder looking. He wasn't a lifter but I figured he was the kind of thug who didn't need a lot of muscle to mess you up. He was short and lean. Except for his flat nose, which had been broken more than once, he had a delicate hollow-cheeked face. His eyes were obscure behind narrow wraparound shades which didn't hide the thin scars that traced through his eyebrows. A silky mustache darkened his upper lip. He was wearing a Frank Sinatra pork-pie hat and a Hawaiian shirt that could hurt your eyes in sunlight. His shoes were steel-toe wingtips and his pants were baggy with big pockets–a nod to the zoot suit glory days. When I was in the army a buddy of mine tangled with a mini-thug like this and came away with a broken collarbone, fractured cheekbone, minus four front teeth, and he pissed blood for a week. Little doesn't mean easy.

"This is one big fat maricón, Forbes. I will give him a *chingazo* upside his head, to start the party," he said, grinning. His short teeth looked like hammered tin. He gave "Forbes" a Spanish twist, pronouncing it *"For*-base."

"Don't pee on your shoes, Victor," Forbes said. "We need to give this muff diver here a chance to cooperate. We don't want to hurt him unnecessarily."

"We *do,* man," Victor said. *"El jefe* would have no *problemas* planting his *chorizito* along with his other body parts in *el desierto."* He patted something in his baggy pocket. Then he added, sober as a network news anchor, *"La vida en la frontera*– it has never been cheaper." It wasn't exactly a bulletin: Life on the border has always been cheap.

Victor was primed. He was savoring this preliminary small talk. He was born to hurt; he'd done it a lot and he liked his job. The white scars that slanted through his eyebrows gave him away: he was an ex-boxer. A welterweight who now took his pleasure in taking big guys down. I could read that much in his eyes, right through the shades. He hadn't moved or made any kind of threatening gesture, but Forbes held up a hand anyway, as if to hold him back. Victor worried me more than Forbes did. Forbes was just a hired goon who took the job because the pay was good and he liked the working conditions. Victor on the other hand would do this kind of work for bullfight tickets.

85

"She put out for you, man," Forbes said. "Don't you have any sense of honor? She fucked you so you'd cash the checks. You can't *process* that? You got a problem with choice pussy and free money?" He grinned as if an amusing thought occurred to him. "Whoa, you got it into your head she thinks your shit is *candy?* What's up with you? You got a mental defect?"

"I thought she fucked me because she was horny," I said. "Her old man couldn't satisfy her. He liked getting spanked better than getting laid."

Forbes took a step toward me, his eyes cranked wide with menace. A thick finger stabbed out of his balled up fist. He aimed it at my face. "Now *see?*" he said, his voice rising to an even higher pitch. "Bad-mouthing the dead–that's exactly the kind of dumbfuck talk that keeps you from being a success. Losers use dumbfuck talk because they think they know something. But losers don't know shit. That's why they're losers. It's like Catch 22. The more they think they know the dumber they are." He labored through this exercise in logic, his forehead crimped by the ponderous machinery behind it.

"You've been reading my resume," I said.

I was acting cool but I wasn't. My heart had picked up extra beats and my hands were sweating. "You want to tell me why my not taking Mrs. Renseller's money is pissing off this *jefe* of yours?"

"You figure it out," Forbes said. "You're the smartass here, it shouldn't be too hard for a genius like you to process."

I moved so that my bed was between me and them. Their boss–their *jefe*–wasn't Jillian. It was someone else, someone who had something to lose because of my not cashing Jillian's checks–which made no sense.

"I'm not so hot at taking orders," I said. "Four years in the

86

army and I never made corporal. I got busted twice for insubordination. Two Article 15 court martials inside a year. Seems like I've got this attitude problem—tell me one thing, I do the opposite."

"Thanks for sharing," Forbes said, "but I don't think anyone's going to make a primetime series based on your personality disorder." He grinned. He was on a roll, proud of his spontaneous displays of wit.

Victor took the thing he'd been patting out of his pants, the secret behind his confident grin—brass knuckles. "This *pendejo's* got a big mouth," he said. "I want to fuck him up a little, *For*-base." The brass knuckles were equipped with a small crescent-shaped blade on the pinkie finger end. Hit and slash. Break a face then slice it open, all in one sweet move. Forbes had started to come around the bed, but now he stopped. "It's Forbes, goddammit, Victor. Not fucking *For*-base. Jesus!"

"No importa," Victor said. "You're so fucking uptight, man. You should loosen up. You should take a vacation in *Mejico,* eat *camerones* in Guymas, eat *tampiqueña* in Guadalajara, eat *panochita* in Puebla. *For*-base sounds cooler than Forbes. Forbes sounds like a dog puking when you say it in Anglo. Foh-orbs." He belched out the Anglo O sounds, over and over. "Foh-orbs, Foh-orbs, Foh-orbs."

Forbes's lightning wit failed him. "Real funny, Mellado," he said. "How about I pronounce your name Mela-Due, Anglo style? Sounds better than fucking may-*yah*-doe."

While they argued about how they should pronounce each others' name, I reached down and pulled one of the Thomas Inch dumbells from under the bed and flung it like a fat black dart at Victor Mellado's head. The 135 pound mass of cast iron drove his head into the wall behind him. The impact sounded like a small detonation. He dropped like a heavy rag doll.

Forbes watched Victor's collapse long enough for me to pick up the other Thomas Inch. I flipped it at his head, end over end, but I missed. The first cast iron sphere hit him in the chest, the second in the gut. Air exploded from his lungs. He tried to refill them but couldn't. He went to his knees. I picked up a loose freeweight dumbbell bar and waited for him to get up but he stayed down. His eyes danced with panic. He tried to take something out of his coat. I didn't let him. I kicked him. He toppled over, his soundless mouth working. I started a back-swing with the steel freeweight bar, then stopped myself. He was finished. I didn't need a corpse in my apartment.

I relieved him of the gun he'd been reaching for–a cheap .32 caliber belly gun–popped open the loading gate and shook out the bullets. I tossed the gun on my bed. My hands were shaking.

"You broke my fucking sternum," he whispered.

"You're lucky," I said, my voice unsteady as my hands. Maybe Güero was right about me. I'd wanted to spill Mr. Potato Head's brains all over my floor. Almost did.

Victor was still out. I slipped the brass knuckles off his hand and tossed it into my kitchen garbage can. Victor had a bad concussion. The whites of his eyes were red.

I helped Forbes to his feet. "Can you drive?" I said.

He nodded. He looked sheepish as a kicked dog. I carried Victor and we all went down to the Mercedes. I loaded Victor into the back seat. Forbes eased himself behind the wheel, his hand over his heart as if he was about to recite The Pledge of Allegiance. "Make your burial arrangements, shithead," he whispered. "You're fucked meat."

"Don't get your shorts bunched up," I said. "After you get

Victor to a hospital, tell your *jefe* you convinced me. I'll cash the checks. I'll cash them Monday. You guys did your job. Tell your boss, whoever the fuck he is, that you beat the shit out of me. You took a few *chingazos* yourself, but in the end you made me see the light. You able to process that, *Forbase*? Make yourself look good at my expense."

He glared at me but there was too much acute pain in his eyes for it to have the effect he wanted. He started the car and managed to steer it out of the parking lot.

I went back to my apartment. My hands were still shaking. Too much adrenaline. I picked up my Thomas Inch dumbbells and did biceps curls until my arms burned and my hands steadied.

There were two messages on my answering machine. The first one was from Rosie Hildebrand. "My tureen don't work again, hotshot. Water spilled over the lip. How're we supposed to use it with water over the lip? Maybe you would like to have yourself a big fat lawsuit. I've got a second cousin who is a lawyer right here in town. His name is Eldon Gary Lofton. Look him up in the Yellow Pages and you'll see I'm not just jokin' around with you."

I imagined drowning Rosie in her toilet bowl. Head held down in the stinking swamp until she stopped twitching. I imagined Bill Hildebrand offering me a glass of Vin Rose in thanks.

The second message was from Jillian. "Don't be at home today. I'm sorry, hon, but they're going to hurt you. Please please *please* cash the checks. I'll try to call them off."

Thanks much, bitch, I thought.

I calmed down a bit. A least she'd tried to warn me.

Maybe she thought my shit was candy after all.

Maybe she loved me.

I could live with that fantasy for a while.

FOURTEEN

I came into the DMZ out of a brisk wind that had sandstorm potential. Güero was lecturing to a table of slump-shouldered drunks. He was born to teach. Losing his job at the university didn't stop him.

"Addiction is a natural state for human beings," he said. "Everyone is addicted to something. You hombres choose alcohol because you have failed to become addicted to the patterns of behavior society rewards."

The drunks nodded, their heads suddenly weighted with this liberating idea. "Fucken society makes you shit carpet tacks," one of the drunks said bitterly.

"And finally it doesn't matter," Güero said. "It all comes to nothing. As Democritus said twenty-five centuries ago, nothing exists except atoms and empty space, everything else is opinion."

"Yeah, but opinion is what busts your balls," another drunk said. The other drunks nodded in sullen agreement, murmuring rebelliously against the social order responsible for their condition.

"Look at it this way: the past once it has happened, is carved in stone. The future, since it grows out of the carved-in-stone past, and will then become the past, is also carved in stone. The relationship is obvious, isn't it? So, what does opinion have to do with it? The game has always been fixed."

"Maybe the past is a springboard into a bunch of possible futures," I said. "You learn from past mistakes, then you correct them. Sorting through the opinions of others is how

90

you figure out your own opinions. That seems even more obvious."

Güero looked up, grinning. "This big gringo is one to talk," he said. "He can't keep a wife or job, but his vanity is intact. What are you doing here so early, *ése?*"

"I came to hear your bullshit. Wouldn't miss it for the world."

"Say that part again about springboards," one of the drunks said, frowning with effort.

"It's the difference between gringo capitalist philosophy," Güero said, "and the older and far more realistic Mexican way of understanding the world. Put your money on the Mexican way, my friends, it will make things easier for you."

I pulled up a chair.

"That's why Mexico is in such great shape," I said.

"*Sí,* we have no Disney World, no space program, no ICBMs, and we have never produced a Frederick Winslow Taylor. We are a happy people though. There's not much happiness evident in gringo America. We know how to have a fiesta; we know how to throw one hell of a *pachanga.* We're the world's top-ranked party animals. "

"Who's this Winslow guy?" a drunk asked. "He that baby-raping serial killer they caught last week?"

"He's the gringo who invented time-and-motion studies," Güero said. "He was the first efficiency expert—the tight-assed *pendejo* who watches you operate your machine with a stop-watch in his hand. He catches you taking five seconds to scratch your balls, he writes you up. You need to go take a piss?—forget about it. Before you know it, you are replaced by the ball-less men who never sweat or need to scratch, and then you are out on the street drinking wine with all the other unemployed ball-scratchers."

One of the drunks made an elaborate show of scratching

his balls. "I love Mexican women," he said, his red eyes glazing over with nostalgia. "I got my first real taste in Chihuahua city."

"It was probably your last, too," said another drunk.

The drunks started a conversation of their own on the merits of Mexican versus American women, and Güero and I retreated to the bar. My saltless margarita was ready for me. It was too early but I was in need.

"Something's on your mind," Güero said.

I told him about Forbes and Victor. Güero whistled between his teeth. "Do you know who these people work for?" he said.

I shook my head. "They just called him *el jefe.*"

"The boss man. Could be anyone. Who have you insulted lately?"

"Besides you? No one."

I couldn't tell him about Jillian Renseller and her dead husband. But even if I could, it wouldn't clear anything up. Jillian didn't send Forbes and Victor after me, I was sure of that. But then who did? And why was my not cashing Jillian's checks important to them?

"Is it about money, then?" Güero said, as if my thoughts were visible. "Do you have some bad debts?"

I felt comfortable talking to Güero. He was a good man to have on your side in a brawl, but this wasn't as simple as a brawl. I knew I could trust him, but I couldn't tell him more. I needed to change the subject. "Then there's my brother," I said.

"The UPS man, the rich lawyer, or the junky?"

"Moses. I need to get him into a de-tox program he can't walk away from. You know of anything like that?"

"Does he want to get clean?"

"Hell no he doesn't."

"Then don't waste your time, *ése*. He's living his life the way he wants to live it. You can't fight that. I meant what I said, addiction is natural. For Chrissakes, there are mountain goats that addict themselves to a hallucinogenic lichen that grows on rocks above ten thousand feet. They ruin their teeth gnawing on it and eventually starve to death because they can no longer browse on vegetation, but eating isn't the number one priority. The head-trip is more important than the consequences of ruining their incisors."

"You're probably right, but I'm going to do it for Maggie's sake."

"You may kill him for Maggie's sake." Güero gave me his inquisitional stare, then said, "There's a place up in the Black Mountains, eighty miles from here. It's been compared to Alcatraz Island. It's in the wilderness—very difficult to walk away from. It's called La Xanadu."

"Sounds Aztec. I like it."

"It's from Coleridge, the junkie Brit poet. You read him in high school. Laudanum junky. Died of constipation. Couldn't shit, but kept chugging down laudanum, the great constipator."

"Can I put Mose in there without his consent?"

"It's kind of a maverick outfit. They operate barely within the law. But the state bureaucracy tacitly approves. People have been sticking their messed-up family members into La Xanadu for years. Some state bigshot committed his son and saved his life, so the story goes. So no one messes with their protocols. They give 'consent' a somewhat flexible definition."

One of the drunks wandered over to the bar. He punched my arm with his feeble fist to get my attention. "Hey stud," he said. "If the past is stone how can it be a springboard? Answer me that. How in hell can *stone* be a springboard, goddammit?"

"You're right," I said. "It can't. You're fucked. Nothing's going to change for you."

His unfocused eyes were glassy. "Hah. I thought so. You had me goin' there for a minute, but I'm a lot smarter than I look."

I thanked Güero for the information, then started for the door. "Wait," he said. "I've got a good one for you." He pulled a newspaper clipping from his shirt pocket. "Listen to this. It's about that retard they executed down at Huntsville. 'Even though he was mentally retarded, the governor refused a stay of execution.' Classic, huh? Straight out of the *Dallas Morning News*. It goes on the wall with the others."

The wall was almost solid with these grammar gaffs. Most ignored them; those who read them thought they were riddles. Only Güero cared. I didn't get this latest one, either. "I guess grammar mistakes aren't carved in stone," I said, acting otherwise.

"Everything's carved in stone. But grammar isn't like history," he said. "It's the way we make sense of history—past, present, and future. Without grammar cognition is not possible. They keep dismantling the language, we'll be back in caves, pronto."

I wondered—almost aloud—if there was anyone left on the planet who was actually sane. I decided there wasn't. Insanity is the price you pay for the gift of consciousness. I thanked him again and headed out.

The world outside the bar had turned gray. The brisk wind had become a gale. It screamed out of the New Mexican desert. The air was full of sand fine as pumice. From the DMZ parking lot I couldn't see across the street to The Baron Arms. I ducked into my car and rolled the windows up tight. My teeth were already gritty and my eyes stung. I sneezed a few times and started the engine. I turned on my headlights and crept across Mesa, hoping a bus didn't slam into me.

The wind, shaped by the open halls, airshafts, and stairwells of the old motel, moaned like voices summoned from hell. I fought it on the way to my apartment, hugging the walls so I wouldn't be pitched over the balcony rail by a sudden gust. It yanked my door free of my hand and slammed it into the apartment wall, denting the sheetrock. I put my shoulder into the door to close it. I could still feel the grit sting my face as it lasered through the crack between the door and the jamb.

There was a message on my machine but I didn't want to hear it. I didn't want to deal with shit-plugged toilets, roach invasions, or referee domestic chaos.

Forbes's gun was still on my bed, along with its bullets. I scooped them up and dumped them into my underwear drawer. There was a streak of blood where Victor's head had slid down the wall. I mopped it up with soapy water and paper towels. Arnold, the nude blonde riding his shoulders, seemed to be laughing at me. *Hey, scheiskopf,* he was saying. *Get a life!* The blonde agreed, the hot vertex of her thighs clamped to the back of his neck. Her laughing eyes were full of mischief.

I made a pot of coffee and sat at the table next to the window. A ridge of pumice made a perfect line across the sill. It was a tight window, but the desert is always ready to reclaim its dominion. I looked at the parking lot below. The cars were pastel ghosts of cars, silhouetted against the asphalt which was obliterated by patterns of moving sand.

By Güero's reckoning, my future looked bad. I wanted to believe I still had a rosy one. I rummaged in a box of text books under the table and came up with a slim monograph on abstract algebra. I hadn't taken a math class in five years.

I had two years before the statute of limitations ran out, after which I'd have to start grad school over again.

I looked at Galois' theory of equations: *"For every given field, an extension field has an associated group whose structure reveals information about the extension."* I wasn't able to call up enough stashed knowledge to understand what this meant. The following paragraphs and pages didn't make sense to me either. I was backsliding badly. I picked up a history of mathematics book and read an essay about Mohammed ibn Musa al-Khwarizmi, the man who invented algebra in 825 A.D. With the desert wind hammering the walls of my apartment it was somehow comforting to read about a man living under a sky full of sand twelve centuries ago who made a stellar contribution to the progress of civilization. Al-Khwarizmi had a future in a time when there wasn't a whole lot to look forward to.

If him, why not me? The heavyweight question of all time.

I punched "play message" on the answering machine. It wasn't a tenant complaint. It was Gert. Gert! Who I hadn't heard from since she bolted. "Uri, for godsakes, you're so over*due!* Judge Whitsall said you're supposed to send one-third of your pay to me. Did you lose my Lauderdale box number? Come on, honey, do the right thing, okay? I hope you're not still P.O.'d. It was for the best, you know. You're way smarter than me, mister! It wouldn't have worked out in the long run, you see that don't you? I wouldn't ask like this, I know you're good for it, but Trey's engine man quit and we need the money right away for a new guy he's looking at. I think you owe me around nine thousand give or take a hundred, I didn't do the math but send nine and we'll call it even. I don't want to notify the superior court clerk in charge of deadbeats, don't make me do that, hon. Okay? What good would you being in jail do any of us? Hey, you watch for the red Camaro at the Gatorade 125 on ESPN. That'll be Trey. You know what his motto is? 'Back off or crash!' It's so *ballsy!* But he might not make the field without a new engine man. So do your best, hon. Really, we need the money. Still love ya."

I dialed the Lauderdale number she left. Her answering machine picked up. "I'm not working, Gert," I said. "Haven't worked since you left. You get one-third of zero, hon. Okay?"

I took a shower. To scrub Gert out of my mind I visualized Jillian on her knees under the driving water. Looking back over her shoulder. Smiling. Her heart-shaped ass raised and receptive. The water-beaded ringlets.

Gert was gone.

I got dressed, then went back out into the punishing wind.

Visibility had gotten worse. The wind rocked my little Ford Escort on its tired springs as if a beefy couple in the back seat were humping their brains out.

I got into the car, started it, turned on the headlights, then headed north on Mesa for the Renseller's fairy tale estate. I needed some answers.

FIFTEEN

The gate was not only unlocked it was wide open. I drove up the steep slalom to the house. In the gray air the many-gabled Renseller mansion loomed huge and eerie, the fairy tale atmosphere gone gothic and sinister. There were two Mercedes, a Chevy Suburban, and a Lincoln parked in the drive, just short of the porte-cochere–Jillian's black sedan, a vintage 300SL Gullwing coupe, the big boxy Chevy, and a new Town Car. The big Lincoln had Mexican plates. They were D.F. plates–*Distrito Federal*–meaning it had been licensed in Mexico City. Jillian was having a gathering of some kind, which explained the open gate. I rang the bell six times before the door opened.

"Uri, what a surprise," she said. She was in silk lounging pajamas. Her feet were bare and there was a martini in her hand.

"Who's there, Jilly?" a man's voice asked from somewhere inside.

"Uriah Walkinghorse," she announced, stressing the syllables of my name for comic effect.

A gust caught the door and slammed it against the doorstop. Jillian's silk pajamas flapped frantically, like a flag in a hurricane. I stepped in and had to put my shoulder to the door to close it. The wind fought back, like a party-crashing drunk.

"Come join us," she said gaily. Her breath held the stink of vermouth. She was smiling in a loose, numb-lip way and her eyes were almost glassy. "I'm having a wee party." She took my arm and pulled me into the foyer. I had to adjust to her short, unsteady steps.

We went into the sitting room. Two men and a woman were seated around a glass-top table. One of the men, silver-haired and tanned, looked like a *GQ* model posing as a tennis pro. The other was a dignified-looking middle-aged Mexican. His hair was combed straight back. It was long enough to end in a matador's three-inch pigtail. He seemed friendly and aloof at the same time, as if he were enjoying himself as an observer, not a participant.

The tennis pro wore an eggshell yellow blazer over a black tee shirt. The crystal face of his thousand-dollar watch glinted with reflected light as he chopped rock expertly against the glass table with a gold-plated pen knife.

The woman snorted the line through a tightly rolled bill. "I love to suck blow past Ben Franklin's nose," she said. She opened the rolled bill and licked the residue dust off Ben Franklin's face. "I like to think the dirty old womanizer is getting a contact high from it. That's why I only use hundreds." She laughed at her own joke. She was a tall, strongly built woman in blue sweats and running shoes. She had butch-cut white-blonde hair and her tan was as deep as the tennis pro's but it had a scorched look to it, as if it had been applied with a blowtorch.

Both men smiled at the woman's joke, but they were distracted. They were studying me.

"Fernie," Jillian said to the Mexican. "This is my friend Uri Walkinghorse. He is *muy fuerte,* like Hulk Hogan." She held

99

my arm up as proof. It was an awkward moment. I felt like displayed meat.

Fernie stood up and extended his hand. Like most Mexicans he did not make his hand into a vise. A firm handshake does not imply strength of character to a Mexican. In fact, it may imply the opposite.

He was a slender man, about fifty. He possessed *elegance,* even though dressed casually in slacks and sport shirt. His brow furrowed with disapproval at Jillian's drunk introduction.

"El gusto es mío," he said formally.

"Igualmente," I said. He smiled at my poor pronunciation, but it was a pleasant smile with no detectable scorn in it. *"¿Estaba un matador, señor?"* I asked.

He only shrugged and held his hands out, palms up. I took that to mean, yes, he'd killed a few bulls, but hadn't made a career of it.

The blonde glanced up at me. *"Que chicotudo,"* she said, smiling. She had big healthy teeth, but her smile was not pleasant. "So this is our big bad stud muffin," she said. *"Ai chihuahua, madre de dios cuídeme!"* She spoke Spanish with a local accent. Her smile faded as she sized me up. She raised her eyebrows dismissively, then vacuumed a second line of coke into her brain.

The Mexican smiled apologetically, as if he were responsible for the woman's insulting manner. He had a receding hairline. His nose was aquiline, his eyes were blue. He was pure Iberian with no Indian blood in his veins. His ancestors stepped off the boat with Cortez and hadn't, in the succeeding centuries, taken Indian wives. In Mexico's caste system, men such as these were the movers and shakers.

"You're the good scout who helped Jilly move Clive's body, right?" said the silver-haired tennis pro. "You did us all a favor, Mr. Walkinghorse." He spoke without looking at me. I recognized his voice. He was the "to whom" guy.

"This is Lenny Trebeaux," Jillian said to me. "Lenny was Clive's right hand man at the bank."

"What's he doing here, Jilly?" Trebeaux said. He studied me as he said this.

"Why does he want to know?" I asked Jillian, returning the insult by looking at him as I spoke to her.

Jillian handed me a drink. "Be nice, boys," she said to both of us.

"Could I talk to you for a minute?" I said to Jillian.

She excused herself and we went down a hallway to the paneled room where Teddy Roosevelt's gunsmith hung over the fireplace mantle, glaring into a future he could not have imagined.

She closed the double doors and kissed me. "I'm a wee bit bombed," she said.

"I noticed."

She pushed herself away from me, both hands on my chest. "You're not going to be a shit, are you? We're celebrating Lenny's promotion. He's taking over as interim bank president. Is that all right with you? Did you cash the checks?"

"I want to know why the checks are so important. Your driver and his friend Victor were going to bust me up because of them."

"I'm sorry about that. I tried to warn you. But you promised to cash them. You've *got* to do it, Uri. Why are you being so difficult?" She pressed herself against me and gave me a sloppy kiss. Her active gin-washed tongue was cold and bitter.

She broke off the kiss abruptly. "Don't you want money? Everybody wants money. What's wrong with you?"

"I told Forbes and Victor I'd cash the checks."

"You told *me* you'd cash them. But you didn't. You lied to me."

She slipped her hand into my pants. "I've got a bad crush on you, you liar," she said.

"Who's the matador?" I said.

"Fernando Solís Davila." She sang the syllables of his name. Her hand went deeper.

"Oh my," she said, touching wood. "Too bad I have company."

"What is . . . does Fernando Solís Davila do?" I was having trouble talking. Her hand was moving.

"He is and does money."

I gripped her forearm, eased her hand from my pants. "What's going on, Jillian? Are you paying me to fuck you?"

She slapped me. When I didn't respond she slapped me harder. When I didn't respond again, she started crying.

"Trouble in here?" said the tennis pro. He came in, his *GQ* face fixed in a hard-guy frown, his tanned jaw rigid. I tried hard to be impressed.

"We're discussing money," she said, wiping tears from her cheeks with the heel of her hand.

"What, you didn't give him enough?" he said. "He wants more, is that it?"

"I don't want any," I said. "I want to know why I'm being paid."

"It was a bad idea in the first place," he said. He stepped next to Jillian and put his arm around her. "What have you told him, Jilly?"

"Not a thing. I begged him to cash the checks, that's all."

She looked confused as the gin-fueled playfulness abandoned her. Her contours fit against the tennis pro in a familiar way I didn't like. Easy to see that Lenny Trebeaux had been— or still was—her lover. Clive wouldn't have protested.

Trebeaux was Clive's right hand man in more ways than one. Jillian let Clive satisfy his needs; Clive let Jillian satisfy hers. I wanted to break something into small pieces. The tennis pro's body came to mind.

"We've given you all the slack we can, Walkinghorse," he said. He stepped away from Jillian and pointed a manicured finger at me. "You don't know what you're dealing with."

I grabbed his pretty finger and bent it backward. He dropped to his knees. His teeth were bared, his eyes shut tight against the pain. "Enlighten me, Trebeaux. Tell me what I'm dealing with."

"With more, perhaps, than a man in your position should desire," said Fernando Solís Davila.

He and the tall, butch-cut blonde woman came into the room. I let Lenny go. Something about Solís commanded respect. He had no nervous tics, no inner turbulence. Easy to imagine him standing in the sun-bright plaza de toros shaking a red cape at a pissed-off thousand pound killing machine.

"May I introduce Clara Howler," Solís said, nodding at the blonde. "Clara is my body guard when I travel en *el norte*. I do not mind her occasional use of the *coca*. If anything, it makes her . . . *mas vigilante* . . . more *alert*." His tone was genteel and mesmerizing, his articulation precise.

"El jefe," I said, mostly to myself.

I nodded to Clara Howler, acknowledging her position of importance. She smiled and stepped toward me. Like a card-carrying moron I extended my hand. She took the opportunity to kick me in the balls hard enough to make my jaw snap shut. "Too late, cowboy," she said. "You should have taken the money."

I doubled over like a folding chair, started to puke. She kicked me again—a sweeping roundhouse kick to the head. I heard Jillian moan. *"No!* Not this!" she said. "I told you I didn't want this!"

I remember the floor rising up to meet my face. I remember Clara Howler's knee coming up to meet my jaw. I remember flopping on my back and rolling into chair legs.

I remember Lenny Trebeaux grunting as he contributed soccer-style sidewinder kicks to my kidneys, his face cramped with concentration, as if he were aiming penalty kicks at a goalie.

And I remember Jillian's tear-streaked face hovering over mine before blackness swallowed it.

SIXTEEN

The unchanging sandstone sky seemed painted on the wide windows of the Suburban. I tried counting miles by counting power poles. But when we entered an area not serviced by electric power I lost my only calculating tool. The red-brown sky—birdless, cloudless—gave no hint of motion.

I was on the back deck, in my shorts, tied up like a bull-dogged calf. The road, if we were on a road, was studded with rocks and cratered by potholes. My head knocked the steel deck with the shock of each rise and fall.

A hot shrapnel of pain ricocheted inside the red walls of my skull. I puked a few times, managed not to drown in it. My tongue was cut—I'd bitten it when Clara drove her knee into my jaw. My jaw wasn't broken. A couple of teeth were loose, but I could yawn wide and bite down hard without doing damage to myself. My throbbing balls felt big as cantaloupes and my ribs and kidneys ached from Trebeaux's penalty shots.

I was tied with unbreakable tape at the ankles and knees. My wrists were tied behind my back with the same kind of tape—strapping tape, the kind that will hold your fenders on in a pinch. My hands and feet ached from a lack of circulation. I kept falling asleep, which probably meant I had a concussion. I'd never been knocked out cold before. Clara Howler was a piece of work.

The radio was turned up loud. *Narcocorridas* thumped in my brain—songs celebrating the drug trade. The driver—Clara—sang along. *Narcocorridas* were hip-hopped *norteña* music, the music of northern Mexico. The Mexican government was trying to suppress the *narcocorridas,* but their popularity was enormous. They were even played in New Mexico, west Texas, and the non-yuppie backwaters of Arizona.

> *me gusta la coca*
> me gusta la mota
> no me ache achi
> aqui en Sinaloa

"Yo cowboy, you awake back there?" Clara yelled.

"Fuck you," I said but I knew she couldn't hear me above the hammering music. My voice creaked like a rusty hinge. The salt from swallowed blood didn't help.

"You're going on a little vacation, *büey.* Last trip of your useless life, cowboy. *Me gusta la coca, me gusta la mota, no me ache achi, aqui en Sinaloa. . . ."*

Before I went back to sleep, I thought, Is that where we are, in Sinaloa? It didn't seem likely. Not with the sandstorm still blowing, the sky raining grit.

I slipped in and out of dream, awake and sleeping. In one dream I was a baby in a buggy. Except I didn't fit. My feet were outside and my head was over an edge and Mama, singing in Spanish, flat didn't give a damn.

Mama wasn't Maggie. Mama was a blonde Amazon with chopped hair. This dream had the three-dimensional feel of reality. I was in a wheelbarrow, a big one, a contractor's wheelbarrow, head hanging over the front wheel, legs draped over the back. Very real. I ran my cut tongue over my teeth and the hurt was still there.

Clara Howler pushed me over rough tiles. Above, the sun was a blood red knot in a gray haze. The driving wind riffled Clara's blond butch-cut. She was wearing shades and gritting her teeth and singing in melodic grunts.

"You're a load, Walkinghorse," she said. "We'll put you on a diet, feed you some Mexican Slim Fast."

She mopped the sweat from her forehead then resumed her labor. I heard a small dog bark. A man said something in Spanish. A woman answered him, and he laughed. We were somewhere in the desert. Definitely not Sinaloa, but probably Mexico. Though it could have been anywhere in the Chihuahuan desert, which included parts of west Texas and New Mexico.

"Ayúdame, Rigoberto. ¿Dónde están Rudy y Luis?" Clara Howler said.

"Fueron al pueblo. The cockfights, *señorita."*

"Shit-birds," she said. "Will they be back tonight?"

Rigoberto laughed. *"Ni con mucho,"* he said. No chance.

Rigoberto was a short, heavily scarred man. He and Clara dragged me into a small adobe house in a compound of half a dozen such houses and dropped me on a cot. I heard a slat crack. Clara went back out and returned with a gym bag. She opened it and took out a syringe case. She filled the syringe from a vial and injected something into my arm without much finesse. "For your pain, Walkinghorse. It's Be Kind To Animals week." I figured it was morphine from the instant drift it put in my head. A drift away from pain and reality, which seemed to be the same thing.

"Sweet dreams," Clara said.

When I woke next I was not on the cot. A leg iron with a

ten-foot chain attached anchored me to a wall. The chain was linked to an iron ring cemented between the adobe bricks. Another length of chain, about eighteen inches long, connected my ankles. The thin mattress I was on had no bed under it, just the red Saltillo tiles of the floor. An army blanket was folded neatly at one end of the mattress. A port-a-potty had been thoughtfully set up within the radius of my chain.

I touched my face. I had a two-day beard. A clay pitcher of water sat next to the mattress, but no food. Clara liked her jokes. Her idea of Mexican Slim Fast was the local water.

It was late afternoon. The winds had died. I crawled to a window, my chains clinking festively behind me. Outside there was nothing but the other adobe houses of the compound and, beyond them, the desert. Someone had taken the trouble to put in some landscaping along the edges the houses–Spanish dagger, nopal, ocotillo, the long sensual stalks of pampas grass. The houses were arranged in a horseshoe pattern that enclosed a tiled courtyard. About a hundred yards away, at the open end of the horseshoe, a white rag flapped on the end of a long bamboo pole. The pole was almost bent double by the wind.

The view from the window was south. The horizon was flat. What I could see gave no hint of my whereabouts. I could have been anywhere. I didn't see the Suburban, Clara, or the men who evidently worked for her. Nothing. I spent the rest of the afternoon trying to pull the chain out of the wall. The ring it was connected to had a thick shaft that most likely went all the way through the adobe and held to the outside wall by a flange.

The ring was about two feet off the floor. I laid on my back, planted both feet on the bricks, and pulled. I didn't feel strong. My quadriceps felt mealy as foam rubber–as if their only function was to pad my bones. They had no tone, no explosive strength. But even if I could have put three or four hundred pounds of tension on the chain it wouldn't have been enough. It would probably take three or four tons to do the job. The effort gave me a pounding headache.

I slept again, and when I woke it was dark. I heard a vehicle grinding toward the house in low gear. I could tell by the sound it wasn't the Suburban, more likely a small pick-up, an old one at that. Both doors of the truck slammed, but only one man came in. It wasn't Rigoberto. This guy was twice Rigoberto's size. He lit a candle and set it on a table. The table and its two chairs were the room's only furniture other than the cot I'd been dumped on.

I smelled food. The big guy went back out, then came back in. He was at least three-hundred pounds but had the footfalls of a cat. *"Algo a comer,"* he said, his voice deep and rough, as if his vocal cords were cut from shoe leather. "Something for you to eat," he translated. He put a styrofoam take-out box on the table.

"Gracias," I said. *"Me gusta la comida Mexicana."*

This made him laugh. "Damn good thing," he said. "Not a lot of Burger Kings around here."

He seemed friendly enough. "Around where?" I asked.

He didn't answer. He went out, his huge mass gliding on those silent feet. The truck started, and drove off. Only one door had slammed—one guy had been left behind.

I crawled to the table, pulled myself up into the chair and opened the box of food. Three tacos, refried beans, rice, a small cup of *pico de gallo*. An almost cold bottle of Negra Modelo beer sat next to the food. I twisted off the cap and took a long drink. I chugged half the bottle. Either they were going to kill me and were being kind to the condemned man, or they were just being kind. I chose the latter explanation. I was hungry enough to eat *menudo* made of roadkill. The heavily larded tortillas and beans were like manna. I chewed greedily through the pain.

I woke up stiff and cold. I pulled the army blanket around my shoulders and crawled to the window. The sun was up and the sky was blue. The sandstorm, which had been the leading edge of a cold front, had blown itself out. An Indian woman came in with breakfast. Tortillas, *menudo,* coffee. I thanked her but she wasn't interested in pleasantries and wouldn't meet my eyes. The tortillas were still warm from the skillet, the *menudo* vile, and the coffee, in a styrofoam cup, was hot. I ate with gusto, with no thought of what a steady diet of such food could do to my arteries. "Gracias, señora," I said again, but she kept her secret eyes averted.

Food and sleep made me stronger. I tried pulling the chain out of the wall again, but it didn't budge. I studied it. It was a little rusty, but had no weak links. The iron cuff around my ankle was tight and had a key-operated lock.

I considered my situation. Nothing made sense. I couldn't be important enough to anyone to make them take this much trouble with me. I was here, imprisoned—for what? For not cashing checks.

Forbes had said, "Figure it out."

I stretched out on the mattress and covered myself with the blanket. I decided the Indian woman wouldn't look at me because of superstition: It was dangerous to look a dead man in the eyes. He might take something of you with him on his way to hell. But maybe she was only embarrassed by the big gringo in his underwear.

I tried to sleep. When I stopped trying, I slept.

When I woke it was dark. Someone was in the house with me. A smokey candle burned on the table. Its flickering light made spastic shadows on the walls. I smelled warm tortillas and beans.

"Come here, handsome," Clara Howler said. "Have some chow."

I dragged my chain to the table and sat.

She looked me over. "You do have one hell of a body," she said. "I respect that. We *are* our bodies, aren't we?"

She was stoned. Her eyes glittered in the candle light. She was smiling but her teeth were hidden in shadow. I picked up a tortilla, filled it with beans, ate.

"Did I hurt you, hunky boy?" Her voice was mocking, but not unfriendly. She had her gym bag with her. She took something out of it. It winked in the candle's flickering light. A silver flask. She put it to her lips and swallowed. I smelled the smokey fumes of tequila. She passed the flask to me. I took a long thankful swallow, then another. It ran to my brain instantly.

"Thanks," I said.

She capped the flask. "They're going to take your meat-house down, Walkinghorse."

I looked blank. The tequila hit was too sweet to give up. I reached for the flask. She uncapped it and handed it back. I wanted to break her neck—I was grateful to her—I wanted to throw her down a flight of stairs—I wanted to kiss her hand. How do you handle yo-yo emotions? Let them ride.

"Meat-house," she said. "That's what my grammy called the body. She was from Liverpool. It's an old English term, goes back to the middle-ages. The old timers knew who and what they were. We've lost the knack. We live in a fantasy world, don't you think? No one thinks of himself as a fucking meat-house."

"Why?"

"Why what? Why don't people see themselves honestly?"

"No. Why are they going to kill me?"

"They don't need a reason. Death is a convenience. Do you know where you are?"

"No.'

"Outside of Samalayuca. Out in the desert. The desert makes a fine boneyard. There's hundreds of convenient kills out there."

"Hundreds?"

"Maybe thousands. There's a major war going on. You've got your head in the sand if you don't know that. But it's always been going on—intensified a bit the last decade or so. Wars need graveyards. Think of this one as the Arlington of the *narcotraficantes*." She laughed at this. She took a vial from her gym bag and dipped a tiny silver spoon into it. She held the loaded spoon to a nostril, pressed a finger against the other one, then sucked in the white powder. She crinkled her nose a bit to ward off a sneeze, then smiled. It was a nicer smile than the one she gave me at the Renseller's. "Damn!" she said. "I do love this shit."

"Why me?" I said. "I'm not involved with drug traffic."

She studied me for a few seconds, then passed the flask. She wasn't sharing her coke. "The fucked citizens have been asking 'Why me?' since day one. 'Why me, Jesus? Why fucking *me?*' You'd think by now they'd quit asking. *A la gente buena, sucedieron las cosas malas.*"

Bad things happen to good people—it came back to bite me. Christ, they were even saying it in Mexico. But maybe the Mexicans said it tongue-in-cheek.

"You speak Spanish like a native," I said.

She took the flask back. "I do a lot of things like a native," she said. "Stand up."

I didn't.

She took a small revolver and something else out of her bag. She pressed the barrel into my throat. I got up.

"Drop them shorts, cowboy," she said.

"Why?"

She pulled back the hammer to full cock. "This thing in your neck is why," she said. I took her very seriously. I knew what Clara Howler was capable of. I dropped my shorts.

"Turn around," she said, "and put your hands behind your back." She nudged the short hairs at the back of my neck with the gun barrel. The other thing she took out of her gym bag were handcuffs. She hooked me up. "You know the Spanish word for handcuffs? *Esposas.* Wives. Funny, huh? Gives you the Mexican pespective on marriage." She tapped my neck again with the gun. "Kneel down, Walkinghorse, as if you were getting ready to say your bed-time prayers."

I knelt. My heart picked up beats, my mouth went dry. I'd seen films of people being executed in this position. The bullet enters the back of the head and launches a gob of blood, bone, and brain as it exits the front. The victim pitches forward, usually into a ditch. A small caliber bullet might not go all the way through the skull, but it would go deep enough.

"What are you going to do?" I managed to ask.

"You got yourself caught in the wheels of a big mean machine, Walkinghorse," she said. "Stay kneeling, but touch the floor with your forehead."

The press of cool tiles against my skull was oddly comforting. I was in an awkward and embarrassing position—ass up, head down—but it wasn't the typical execution position. Which gave me foolish hope.

She touched my balls with the cold gun barrel. They shrank away from it. "I'm sorry I nailed you little guys," she said. "I don't like to make that particular kick, believe it or not. There's something intrinsically unsportsman-like about breaking a guy's eggs, don't you think?"

Crazy, she was crazy. I was bare-assed on my knees and a crazy woman was apologizing to my balls while tapping a gun barrel against them.

She reached between my thighs. She took my prick in her hand. "Tiny Tim," she said. She began to massage heat into it. She had outdoor hands, hard as leather. "Come on," she said, "say hello to mama, mister chubby." The brainless thing responded. But then I felt cold steel touch my sphincter.

"This little piece," she said, "is a Ruger .22. Not much in a firefight. But it's loaded with Stingers. Imagine the kind of mischief a .22 hollow-point mini-mag would do up your ass. Makes an intriguing picture, doesn't it?"

She kept stroking me and the brainless one kept rising to what it believed was an occasion. I didn't share its optimism. "Jesus Christ! Don't do it!" I said.

"I like religious men," she said, stroking harder.

She pushed the barrel in a full inch. I felt the raised front sight tear my sphincter, felt blood tickle my thigh.

"If you're going to kill me shoot me in the head, goddamnit," I said. My voice failed this bit of bravado. It cracked.

"You really want to die, tiger? Sorry, but I can't oblige. I'm not your scheduled executioner. Fernie's very particular about job assignments. Victor Mellado gets to do you—it's a Mexican revenge-code thing. But, hey, accidents happen. Bad things happen to good people."

A body spasm made me buck away from her. I couldn't help it, but it could have triggered the gun. "Be careful with that thing!" I said.

"Stay cool, big boy," she said. "The trigger spring needs a deliberate pull. I personally don't like hair triggers. It won't go off unless I want it to."

She laughed, then eased the gun barrel out—careful as a nurse removing a catheter. She turned me over. Somehow she'd managed to pull off her clothes. Her pubic hair was dyed purple and shaved into a rectangle the size of a dollar bill. She climbed on top of me and took me inside her. She had compact Amazon breasts, the dark nipples long and erect. Above me, her face was smiling with all its teeth. My cuffed wrists ground into the small of my back as she rode me. We came together, like old lovers, aware of each other's rhythms and twists.

She got up and dressed. "And you thought I was a dyke, didn't you?" she said.

"I still do." I sat up, hoping her sadistic need had run its course.

"You're half right. I've fucked your little friend."

"What little friend?"

"The one who's been standing between you and the grave."

I watched her lace up her running shoes. Watched her snort another spoonette of coke. I didn't know what she was talking about.

"Renseller," she said. "Jilly Renseller. I fuck her brains out now and then. She is one *ruca loca en la cama*. I give her sustained multiples. Women do women so much better than men do women."

She uncuffed my hands while holding the pistol against my throat. "Am I too brutal, Walkinghorse? Did I give you a little *susto*? Maybe you needed it. I love her, you know. She's *mine*, you big prick. Am I jealous, am I vengeful? A tad, yes. In any case, terror is a good purgative. It clears out the bullshit. Your head feels so much clearer, right? Terror helps you separate your priorities. It also prepares you for *sustos* to come."

"You're fucking nuts," I said.

"Be honest with yourself. You caught a thrill, didn't you? Don't be ashamed. Everyone's got a little perversion locked away in their dark little hearts, don't you think?"

115

I thought of Clive. I thought of the Farnsworths. I thought of Jillian in bed with Clara Howler. It made the arteries in my brain throb.

"What was that about Jillian standing between me and the grave?" I said.

"You don't get it, do you?"

"There's very little I get."

"You're a naive guy, Walkinghorse. I kind of like that in a man provided he isn't also stupid. Naive and stupid is hard to take."

She picked up the candle and carried it across the room. "Did you notice this picture?" she said.

She held the flame under a bad painting of a man with thick black hair. It was on the wall opposite the table and chair, but I'd hardly noticed it. It wasn't something that held your interest.

"This is the narco saint, Jesús Malverde. He moved leaf, flake, and *mota* from Sinaloa into the States a hundred years ago. This is a very old and well-established business. It's taken very seriously here."

"Saint?" I said.

"As important to the Sinaloans as Patrick is to the Irish. He was a kind of Robinhood, he shared his take with the poor. Sinaloans have always been poor as church mice."

"I'll say my bed-time prayers to him," I said.

"Be a smart-ass. It gets you *en ninguna parte*–nowhere. You're a nice screw. I hope they change their minds. But it's not likely. I think you need *un milagro*. Pray to Jesús Malverde, maybe you'll get one. *Adios*, tiger."

"Let me have your flask one more time before you go," I said.

She gave me the flask. It was still half full. I raised it to the narco saint. His calm black eyes met mine. The dead have no trouble meeting the eyes of the dead. I looked away first. Then I drained the flask.

SEVENTEEN

The *milagro*–the miracle I didn't pray for but got anyway– was sleep. A long, dreamless tequila sleep. The roar of lawnmowers ended it.

The unlikely roar threw me–I didn't know where I was. I pictured wide, generously-watered lawns, lush green land-scaping. I ran through all the places I'd lived in the past twenty years, the rented houses, the apartments Gert and I had shared, the Scottsdale condo I once house-sat for a friend, my little room in The Baron Arms, but nothing matched the stark whitewashed walls of this place. And lawnmowing on this scale didn't fit in with any of them. The chain on my leg broke the memory block.

I crawled to the window. No lawnmowers. A twin-engine Cessna was taxiing toward the houses. It had landed beyond the courtyard of the compound, and now it was sitting at the open end of the horseshoe. I realized then that the bamboo pole with the white rag attached was a wind-sock, giving pilots wind direction and intensity. This place–stash houses, I figured–had a makeshift airport.

Five men carrying automatic weapons came out of the plane and took up casual positions in the courtyard. A sixth man– the pilot–off-loaded a few dozen plastic-wrapped packages the size of shoe boxes and brought them into the house on a hand truck. He stacked them neatly, with reverence, against the wall under the painting of the narco saint. If this had been a Sunday, you might think you were in church, watching a priest prepare the Eucharist for consecration. He glanced at me without interest, then went back to the plane. He revved

117

the right engine, which turned the Cessna around smartly, and took off, raising a mini-sandstorm. I watched the plane fly south until it was a silver gleam in the bright air, then nothing. The armed men who had gotten off the plane, stayed behind.

Rigoberto, the man who had helped Clara Howler carry me into the house, came in.

"¿Qué pasa?" I said.

He was carrying a rifle, an ancient Springfield, World War I vintage. He leaned it against a wall. "You want to play some cards?" he said, yawning.

He sat down at the table and waved me over. I sat opposite him. "Five card draw," he said. He gave me a few dozen kitchen matches, kept the box for himself. "We play only for big money. Each stick will be one-thousand *dolarucos.*" He grinned at the absurdity. "The winner is to be a rich man." He shuffled briefly and dealt out two hands. He arranged his cards carefully, frowning at them like a scholar studying an old text. A smile split his leathery face. A gold upper bicuspid gleamed. He looked at me, his black eyes serious but also festive under his shaggy brows. "We are going to be hit," he said, finally answering my question. *"Pero,* you have nothing to worry about."

"Who's going to hit us?"

He shrugged. "It could be anybody. Maybe some *maricónes* from your DEA. Maybe some *panchos riatas* from Tijuana. Maybe Italian gangsters from Chicago." He laughed at this last possibility. "Who kills you—*no importa.* Dead is dead."

Rigoberto was calm about the prospect of doing battle. He was a little man, a *mestizo,* but mostly Indian. His face bore the emblems of a warrior—the most impressive was a thick scar that ridged his face on a diagonal from above his left eye down across his nose and ending at the back of his right jaw.

118

It looked like someone had tried to divide his head with a machete. Half his left ear was gone, a perfect split. A shred of earlobe hung down like a meaty teardrop.

My Spanish was only fair, not quick enough to hold my own in a conversation, but Rigoberto spoke serviceable English. Even so, we played the game in silence, except when he won a pot. Then he'd hoot a complex obscenity and smile his gold bicuspid smile. Like most warriors, he was a simple man who took joy in simple pleasures.

We played three or four games before he spoke again. "I hope you are not going to take it too personal," he said.

"Take what personal?" It was an unnecessary question; his eyes said it all.

He nodded at the Springfield leaning against the adobe bricks. "I think you are an okay *büey* for a gringo, so it will give me no pleasure." He didn't have to add: *to shoot you.* Rigoberto had been given the assignment.

"What about Victor Mellado?" I said.

He shrugged. "He's killing somebody in Califas, I think. Much is happening, you know?"

I swallowed hard. For some stupid reason his friendliness had made me feel optimistic about my chances of getting out of there alive.

He shrugged, a familiar Mexican shrug that said volumes. It signified the entrenched fatalism of the Mexican soul. I thought of Güero. The future is carved in stone. So why worry? The Mexican shrug said it best.

"Business is business," Rigoberto said. "Sometimes you do things for *el jefe* you would not be very happy about doing if it was only for yourself. But this is the way it is everywhere, even in your country. *Lo siento, ése.* I hope you will not think badly of me. Tell Jesus when you see him that Rigoberto Acosta Nuñez was not a *pendejo.* When I shoot you, I will be

119

very careful to make the bullet enter your heart. Unless you want it in *los sesos.*" He tapped his forehead. "You know—the *brains.* I will personally bring you a big steak dinner first. Do you like it red in middle or burnt up? Mushrooms on top? *Cebollas?*"

I shrugged. It wasn't the Mexican shrug. It was the purely American *I'm-so-fucked* shrug. Food was the last thing on my mind.

"And tequila," he said. "You can have tequila. A *chingón* liter!" He grinned a good-natured grin. It was hard to dislike him.

He laid down a full house, kings over sevens, and scooped up the matchsticks heaped in the middle of the table. *"Ai, dios* forgive me, I am *un hombre rico,"* he said, smiling again, but less broadly.

At one point he turned to the window, listening. *"Un camión,"* he said. *"Un troque,* more maybe. Big Fords. *Sí, Fords. Ford troques.* Big ones."

I listened but didn't hear anything. A moment later I did— the far away sorrowful moan of a transmission in low range. The moan got louder; its pitch rose. The men outside began to shout instructions to each other. One of them let loose a long stuttering burst from his weapon. More joined in. Then I saw the trucks, four of them. About a dozen men in black ski masks and camouflage fatigues jumped out of the beds. I'd seen them before, in a hundred movies. I guess they'd seen the movies too.

I saw the flashes from the barrels of their guns. They also had automatics. A soundless bullet from one of them made a neat hole in the window and spattered dust from the wall opposite.

"Get me out of these fucking chains, Rigo!" I said. "I don't want to die chained to a wall!"

"No es posible, man," he said with real regret. *"Señorita* Howler, the *manflora,* she took the key with her."

I tossed my cards on the table. "See you later then," I said. I crawled back to my mat and hunkered down low against the adobe wall, making myself small as possible. Rigoberto picked up his rifle and broke out a window pane with the barrel. He expended his clip in a few seconds. Outside, someone yelled, *"¡Cada chango a su mecate y a darse vuelo!"*– Every man for himself.

The fire-fight didn't last long. The attackers had more firepower; they outnumbered the defenders. The shooting outside died down. Someone yelled an elaborate obscenity. Rigoberto yelled obscenities back. One of the men kicked open the door. He pointed an AK-47 at Rigoberto, told him to get on his knees, hands behind his head. He wore a Dodgers baseball cap.

Rigoberto sneered. He remained standing. *"Chinga tu madre, pocho,"* he said.

The man returned the insult and fired low, into Rigoberto's upper thighs and groin. Rigoberto went down. He released a long closed-mouth growl, but did not scream.

The man fired again, this time aiming at the lower abdomen. He was satisfied with that. He slung the AK over his shoulder and pulled off his ski mask. He was young, no more than twenty, his smooth brown face shined with sweat. He was hyped by the kill, but it wasn't a kill yet. Rigoberto writhed on the floor in a lake of his own blood, grunting hard but holding back his screams.

"Finish him off for Christ's sakes," I said.

He looked at me, noticing me for the first time. My condition amused him. He laughed. "Why?" he said. "The asshole said a dirty thing about me and my mother. He needs to suffer for it before he goes to hell. He suffers well, *tiene huevos*. He's got balls, this Mexican hero, but now he won't be able to fuck his mother or anyone else with no *pito* and no *huevos*. Maybe he'll fuck her *puta* ass in hell." He glanced over at Rigoberto who was now pretty much out of it—his eyes were unfocused and he'd stopped grunting. "Is that what you are going to do, *joto?*"the gunman said to the dying man. "You going to fuck your *mami* in hell?" He spoke east L.A. American—a *pocho* from *eastla* with a lot of attitude.

"Now tell me," he said, turning to me, "who the fuck are *you?*"

"I'm a prisoner waiting to be shot."

He lit a cigarette. "No shit? What for? You work for the *chilango* money broker and you fucked up? Maybe you are DEA. Is that what you are, undercover DEA cocksucker who got caught?"

"I'm a plumber," I said. An absurd thought struck me: the Hildebrand's tureen had been plugged for days. They were probably living in a lake of sewage by now. My answering machine must have been clogged with Rosie's complaints.

Then he saw the packages under the narco saint. "Yo! *Feliz* fucking *navidad,"* he said. "All wrapped up pretty." He brought a package up to his face and inhaled as if he could smell its contents. "Six mil on the street. Maybe seven. It's—what do you call it—a windfall? We didn't come for this, we came to waste the motherfuckers. We came to make a fucking statement, you know?"

He was happy. I was happy he was happy.

Another man came in. He pulled off his ski mask. He was full-bellied, older, balding. He had the air of authority. He saw Rigoberto, inspected the body, gave the young *pocho* a hard look, then calmly fired a bullet into Rigoberto's forehead. The body flexed, as if a cattle prod had touched it, then relaxed. Rigoberto's hard time on planet earth had officially ended.

"*¿Quién es?*" the older man said, pointing his rifle at me.

"*Dice que es un prisionero, jefe,*" the *pocho* said.

The older man walked over to me. He poked my chest with the barrel of his AK. It was still hot. "Why are you their prisoner?" he said.

"They didn't tell me," I said.

He stared at me, looking for attitude.

"Seriously, *señor,*" I said respectfully. "They didn't tell me."

He lit a cigarette and went outside. The *pocho* drew a hunting knife from the sheath on his thigh. He tested the hone of the blade against his thumb. He squatted next to Rigoberto's head and cut off his ears with the precision of a butcher trimming a steak. "Shit, look at this," he said, holding up Rigoberto's half-ear. "Some asshole fucked this one up." He put the ears in his pocket.

"Jesus Christ," I said, disgusted.

He came over to me, looking mean. "You got a little *problema?*" he said. "You are in no fucking position to have a problem, man. The ears, they confirm the kill. This *pendejo* is number seven. Seven is my lucky number. You believe in luck?" He turned away, chuckling to himself, not expecting an answer.

"I believe in both kinds," I said. "Bad and good."

The *pocho's* boss came in carrying bolt cutters. He cut the chains off my legs. As far as I knew my prospects hadn't improved, but I thanked him anyway.

He gave me a cigarette. I'd given up smoking in the army, but I wasn't about to jinx this piece of good luck by turning him down.

"There's an old Arab saying," he said, studying me through the smoke. " 'The enemy of my enemy is my friend.' You are free to go, whoever the hell you are."

123

EIGHTEEN

The afternoon bartender, Mando Ojara—another descendant of a *patricio*—didn't recognize me. He saw my clothes, not my face. My pants were baggy and wide, the wide-body pants of a three-hundred pound man. The belt that held them up was tied-together laces I'd stripped from the shoes of the dead. My shirt was torn and spattered with blood. The army brogans I'd taken off a corpse were too small. I'd had to cut the toes out so I could walk.

"It's me, Mando," I said. My voice was hoarse, my throat scratched with desert sand. "You've been making saltless margaritas for me for years." I had a beard, my grimy hair hung over my ears. I smelled of blood, sweat, and shit. Maybe of gunpowder; maybe of Clara Howler.

Mando finally agreed to recognize me. *"¡Cielos!* Walking-horse! What happened to you, man?" he said. "I was about to escort your *mugriento* butt back out on the street." Mando, a good Catholic, was careful with his expletives. *¡Cielos!*–Heavens!–was the strongest he allowed himself.

"I got lost," I said. It wasn't exactly a lie. "What day is it?"

"What *day* is it? It's hump day, man."

"Wednesday? I thought it was Monday."

"Where did you get lost, on the moon?" Mando said. *"Cielos,* man. Next time, take one of those global positioning things with you."

Mando was short, dark, his nose beaky, his almond eyes Mayan and insular. His Irish heritage, what was left of it, had been relegated to subtler aspects of his make-up. He leaned toward me a few inches, opened his nostrils. *"Ai chihuahua,* you need to take a *bath,* Walkinghorse," he said.

"A drink first, Mando, *por favor."*

He made me a generous margarita. I swilled it down.

The DMZ was mostly empty. A pair of transvestite prostitutes in sequined dresses sat at a table, heads close together. One had lemon yellow hair. His skin was bleached of all color. The other was dark, a *morena.* His jet hair shone with metallic blue highlights. They were both pretty and more jumpy than they needed to be. Their act was a good one, but they were new to the DMZ and might have been wondering if this was one of those places where it wouldn't work. *No problema.*

A young guy wide as a door pulled a chair up to their table. His scrubbed-pink scalp gleamed under a blond crew cut. He was wearing boot-cut jeans, a rosy pearl-buttoned cowboy shirt, and squeaky new snakeskin boots. He looked like material for the University's freshman football team but was, more than likely, a trainee from Fort Bliss.

"One more," I said to Mando. I dug in my pockets. I only had pesos, the value of which seemed to be growing less and less by the day. I dumped them on the bar. "Put the rest on my tab, Mando. I lost my wallet."

Güero had put up a new sign in my absence. It was taped to the mirror, above the bourbon bottles:

> Wandering too long
> without map or water,
> the unforgiving desert
> took a terrible toll.

It seemed to be meant for me—one of those coincidences

that you can't believe has no meaning. I raised my second margarita to the synchronistic grammar gaff.

I *had* wandered too long in the unforgiving desert. My face in the mirror was a toxic shade of vermilion, burned by the ultraviolet sun. The wind-parched skin around my eyes and mouth was cracked. The whites of my eyes were streaked red, the lids swollen. My puffy lips bled if I made them smile or smirk. Not that I had anything to smile or smirk about. I looked like a sixty-year-old desert rat. No wonder Mando hadn't recognized me. *Cielos,* I didn't recognize myself.

I'd taken my clothes from the fly-covered bodies of the dead, stopping when I needed to get control of my gag reflex. The dense stink of death caught in my throat and made me retch. I walked a few hundred feet away from the scene now and then to brace myself with lungfuls of clean air. The bodies hadn't stiffened yet, and relieving them of their clothes wasn't difficult. I took the pants off the big silent guy who'd brought me food. He'd been shot in the head and throat—his pants were stained with urine, involuntarily released when he died. He'd also filled them with shit. After emptying them, I'd turned them inside out and cleaned them as best I could with handfuls of sand. The pants were too big in the waist but the length was right. I took the shirt off someone who'd been killed with a single shot through the left eye. There were a few spots of blood on the collar. Another, in the shape of a lopsided star, decorated the left breast pocket like a badge of honor. The back of his head was gone, but the volume of blood and brains had miraculously cleared the backside of the shirt. The brogans were almost new, but a size small. I took a knife off one of the dead men and cut out the toes. I went through their pockets, looking for money, and came up with about fifty pesos. I retched some more, then vomited.

I started walking north on a road I now recognized as

highway 45, a toll road. I passed through the village of Samalayuca. Men sitting on the shaded porch of a *tienda* stared at me but didn't speak. They no doubt heard the noise of the fire-fight, and wanted no part of it or its survivors. A dog barked but kept its distance, discouraged by the smell of death, which worried it.

After a few hours I reached one of the new *colonias* on the far southern outskirts of Juárez. I boarded a *rutera,* a bus that carried *maquila* workers to and from their jobs. The *maquilas*— mostly American-owned high-tech factories that once were part of the American industrial landscape—made northern Mexico look prosperous. But the workers who rode the *ruteras* made five dollars a day with no benefits. The status quo of Mexican poverty was maintained by the *maquilas.* The *maquilas* increased the number of poor by attracting immigrants from the Mexican interior as well as from Central America who hoped, mostly in vain, to find work in the splendid factories on the border. Scrapwood *colonias* of the hopeful sprouted in the outskirts of the city—*colonias* without power, water, sewers, medical care, schools, and bread. A number of the inhabitants died every winter from carbon monoxide-spewing kerosene heaters. In the summer they died of cholera and typhoid. Tuberculosis and polio were making a comeback in these areas.

The *rutera* took me within a mile of a bridge that crossed the Rio. The border guards gave me some long, curious looks, asked the usual questions, reluctantly let me into the richest country on earth. I walked the rest of the way up Mesa, about two miles, to the DMZ.

I finished my drink and was about to ask Mando to make me another, when the big kid sitting with the transvestite whores roared as if he'd been ice-picked in the eye. He'd been sucking the tongue of the lemon yellow blonde and squeezing his silicon *chichis,* while the *morena* massaged his steaming crotch. The kid, who looked like he might have come from the northern mid-west, was awash in wonder at life on the border. He was probably asking himself, How lucky can a guy get, hey?

But as he groped the blonde he found hardwood hiding under the sequined dress. He'd been sitting between the two, slurping up tap beer and regaling them with stories of his wild and carefree teenage days. When he processed the implications of the surprise in his hand, his face drained of color and the stories stopped dead in his hanging jaws. He exploded upward, knocking over the table and kicking the blonde away from him as if she were a rabid gargoyle. He howled with fear and disgust, then started in on them with boots and fists. Mando vaulted over the bar and cooled the kid off with a professional stroke of his lead-filled leather sap.

I helped Mando carry him into the men's room. We sat him down against the wall opposite the urinals. His big pink head rested on the damp tiles. The kid stayed cool for about ten minutes, then crawled out of the men's room. He made it to his feet, then staggered out of the bar. The transvestites weren't hurt badly. They'd dealt with rougher trade than the kid and knew how to slip punches and dodge kicks. The kid was lucky one of them didn't open him up with a switchblade. They fixed their make-up, adjusted their clothes, thanked Mando in impeccable Spanish, and marched out with the dignity of visiting royalty.

"These gringo kids," Mando said. "They act like they just got off the bus from peckerville."

I finished my drink, thanked Mando, then headed for The Baron Arms, hoping that my apartment hadn't been cleaned out by thieves. I'd been gone almost a week. I felt good but suddenly shaky. I inhaled the sights and smells of Mesa Street; I inhaled my freedom. Halfway across the light changed and I was stranded on the traffic island. A car slowed and the driver handed me a dollar. The next car also slowed and the guy behind the wheel gave me a scornful look. "Get a job!" he yelled. "You're healthy as a fucking ox! Go to work!"

The next car was trapped by a red light. The driver ignored me, but the kids in the back seat tossed a bag of jelly beans to me. *"Gracias, niños,"* I said. *"De nada,"* they chimed.

I waited through several light changes before I left my post. I'd collected six dollars and a bag of jelly beans in ten minutes without having asked anyone for anything. The kindness of strangers—nothing to depend on, but always amazing.

I passed by The Healing Witch, the herbal medicine shop. A man who looked as bad as me squatted near the entrance. No fool, he knew the people who could buy herbal remedies probably had money. He had a crutch and a sign

Disabled Vet, Please Help.
God Bless you and yours.

I decided to give the money to him since I'd collected it on his turf, but a woman got to him before I did. She'd driven up in a new Camry. She was young and good-looking and she began haranguing him before he realized who she was talking to. He tilted his head back and squinted up at her. Her face shined like focused sunlight, bright enough to incinerate bugs. The beggar flinched; he began to sweat. His brown, gap-toothed smile did not disarm her. She was dressed in black tights, white silk blouse, and black suede high-heeled boots. She spoke of the ideal Christian man, the importance of decency, and the rewards of hard work. She scolded him for using God's name to support his degenerate life. The beggar assumed a defensive posture, arms folded against his chest. He wagged his shaggy head side to side, looking for rescue, but the woman was relentless, full of passionate intensity. She squatted without fear in front of him on her exquisite haunches, instructing him in what Jesus requires of the American man. The beggar finally caved. His head dropped down, chin on chest–as if he'd realized that submission was the only way to get rid of her. The woman took his hand in hers and began to pray. She instructed him to pray along with her. "Jesus, this unclean man cometh before thee. . . ." she said, as prologue, and then went on for a full minute.

They prayed together, the bum mumbling darkly, the woman's clarion voice rising furiously into the eaves of The Healing Witch. Then she rose and strode into the store, her heels snapping against the concrete walk like exclamations.

"You okay?" I asked the bum.

"The bitch didn't give me a fucken nickel," he said. "She wears fuck-me boots and prays to Jesus, go figure."

"Sign of the times, amigo," I said.

I gave him the money I'd collected. "This is yours," I said. "I got it on your turf."

"Hey, thanks man." He pulled a bottle of Mad Dog from his bindle and offered me a hit. I declined.

"You sure? You look like you could use something, brother. I got a stick of reefer if you want it."

"No. I'm okay," I said. I had to hear myself say it to know it was a lie.

I felt weak and sick, and it seemed that I would not be able to rid myself of the smell of death.

130

NINETEEN

My apartment door was open. The place was trashed—dresser drawers scattered around the room, the contents heaped together on the floor. Bed overturned, sheets and blankets heaped in a twisted pile. Even the carpeting, where it met the walls, had been ripped up. The kitchen cabinets were open, the shelves dumped. Glass shards littered the counter, the sink was full of packaged food, broken bottles, vitamins, and mouse-size water roaches.

My picture of Arnold with the naked blonde clamped to his shoulders was on the floor, the frame broken, the photo ripped in half. Revenge of the huffers, I figured. I added to the mess by firing a skillet at the wall, imagined it skulling a huffer. Oddly enough, my big TV and VCR were untouched. *Un milagro.*

I needed to get out. No matter how humble, home is home, and home is all you have. I promised myself: This violation was going to be the last. My ring of keys was still hanging on a hook inside the circuit breaker box at the back of the closet. At least they hadn't found those. If they had, all the locks in the complex would have to be changed. I tried to be thankful for these small miracles. My clothes were pretty much intact, too. I grabbed my sweats, socks, and gym shoes.

I went into the bathroom and opened the medicine cabinet. Another surprise: nothing was touched. Not that there was much of huffer-interest in it—some old cosmetics Gert had

131

left. I kept these pink and beige jars and tubes, thinking she'd be back and would want them even when it became clear her absence was permanent. I'd been meaning to dump them for some time, but was hampered by a reluctance I didn't want to look at too closely. Sentimentality, I guess. Loneliness, maybe. But not hope. Hope doesn't keep. Like day-old coffee, it leaves a bitter, metallic taste in your mouth. Hope is the spiritual equivalent of drinking your own bile.

Among the emollients, blushes, blemish concealers, creams, and oils, were Seconal caps. Red devils, she called them, and there were half a dozen left in the vial. The huffers either missed them or they looked down their noses at mere pharmaceuticals. Bayer, Pfizer, Roche, had nothing in the brain-melting area that matched up with lacquer remover at fifteen dollars a gallon. I grabbed a towel off the rack, a fresh bar of soap, and cleared out.

I opened an unused apartment two doors away. I stripped out of the dead men's clothes, swallowed two red devils, and took a long shower hot enough to boil death out of my skin. Then I laid down on the bare mattress and case-less pillow.

When I closed my eyes I saw Rigoberto's ears, the knife in the *pocho's* hand as he sawed them off close to the skull, the fly-specked dead floating across my field of vision like shapes on a river. The face of Jesús Malverde, the narco saint, looming above it all, his 19th century eyes sad, as if he could see Mexico's future.

Then the red devils kicked in. They opened the door on a tranquil black sea. I fell into it.

Clara Howler took hold of my ears and turned my head left and right, to confirm my helplessness. From the neck down I was paralyzed. "You are nine-tenths dead," she said. She sat on my chest and cut off my ears with a hunting knife. She held them up, dangling them before my eyes. They were bloodless as white wax. "See," she said. "It's no big deal. It's just meat. We're all just meat, carnal, nothing more." She hiked up her skirt and straddled my face. I felt myself sinking under the damp weight of her jungle heat. I tried to scream but my lungs could not draw air. She was drowning me with her body. Then I was running, running through deep sand, voices raging behind me, the voices of dead men begging me to bury them before it was too late. Too late for what? I yelled. Hurry, they said. Hurry.

I sat upright in bed, the phrase *too late for what?* moving my lips, my heart accelerating. It was morning–but of what day? I felt as if I'd been asleep for a week but I didn't feel rested, my head stuffed with sawdust. I rolled out of bed, crawled to the bathroom. I climbed into the shower and turned on the cold water. I sat there until my heart slowed. My head cleared. I was cold enough now to want to be warm, my panic overruled by the need for physical comfort.

I went back to my place and cleaned it up. I made a pot of strong coffee, sat at my table overlooking the parking lot. I was grateful to be alive but wondering how long that condition would last.

My life wasn't worth much in the general scheme of things, but it was all I had. I still believed I had a future–a vague, unspecific future, but still a future. Maybe I'd finish my master's degree. Maybe I'd go to work for an up-and-coming high-tech company, a company so generous with stock options for its employees that they could retire as millionaires. Maybe I'd meet a good woman and marry her. Maybe I'd enter the righteous middle-class life: split level happiness in green suburbia, pacified by the constant hiss of minivans gliding down wide, tree-lined avenues.

The more of these images I invented the more cartoon-like

they became. Who did I think I was kidding? I wasn't going anywhere. I had all I could do just to hold on to the status quo, to keep myself from backsliding and winding up on the street.

I hammered the table with my fist, making my coffee cup jump and slosh over. "Fuck *you!*" I yelled, as if singling out the culprit responsible for my misery. Maybe it was Gert who'd left me for the stock car racer. Maybe it was Jillian—Jillian who'd made me think I could have a relationship with a woman again. Or *el jefe* and his butch bodyguard Clara Howler. Maybe it was the Farnsworths who'd got me into this mess in the first place. I could point my finger at a lot of people, but it finally all came down to me: I'd fucked up my own life for no apparent reason.

Maybe it was genetic—my real parents might have been carriers of the Fuck-Up Gene, soon to be identified by the genome project. Maybe it was Sam and Maggie, the way they raised us to be self-critical, always aware of our faults. Maybe I was too aware of mine. But that didn't explain Isaiah, Zipporah or Zacharias. Nature or nurture? It was a toss-up, since the successes of Isaiah, Zack and Zip were offset by the major and minor catastrophes of Moses and Uriah.

I put on my sweats and carried the dead men's clothes to the dumpster, along with bags of huffer rubble. A small surprise was waiting for me in the parking lot: my car. It was not parked in my slot, but it was *there*. Someone had even washed it. It was unlocked and the keys were in the ignition. Jillian, or one of her friends, didn't want a dead man's car on her property. Reasonable enough. They were careful people, even though chances were slim my body would ever be discovered in the *narcotraficantes'* graveyard.

There were two more surprises. Jillian's checks were gone. And Forbes's cheesy .32 was gone. It's easy to break into these apartments. I had to be inventive to keep the important stuff out of the hands of ordinary thieves. I'd kept the checks in the freezer compartment of my fridge, under the ice cube trays. They were not there. And Forbes's belly-gun was not there either, where it had been pretending to be a steak in its opaque freezer bag.

The huffers wouldn't have known what to do with the checks, except maybe use them for toilet paper. To them, it might have seemed a species of high-concept revenge to wipe their asses with promisory notes they didn't know how to convert into cash. And huffers don't use weapons as a rule. Their dope is cheap, too easy to lift off supermarket shelves to justify armed robbery. They lived on the streets and ate at the Rescue Mission, when the solvents hadn't killed off their appetites completely. A gun to a huffer was a liability. The cops pretty much left them alone, but possession of a gun might land them in the pokey for a few months. No glue, no thinner, no aerosol spot-removers there. This, along with the fact that huffers haven't got enough brain cells left to look for goods in a clever hiding place, such as a refrigerator, made me re-think the break-in.

Whoever came in wanted the checks and the gun. He looked in all the obvious places first, conducting a crazed search, like a junkyard dog turned loose in a steakhouse dumpster.

Forbes.

Forbes had taken the checks and reclaimed his gun. This also explained the violation of Arnold and the naked blonde riding his neck: Forbes was a slob who could not abide the idea of physical perfection and sexual success. The picture pissed him off, and the memory of it was probably still pissing him off.

The checks were the only thing that connected me to the

Rensellers. The gun, which was registered in Forbes's name, connected me to Forbes and thus to Fernando Solís Davila.

There was one other item. I called the Farnsworths. Jerry answered.

"This is Walkinghorse. I need to talk to you," I said.

"Uri? Can't talk right now. We've got a gig going. Mona called you. Don't you check your messages?"

"I've been out of town."

"Look, Mona's with a major client right now and I'm going to assist her. It's a first for me and I'm a little nervous. I'll be in grandma drag. This guy wants to be paddled with a spatula by granny while munching on Mom. Mona's playing Mom. Demento city. Isn't America great? What's up?"

"Has anyone broken into your house recently?"

"How did you know?"

"They only took the video tapes of Renseller, right?"

I heard him suck wind. "You son of a *bitch*," he said. "It was you, wasn't it? Or someone you put up to it. We told you there was nothing to worry about. The whole thing is history now, anyway."

"It wasn't me. It was Jillian's friends. They want to make sure Clive Renseller's tacky death is undocumented."

He didn't respond. I could almost hear the worry wheels turning under his red Mohawk.

"I'm part of the documentation," I said. "They won't mess with you. Mona's not going to tell anyone how Renseller died. She makes too much money to risk exposure. The last thing *Mind Me!* needs is the publication of a clientele list. I'm the only one who might have a reason to meet the press."

"Uri, for Christ's sakes! Don't do it!" Jerry wasn't cool. His emotions were all up front. It kept him honest. I liked him for that.

"No sweat. The tabloids might give me a thousand, but *el jefe* wouldn't fail twice to bury me in Samalayuca."

"El who? Bury you *where?"*

"You don't want to know. Why did Mona call me?"

He sighed. "Job offer. Mona wants to put you on the staff full time. She'd pay you a grand a week."

"Not my kind of work, Jerry."

"Don't be hasty. Think about it."

I hung up.

For the first time I noticed the red light on my answering machine. It was blinking fast, which meant I had a half hour or more of messages. I played them while I put on my best—and only—suit.

TWENTY

I paid four hundred dollars for the suit five years ago. It was wool, a light overcast gray with subtle black pinstripes. Gert picked it out. It even had a vest. It was a tight fit, but I looked better than good in it—I looked prosperous, confident, able to face the world on equal terms. My shoes were Florsheim wingtips, shoes I hadn't worn since our wedding. The feel and smell of the suit and shoes brought back memories I didn't want to deal with just now. *No problema.* Gert's message took care of any uninvited nostalgia.

She was sending lawyers after me. Trey didn't make the field in the Gatorade 125 and he was royally pissed. The next race was in North Carolina and if he didn't get a good engine man before that he probably wouldn't make that field either. I had no right holding back the money that would let Trey hire a good engine man. Didn't I understand? These engines run at eight-thousand rpm all afternoon long and they have to be *tight.* Her tone was shrill, the voice of a frantic bill collector. Then she switched to a softer tone. "And to top everything," she said, "we're preggers. We really need the money like *yesterday,* hon. You *can* understand that, can't you? OB-GYNs don't come cheap. Neither do anti-nausea pills and lawyers. Expect to hear from Rooney and Vesco."

All the time we were together she'd been on the pill. She hadn't wanted any babies. Babies were a responsibility and

138

hindrance she wasn't ready to deal with. I didn't want babies either. We were together on this. There would be time for babies later on, when our lives became more settled, when we had a house of our own and a reliable income. She was almost ten years younger than me, and we agreed there was still plenty of time on her biological clock. But now she and the stock car racer had decided to make a baby even though they lived on the road and depended on his track winnings and the generosity of sponsors for income.

Or maybe she needed the money for an abortion. If she had said "I'm pregnant" rather than the cute and plural "we're preggers" that might have been a reasonable assumption. *"We're preggers"* meant the pregnancy had been deliberate, something they both wanted. Which added to my black state of mind. I was not a suitable maker of babies; Trey "back-off-or-crash" Stovekiss was. I laughed; it sounded like a bark.

I thought of the man and the woman who had conceived me, brought me into the world, then left me on a stranger's doorstep. I wanted to ask them, *Why?* Why did they not want their baby? What was it about me that made them think they could not love and provide for me no matter what their circumstances? And then the obvious next question: Why didn't they abort me if they didn't want to raise me? Why did they let me grow up into a middle-aged non-entity who was in the process of aborting his so-called life in his own stupid way?

In my blue funk, this anonymous pair became Gert and Trey Stovekiss. They stood at the edge of a roaring race track, wearing simpleton smiles, smiles without irony or brag or even meanness. Mindless conceivers of babies, populating the world with the unwanted. His arm was draped over her shoulder and his hand rested carelessly on her full breast. *Preggers,* for Christ's sake.

At that point I realized my thoughts had taken a warped turn. Demento, Jerry Farnsworth would say. The flipside of self-pity is destructive rage.

The message from Mona Farnsworth had been brief and to the point. "Uri—or should we just settle on Strobe?—I think we can use you on a regular basis. The money will be very good. Jerry and I have cooked up some terrific new scenarios. Are you up to dispensing body fluids on the clientele? Call me."

Six furious messages from Rosie Hildebrand had followed. Her tureen runneth over. She and Bill had to walk down the street to the Shell station to relieve themselves. She threatened a lawsuit. She threatened to call the board of health. She threatened to withhold her rent. She threatened to nail a dead fish to my door. I didn't want to deal with her. I called a plumbing shop and told then to send the bill directly to the owner of The Baron Arms. That would jeopardize my job, but I was past caring.

I checked myself out in the bathroom mirror. I'd kept the beard, which was long enough to run a comb through, and my hair was over my collar. In this banker's suit, my state of mind made me look like a cold-blooded loan officer about to throw a family out of the house they had quit making payments on. I added sunglasses to this image, escalating it. A loan shark looked back at me, ready to break someone's legs for reneging on the vig.

Down in the parking lot, a teenage huffer was kneeling next to my Ford. He had the gas cap off and was sniffing the benzene-rich gasoline fumes. I bent down to him and yelled in his ear but he didn't move. He was glued to the gas intake hole in the car's fender. I picked him up by the belt and set him down next to someone else's car. He looked at me. There was nothing in his eyes, not even anger. Fifteen years old going on eighty. He went to the dumpster to look for discarded spray cans. A spook in the making. I screwed my gas cap back on and drove across the street to the DMZ.

Güero was there. "Nice threads, man," he said. "You finally get a real job?"

"No job. I got married in this outfit."

He looked at me for a long moment, but made no comment.

He wiped down the bar in front of me. "Where've you been, Uri?" he said. "You've been missing your afternoon margaritas."

"I took a Mexican vacation."

"Vacation from what? Your life is a vacation."

"Don't rub it in."

I told him about my stay in Samalayuca.

"You've got a guardian angel, *ése*. Someone up there is looking out for you. You'd better quit playing with those people."

"Would if I could," I said.

He fixed me a margarita. "I'm not going to ask you how you got mixed up with *traficantes*," he said. "I don't want to know. But you'd better lie low. I'd go north if I were you. Way up north, like Saskatoon. Maybe south to Australia."

"I've been lying low all my life," I said. "Like there was something coming after me from day one, something that knew I should have died in a garbage can forty-two years ago." I realized it was true. Saying it made it clear, as if the notion had existed only as a vague theory.

"You okay, man?" Güero said. "You look a little wild. You're not turning into a *loco*, are you?"

"I've been in hiding, Güero. I'm tired of it. I might as well be dead, don't you think? What's the difference—dead or in hiding? I used to think that having a body like this was protection."

He looked at me. His inquisitioner's eyes judging my fitness, my sanity. "Protection from what? Meat doesn't stop bullets."

"Demons, I guess." I started to laugh at myself, at this confession.

"Demons are inside, *ése,*" Güero said. "Maybe your muscles keep them in. You want the name of a good *curandera?* Or maybe a gringo shrink? I hear the Freudians are making a comeback."

"First things first," I said.

"Whatever," he said. "I've got my own problems." He looked sad then, his eyes distant.

I didn't ask him what his problems were. I only had time for mine.

I headed south on Mesa toward downtown. I had no plan. I was pissed off and a little suicidal—a mental state that makes planning beside the point.

I blasted my horn at the driver ahead of me who was riding the brakes of his silver Cadillac. One foot on the gas, the other on the brake. He needed to go forward, but he wasn't taking any chances. Nineteen miles an hour in a 40 mph zone. He ignored my horn blasts. I couldn't see him—probably a tiny old man whose head didn't clear the headrest of the driver's seat. I'd seen them before: shriveled and rich and careful, riding their brakes, and always behind the wheel of a Cadillac. I leaned on my horn but the driver was secure in the insulated plush of the Caddy.

I found a parking place next to the civic center. The roof of the civic center was a sombrero half the size of a football field—the city fathers' idea of a tourist attraction. The sombrero suggested the festive nature of El Paso and our sister city across the river. A monument to simpler times. The festive nature of the two cities separated by the polluted waters of the Rio Grande had gone the way of the passenger pigeon and the quickie Mexican divorce.

Cibola Savings and Loan loomed three blocks away, a twenty-eight story monolith of green glass and black steel with no tourist-attracting niceties. The slanted roof faced south, suggesting top-floor luxury suites with solariums that in winter were full of light and warmth and optimism.

I'd read something about this building. It had been constructed in the early eighties by speculators. When the Reagan administration deregulated the banking industry, big loans were handed out like complimentary mints to almost anyone with an investment plan that wasn't patently insane. Office buildings, condos, theme parks, housing developments sprung up everywhere. Then the economy flat-lined. Loans went unpaid and banks collapsed. Buildings like the Cibola were put up for sale by the government's bank bail-out teams for a fraction of the defaulted loans. When the Cibola was picked up for less than a million by a group representing a Mexican holding company, the op-ed section of the paper seethed with outrage. A building that cost close to ninety million had been practically given away by the government, and the eternally screwed taxpayers were left to make up the losses. Nation-wide, taxpayers shelled out close to a trillion dollars for the bankers' fiascoes. Bottom-feeders favored by the bail-out teams grabbed major properties for dimes on the dollar, and rumors of sweetheart deals and kick-backs persisted for years. Then the economy got hot again and the public discussion was ended by the usual public amnesia.

The sun was muted behind strings of high, skinny clouds, and in this light the glass walls of Cibola took on the green hues of money. This architectural nicety, more subtle than the civic center's concrete sombrero, was meant not to attract tourists but large cash deposits.

I went in through gold-flecked glass doors and was greeted by an elderly man in a maroon jacket with brass buttons and gold epaulets. "Good day, sir," he said. "May I direct you?" His tone was hushed, his manner confidential. His greeting carried this message: your privacy will be honored, your importance acknowledged, the gravity of your business will be taken with the utmost seriousness.

"Where's the *jefe's* office?" I said.

"Sir?"

"The boss. *El presidente.* The man."

"In the Penthouse, sir. Top floor. I assume you are with the Helmstrom Group?"

I nodded. "Assistant Chief financial officer," I said. "In charge of hostile takeovers, imaginary satellite companies, creative number juggling, and other lucrative fantasies." A hesitant smile made his thin lips twitch while he concluded I was quite the joker for an assistant CFO. I gave him a two-finger salute, honoring his maroon military costume. I gripped the stringy trapezius muscle between his shoulder and neck and gave him a jolly little shake. The epaulets quivered. The patronizing gesture from a man of my stature touched him. His eyes grew weepy. He bowed.

I felt as if I'd walked into an old-world cathedral. You could almost smell the incense. The tellers sat behind old-fashioned cages—carved oak bars and pebbled glass. They listened to their customers' whispered requests as if they were priests receiving confessions. All that was missing was a padded kneeling-rail and the murmur of penitential prayers.

The floor was black marble flecked with gold, and a dozen marble columns rose up to meet a vaulted ceiling painted with Italianate frescos. Opposite the tellers were a series of spacious alcoves where loan officers sat behind ebony desks fat as tombs. The walls of the alcoves were draped with gold damask and hung with paintings that resembled the religious art of the early Italian Renaissance. Customers, even those of considerable size, looked diminutive before the massive black desks. The chairs they sat in were lower than the chairs of the loan officers who interviewed them—which gave the loan officers physical and psychological advantage over the petitioners. The impact was clear and probably intentional: the money-changers had taken over the temple.

I looked for the elevators, found them, boarded one along with a guy in a thousand-dollar suit. He was carrying a briefcase that made him lean slightly to one side, as if it were filled with gold bars. His fifty dollar haircut was an object of art in itself. He had predator eyes, pale gray and unblinking. His suit was a slightly darker shade of gray. If a fox chose to be human, this is what he'd look like.

"Helmstrom group?" I said. The human fox nodded, too preoccupied with the weight of his business to respond. He punched P for penthouse. The elevator stopped at the 27th floor, one shy of our goal. The human fox studied me as we waited.

I punched P again. The doors to the 27th floor remained open.

"You've got to enter your PIN," my fellow traveler said, pointing to a keyboard matrix above the panel of floor buttons. "No PIN, this is your last stop."

"Pin?" I said. The reference seemed Biblical. Easier for a rich man to pass through the eye of a needle than enter the gates of heaven. Pins and needles. We sit on them, waiting for the cosmic ax.

"You don't have a personal identification number, you get out here, on twenty-seven. There's no public access to the penthouse." He punched in his PIN and held the door open for me.

"Give 'em rabies," I said, winking, as the doors closed on his unresponsive vulpine stare.

I got out into a carpeted hallway lined with office doors. Several of the doors opened into conference rooms. Oval tables with a couple of dozen chairs. Podiums. Projector screens. One of the conference rooms was occupied. I cracked the door and peeked in. Suits speaking to suits. Suits taking notes. Suits snapping open brief cases. Suits picking their noses. Suits arranging their postures and expressions to reflect their boredom with and their superiority to the other suits.

At the end of the hallway, beyond the conference rooms, was a door marked "Fire Exit." On the other side of it there was a narrow stairwell. I went in, then climbed the narrow steel stairs to the penthouse. A "No Admittance" sign was pasted on the fire door, but the door, of course, wasn't locked. What good is a locked fire exit?

The door opened easily. It opened into an oasis, a tropical green paradise. A real parrot in a real banana tree looked at me and said, *"¿Que pasa, compa?"* as it dropped a small hail of white turds.

TWENTY-ONE

The penthouse didn't have the cathedral-like atmosphere of the main floor. It was a tropical Eden, a jungle with Saltillo-tiled corridors walled in by rows of waxy banana palms. The palms were intermixed with birds-of-paradise trees and wide fans of lacy fern that rose languidly from beds of thick-leafed flowering succulents. Among all this equatorial green were banks of lurid red and yellow flowers that hung open like a thousand obscene mouths ready to swallow anyone's idea of innocence. Overhead, the slanted glass ceiling admitted a half-acre of bright, milky sky. It should have been hot and humid in the Penthouse, but air-conditioning kept the atmosphere civilized.

Off the main corridor were adjoining corridors that led to conference rooms far plusher than the ones on the twenty-seventh floor. Most of them were empty. One wasn't. The Helmstrom group sat in Eames chairs at carved tables made of red and yellow jarrah. The guy I shared the elevator with was making a presentation. He looked energized by a thrilling idea, as if he were plotting a blitzkrieg invasion of Poland.

I walked to the far end of the jungle. The corridor ended in a T-section. To the left and right were large suites—the main offices of Cibola Savings and Loan. I picked the one on the left. The door was inscribed in gold-leaf:

Branch President

I went in without knocking.

Clara Howler didn't quite recognize me in my suit, beard, and shades. When she did, she got out of her chair as if she'd been goosed with a cattle prod. I took advantage of her surprise. I stepped in close and punched her hard under the heart, just below the ribs. She still managed to aim a kick at my head. The kick had nothing on it. It was more gesture than kick. I caught her foot mid-way through its arc and flipped her. She went down hard, her mouth opening and closing like the gill of a beached fish.

In spite of what she'd done to me, I felt a twinge of shame. She was wearing a skirt and blouse and slingback sandals. Her hair had grown out a bit and she was wearing make-up. She even had earrings on, sapphire teardrops. She looked feminine, even pretty. She didn't seem dangerous. I knew better. A coral snake doesn't seem dangerous. The twinge of shame passed.

It was a big office with glass doors that led out to a wide, open-air deck. One corner of the office had been set up as a mini-gym. Lenny Trebeaux had been working out on a speed bag. He was wearing sweats and padded gloves. His thousand dollar banker's suit was hanging on a rack behind the speed bag. The bag was still oscillating though Lenny had stopped rolling punches into it. He came toward me, gloves up, feet moving in a tricky little dance. "I boxed in college," he said.

"Then you'll remember how it feels to get your ass kicked," I said. This made him laugh.

"Muscle boys are all show," he said, "pretty to look at but no hand speed or finesse. In the ring they're easy to take down."

"We're not in a ring," I said.

His grin was confident. He stepped up to me and landed half a dozen jabs and a flimsy hook. He finessed a little bob and weave, demonstrating his ring savvy, then came at me again with more textbook jabs. He feinted with his right, hooked again with his anemic left.

"Now do the Ali shuffle," I said.

He threw a wild overhand right. I caught his fist, yanked his arm down, twisted it, pulled it up behind his back, and snapped it at the elbow. He screamed, then fainted.

"How the hell did you get out of Samalayuca?" Clara whispered. She still couldn't pull in air.

I took the laces from Lenny's gym shoes and tied Clara's hands behind her back. I tied her ankles together with the laces from his street shoes. Then I picked her up and put her back in her chair. She was breathing again, in ragged gasps. She coughed up a little blood.

"You mean how did I return from the dead? I could be a ghost, Clara."

"I don't know how you got away," she said, "but you're pretty stupid to come here. What do you want?"

"What does any ghost want? I want to haunt the living. I want to make them shit blood."

I searched Lenny's desk. Among the usual desk paraphernalia was a .40 caliber Beretta semi-automatic, a cell phone, and a Palm Pilot. I slipped the gun into my jacket pocket.

"If you had any brains you'd have lost yourself in Mexico," Clara said.

"I've got brains enough to get lost anywhere," I said.

"Whatever that means," Trebeaux said. He'd come to, but his face was paler than the wan sky that pressed down on the glass ceiling. Even so, his manner suggested that he'd regained the advantage. It was a pose he specialized in. "I suppose you came here to ask questions. Ask away, Walkinghorse."

"He doesn't know what to ask," Clara said.

"The checks," I said.

"Jesus, you have to ask about *them?*" she said. "You're still in the dark?"

"The checks were Jillian's idea," Trebeaux said. "Jillian has a sentimental streak–a liability among her many fine qualities. The bank was going to disappear you, but Jillian begged for your life. She got her way. Solís is fond of Jillian. Hell, we're all fond of Jillian."

This last remark made Clara laugh cynically. "Jilly's a fucking gem," she said.

"The checks would what?–buy me off?" I said.

"Buy you *off?* We weren't buying anything," Trebeaux said. "We were putting you in a locked box." He'd managed to get up and sit in his leather exec chair. He was sweating profusely. It dripped off his chin. His eyes were dilated and dreamy. He was in shock.

"I don't get it," I said. "What locked box?"

Clara laughed. "He still doesn't get it," she said. "I think we should have that inscribed on his headstone."

"If you were accepting money from Jillian," Trebeaux said, "it could be argued that it was dirty money. Payoff money."

"Blackmail," I said.

"Bravo. Soon as you cashed the checks, you'd get the message: You talk about Clive Renseller's sick little hobby, you get charged with blackmail, a felony. But you had to cash the checks–there was no noose around your neck until you did. Jilly dreamed it up. She didn't want you dead. She had a little crush on you. Go figure." He started to fade again. I got him a glass of water from a dispenser in the mini-gym.

"It was a bad idea to begin with," Clara said. "Everyone knew that, but Jillian prevailed. When you didn't cash the

150

checks the bank went back to plan A. How the hell did you get out of Samalayuca?"

"Walked," I said, leaving the rest of it hanging. It was a good feeling, knowing something that these people didn't.

"*¡Qué milagro!*" Clara said.

"Right," I said. "It was a miracle."

"You're going to need another one," Trebeaux said.

"Why do any of you care about Renseller's fun and games getting public attention?" I said. "That kind of crap is pretty common these days. The citizens are shock-proof."

Trebeaux shook his head as if he were dealing with someone who had severe mental impairment. It was a good act, but his eyelids were fluttering and his head tipped back and began to loll. "Did you *look* at this bank?" he said. "It's the classiest bank west of the Hudson. We're beginning to attract Fortune Five Hundred people. *Old* old money. The community loves us. The mayor made it a point to kiss Clive's ass publicly. No one wants to tarnish the image, Walkinghorse. Image in banking is part of our assets, a very large part."

"I was going to get buried in Samalayuca because of *image?*"

"Here's something you ought to get used to," he said, rallying. "You're an expendable kind of guy. You have no value. Feel free to take that as an insult, but I don't mean it that way. It's just a fact. There are billions like you out there." He noted my expression. "What, you don't think so?" he said. "Look what's happening in Africa. Millions dying of AIDS and millions more who will. Do you give a shit? Does anyone in the USA give a shit? Of course not. Those folks are expendables. Well, here's the point: Most of humanity is expendable."

"That's a hell of a philosophy, Trebeaux," I said.

He leaned to one side in his chair as if leaning away from the pain. "It's not a philosophy. It's a description of reality."

He was serious; his brow furrowed with the weight of insight. It was almost comic. Maybe the world was in the process of becoming a vicious cartoon and men like Trebeaux were the principle cartoonists.

"God save the Rainmaker," I said, remembering sad old Clive Renseller face-up under Mona's sturdy haunches.

Trebeaux scoffed. "Rainmaker my tired ass," he said. "That's an in-house joke. Renseller was pure figurehead. The bank liked his looks, his public style. He was a work of corporate art. He was useful as an image, period. If anyone's a rainmaker around here, it's me. I brought in all the straight dollars, kissed all the straight asses, fucked the unfucked wives. Clive got the credit. The truth is, Clive couldn't sell dogshit to blowflies. He looked like God but he was a dim bulb."

"So Renseller was expendable, too."

"Sure he was. We all are, at some point. But he had value as long as his public image remained untainted. You on the other hand have no value for anyone."

I needed more equity. Breaking his arm and disabling Clara wasn't enough. I took the gun out of my pocket. "Let's see how expendable you are, Lenny," I said.

"Wait now," Lenny said, raising his good arm. "This could still work in your favor. We could come up with something. You look good in that suit. Maybe we could find you something here at the bank. Fernando has all the money in the world. It comes here in truckloads. He's a broker, Walkinghorse, if you understand what that means."

I didn't but wasn't about to ask. I didn't care.

I thought of Jillian, of Trebeaux fucking her. I thought of Gert, pregnant with Trey Stovekiss's child. I thought of King David fucking Bathsheba then sending his good soldier Uriah off to be killed so that he could add Bathsheba to his harem. I thought of Rigoberto who died for people who didn't know him and didn't want to know him. I thought of his ears and the *pocho's* knife. I thought of the bullet that proved Rigoberto's expendability.

These thoughts opened a volcano of mindless rage I could not cap.

Trebeaux started mewling. "Walkinghorse, please, for the love of Christ, calm down. Think of your future. We can fix you up so that you'll never have to worry about money again. Believe me, none of what happened to you was my idea!"

"Right. It was the bank's idea. You're just an expendable cog in the great green wheel." I put the gun back into my pocket. I stripped the belt out of his street pants, wrapped it around his ankles and cinched it tight. I carried him out to the open-air deck. The railing was wrought iron interspersed with spear-point posts. I hooked his belt on a spear-point, then dropped him. He hung there by his ankles, three-hundred feet above the busy street. It was a windy day. The high-pitched sounds Trebeaux made blended with the moaning wind and traffic noise below.

"Clara should work her way loose in a few minutes, Lenny. Then you'll find out if she finds you expendable or not." I said this while looking at Clara. Her expression was calm, even amused. She might have been at a tea party.

"Gee, Walkinghorse," she said. "You put a crimp in J.P. Morgan's day. He's not going to make his pep talk to the Helmstrom group, one of the biggest money-laundering fronts on the continent. They're breaking ground next week for the new Upper Valley theme park—Sand and Sky, I think it's called. You can clean a lot of tainted cash in a big fancy-ass theme park."

She didn't think much of the banker and didn't mind letting him know it. She worked for Solís, not Trebeaux. It didn't matter what Lenny thought of her. She was muscle, not brain, though I think she had a double-digit advantage over Lenny when it came to I.Q. points.

I started to walk out.

"Wait," Clara said. "I need a toot. Look in my purse. There's a vial of blow in there. Give me a break, okay?"

I remembered the flask of tequila she gave me in Samala-yuca, my gratitude for it. I opened her purse and found the vial along with her coke spoon. I filled the spoon and held it under a nostril. I pressed the other nostril shut. She vacuumed it up.

"Thanks, *vato*," she said. "I'll fuck you again sometime. I mean consensually, if you live long enough. You get to ride on top next time. What do you say?"

"I'd rather ride a cobra," I said.

TWENTY-TWO

I drove back to The Baron Arms. The first thing I did was move my stuff to another apartment. If anyone was going to come after me, they were going to have to hunt through the entire complex. I had Trebeaux's pistol and intended to sleep with it. Maybe I'd buy a shotgun for added splatter power.

Before I unplugged my phone and answering machine, I checked my messages. The first was from Zipporah. "Sam's in Providence," she said. "Meet us there this evening at six, if you can. Zack's flying in from Brussels. They're going to operate tomorrow. It's fifty-fifty, the doc says."

The second message was from Dale Rooney of Rooney and Vesco: "You appreciate, do you not, Mr. Walkinghorse, that jail sentences can be imposed for non-payment in alimony settlement cases? The court has confirmed the referee's report and granted the motion to punish you for contempt. You can avoid these proceedings by simply paying Mrs. Walkinghorse what the referee, the honorable Kenneth G. Skinner, has determined you owe her. The amount, as of this date, is eleven-thousand one-hundred sixty-seven dollars and nine cents. If you do not comply with the terms of this judgment, an order of commitment will be issued and you will be put in jail. I do hope you understand the gravity of your situation. Do the right thing, Mr. Walkinghorse."

I did the right thing. I drove to Providence Memorial and met Zipporah in a smoking room adjacent to the main lobby of Providence. "He's in pre-op," she said, stubbing out her cigarette. "Maggie and Isaiah are with him. He looks like shit. I don't think he's going to make it through the operation."

We went up to the fifth floor where the operating rooms were, then to the neurosurgery wing. Sam was in a ward of a dozen or so beds. Each bed had a privacy screen around it. Maggie sat next to Sam, holding his hand. Isaiah stood behind Maggie, his big hands on her shoulders.

Sam was out of it. They were giving him morphine. An IV drip was plugged into a heplock in his forearm. Maggie looked at me. There were tears in her eyes. "He was in terrible pain, Uriah," she said. "It came on suddenly. He said his head was trying to split open, as if there was something inside it trying to get out."

"He doesn't like the morphine," Isaiah said. "Says it makes everything blur over. He always liked to keep a sharp eye on things."

Sam opened his eyes and looked in my direction. "Where've you been?" he said. He didn't mean me. There was too much expectation in his eyes. I usually got a quick glance and a lecture, not a lingering appraisal. I said nothing.

"He's been looking for Jesus," Isaiah said. "Seems the drugs have dimmed his spiritual eyes."

"Spiritual eyes," I said.

"That's what he calls them. When he can see Jesus, I mean."

I pulled him aside. "Let's go outside a minute," I said.

We left pre-op and sat down in the heavily cushioned chairs of the waiting room. I didn't exactly know how to begin.

"What?" Isaiah said after a minute.

"I know you think Mose is a lost cause," I said.

"I never said that."

"But you thought it. We all did. Me especially, because I've seen him."

"But now you're thinking differently?"

"I'm thinking differently." I meant it in a broader sense. Isaiah seemed to grasp this.

"Enlighten me, Uriah," he said.

"There's this place way the hell up in the Black Mountains called La Xanadu. It's a private re-hab clinic known for bending the rules. I want to put Mose into it. More for Maggie than for Mose."

"And you think they'll get him off the junk?"

"It's worth a try."

Isaiah sighed. "You can't make a cat quit tearing up the sofa unless you de-claw him. They going to de-claw Moses? I don't think so. Besides, where are you going to get the money for it? Private clinics don't take in bums, and that's what Moses is, Uriah, a bum."

"I think I can get the money," I said. "But I'll need your help." It wasn't clear to me yet how I'd pull it off, but the impulse that made me say it seemed to have some conviction behind it.

"We going to rob a bank?"

"No. I mean I'll need your help in taking him up there."

"You mean you want to kidnap him."

"Abduct, kidnap, forced escort, a drive in the country. Doesn't matter what we call it, we'll just see to it that he gets there."

Isaiah took a deep breath and let it sigh out. "You work it out, Uriah. I'll help if I can."

"Great. That's what I wanted to hear. Maybe we can do this in a few weeks."

"If he doesn't OD by then."

"Right."

We went back to pre-op. Sam was in a morphine doze. Even though he was mostly unconscious, his pain was visible

157

in his worried brow and the drawn white skin around his eyes.

I kissed Maggie and Zipporah, shook Isaiah's hand, and left.

In the neurosurgery wing a man in a hospital bathrobe stopped me. "You got a cigarette, my friend?" he said. I knew he was speaking to me because he'd put his hand on my arm, but he was directing his attention at the empty space immediately to my left. All he showed me was his full left profile. "I could kill for a pack of Benson and Hedges."

"I don't smoke," I said.

"Shit, you're one of *them,*" he said. "The new storm-troopers. Pretty soon they'll set up concentration camps for us die-hard weed beaters."

He looked normal enough, handsome even, but when I moved to face him he turned away, offering his left profile only. "I haven't had a goddamned cigarette since the operation," he said. "That's ten days now."

"The gift shop might sell cigarettes," I said.

"Not a hospital gift shop. Not these days. Where you been, man, on Mars? Smokers are the modern day lepers."

He forgot himself. He turned to face me full-front. The right half of his head was gone. The eyehole was sewn shut. Where the cheek bone should have been was a deep concavity. His skull on that side was hairless and flat as a board. A thick wound tracked with sutures made a red horseshoe from the empty eye socket to the bony area behind his ear hole.

"Jesus," I said.

He grinned with half his mouth. "Brain cancer," he said. "The docs took half my brain and some of the skull bone. I'm working with the left side only. I'll still be able to count beans when I get out, but no more poetry writing! No more playing grab-ass with the artsy-fartsy crowd! No sir!" He laughed at the absurdity of these notions. His laugh sounded like gravel falling through a drain pipe. "Hell, I'm a CPA so it's no big loss."

He turned the handsome side of his face to me again and spoke to the wall. "You roll with the punches, bud. But if I don't get a smoke pretty fucking soon I'm going to flip what's left of my lid."

I left the hospital, wondering why I'd asked Isaiah to help me kidnap Mose. I didn't have a plan. I'd committed myself to something, and didn't know what it was or how I was going to carry it out. Maybe my life had reached a turning point. Maybe I was just hoping my life had reached a turning point.

TWENTY-THREE

I spent the night in 34A. It wasn't a good night. My neighbor was a nocturnal type. Lots of comings-and-goings, door-slammings, occasional shouts, the endless percussive thuds of hip hop. I woke several times from half-sleep with the gun in my hand, aiming at the noise. I'd been having bad dreams. Images from them drifted through the room like targets.

I got up before sunrise and made myself a yogurt shake. I hadn't had a decent workout in weeks, my diet was screwed, and I looked bad. I'd added tallow to my waist and my arms felt mealy. I tried the Thomas Inch dumbbells, but I crapped out after cheating my way through a set of biceps curls and triceps presses. My rotator cuffs ached and I felt a stinging burn, as if a thread of electrically charged wire ran from the back of my neck to my elbows. My old back injury throbbed like an abscessed tooth. I checked myself out in the bathroom mirror. My pecs had lost tone and were sagging a bit; my deltoids looked wasted; there were early signs of leaflard at the jaw; my abs were blurred by new fat. The equipment was definitely on the skids. I showered, dressed, had a second breakfast of scrambled egg whites and toast, then drove out to the airport to pick up Zacharias. Isaiah and Zipporah were working, so the job fell to me.

Zack, the youngest of Sam's and Maggie's adoptees, intimidated me. He was pure genius embedded in a no-nonsense personality. He could read and write before kindergarten. By the age of ten he'd mastered analytical geometry, calculus, and could play *The Flight of the Bumblebee*

160

on the violin. He was a good kid, but a born skeptic. "If Adam and Eve were the first human beings," he once asked Sam, "and if Cain and Abel were their first children, then how did Cain find a wife in the land of Nod? Was Nod a place like Eden? Did it have its own Adam and Eve? And how could Adam live to be nine-hundred and thirty years old? It doesn't make sense, Daddy."

"Sense is overrated," Sam said, dodging the issue—or maybe expanding it. "God's ways are not geared to man's ability to understand them. Remember, son, God is not a rational being." Zack's Korean eyes widened as if this was the scariest thing he'd ever heard. But he wasn't buying any of it and so didn't follow up with a set of new questions raised by Sam's notion of an irrational God.

Zack never questioned Sam or the Bible again: he'd outgrown both of them before his teens. He became a Buddhist when he was twenty but kept the conversion from Sam and Maggie. He went to Stanford on a scholarship and got his law degree at the University of San Francisco. He now worked for an import-export conglomerate, making deals that danced around World Trade Organization mandates. He didn't have much time for family matters, but even if he did he probably wouldn't have come home except for emergencies. He wasn't exactly aloof, he just lived in a larger, more logically structured and far more sophisticated world.

He came off the plane looking grim. I waved above the crowd. It took him a few seconds to recognize me. I hadn't seen Zack in ten years. He was just under six feet tall and heavier than I remembered—a side-effect of prosperity. His bristly hair was black as liquid tar and combed straight back. He was dressed for flying—khaki slacks, pullover shirt, sandals.

"Fucking airplanes," he said. "I've been in the air for the last fourteen hours. Your intestines get knotted up when you sit that long. I would have taken the Concorde but there was no way to get a seat on short notice. How's Sam doing?"

"I don't think he's going to make it," I said.

He set down his carry-on bag and shook my hand. His grip was firm and confident. "And how're you doing, big brother? You look a bit tapped out."

"Getting by," I said.

He knew it was an evasion, but didn't follow up. We exchanged more pleasantries on our way out to the parking lot–life in San Francisco, life in Europe, life in general. He was more talkative than I remembered. I guessed that was a result of his success in the larger world. On the way into town from the airport he told me about a Korean couple in Brussels who mistook him for a countryman and started speaking to him in their language. Zack speaks five languages, but not Korean. He answered them in border Spanish, his second language. It was a reflex. In border towns you get used to people addressing you in Spanish. Your reaction is to call up what you know of the language and respond as well as you can. The Koreans surprised him, and Zack reverted to the border-town reflex. *"¿Mande?"* he said to them. They were pointing to their tourist brochure, at a full-page glossy of the little brass boy pissing in the fountain at *Rue de l'Etuve.* *"No valedón esa transa,"* he said, instructing them not to bother with it. But his indecipherable reply left them open-mouthed with astonishment.

He went on for a while, then lapsed into silence. I was curious about him and took the opportunity to ask a direct question. "What exactly do you do, Zack, traveling from country to country?"

"To put it in a nutshell, Uri, I look for loopholes in export-import laws then design ICPs–internal compliance programs– to keep my clients one step ahead of the regulators. My clients are multi-national in structure. The idea is to get goods from point A to point B without triggering certain encumbering restrictions imposed by the transnational trade barriers."

"Thanks for keeping it simple," I said.

He saw that I was annoyed. "The technical details are boring, Uri. International legalese is as dull as the local kind. The bottom line is, I help the rich get richer."

This made me think of Dale Rooney's threat. I was annoyed enough now to be blunt. "How much money do you make, Zack? Are *you* rich?"

He laughed. "Rich is a subjective term that needs qualification, Uri. I make a shitload of money and I've got a couple of seven-figure annuities I'm still feeding, but am I rich? No, not even close. On an absolute scale in a world of very rich people I'm just a waterboy. The rich stay put, they don't have to book overnight flights to Buttfuck, Turkestan or wherever at the whim of dyspeptic old men in pinstripes."

The timing was probably bad, but the timing would always be bad for what I had to say. "I'm going to force Moses into a re-hab clinic up in the Black Mountains. It'll be expensive." I took a couple of breaths.

"And?"

"And can you contribute a few grand to the cause."

"A few grand down a rat hole you mean."

"I'm doing it for Maggie, Zack. Maggie needs something good to happen."

"Don't we all."

"You don't exactly look fucked-over by bad breaks."

"The answer is no, Uri."

"He's your brother, Zack, sad sack of shit that he is."

"Don't give me that 'he's your brother' crap. We're a bunch of mongrels who were lucky enough to be taken in by a Bible-crazed lunatic and his sweet wife when we could have been stuffed into the nearest dumpster in our diapers, but don't tell me Moses is my fucking brother. He's an unreformable loser and you know it. And don't tell me you have any real hope of turning that asshole into a straight arrow."

I got off the freeway at the Mesa Street exit and headed into town. The silence between us was thick enough to cut. Zack finally broke it.

"All right," he said. "Here's how we'll do it. You have Moses write to me. Let him ask for the money. I want him to tell me, in writing, that he wants to take the cure. Then I'll finance the whole trip."

"Your money's safe, Zack. You know he won't do it."

"If he doesn't want to clean up, he won't. You should know that."

"I'm thinking of Maggie," I said.

"Good. Think of her. Straighten your own life out. That will go a long way toward making her happy."

What did he know of my life? "Mose was her first baby," I said. "A mother can't forget her first."

"When you started pumping iron—I guess you were about sixteen—I hero-worshipped you. My big brother, the muscle man. By the time I was in high school, I could see—hell, anyone could see—that you were going overboard. You were obsessed with it, Mr. West Side. And it looks like you still are. But what else have you done? How long do you think you can keep a sculpted body? Until you're sixty? Seventy?"

"We were talking about Moses, not me."

"Write him off. He's written the rest of us off, including Maggie."

The dull roar of downtown traffic filled the silence between us. Zack had put on a pair of Italian shades. He looked around at the city he'd grown up in. He hadn't been back home in ten years and the city had changed a lot in that time.

"Prosperity," he said. When I didn't respond, he said, "It's here, too. The whole damn world is suffering from it."

"What do you mean, 'suffering'?"

"The higher you fly, the farther you fall. Boom and bust. It's the old fever, but the ride up has been exceptionally steep and long-lasting. It's historic, and the collapse will be historic, too. We're in a collective delerium right now. But the big boys will get a little too greedy again, as they usually do, and things will begin to erode. The economy here on the border has always been iffy. But in a way the folks here are lucky. The local economy will always survive on the drug trade."

"You say that like you approve."

"My approval or disapproval has nothing to do with it. We're talking about the massive influx of cash. This area used to be called the Sun Belt. Now it's called the Laundry Belt. Banks from San Diego to Miami are stuffed with laundry. Nobody objects. It keeps the communities thriving."

"What do you mean nobody objects? What about the law?"

Zack studied me for a few seconds to see if I was serious. I snickered a bit to make him think I was playing the rube on purpose. He wasn't buying. He laughed at me.

"Uri, all these laundromats have massive year-end surpluses," he said. "These surpluses run into the billions. And no one asks them to explain. If a citizen tries to make a deposit of more than ten grand in cash, all the alarms go off. The citizen will need a damn good explanation ready about where the money came from. The banks aren't subject to that kind of scrutiny. A bank surplus just means the organization is sound and that its execs are sharp businessmen. Why do you think the banks lobbied hard for NAFTA? They knew their vaults would fill up with truckloads of drug money from across the Rio."

We were close enough to see the Cibola building. I slowed

down and pointed to it. "There's Cibola Savings and Loan," I said. "Mexican owned. They've got their hand in some major building projects here in town."

Zack laughed. "Nervy bastards! Calling their laundromat 'Cibola,' the fabulous land of the seven golden cities! You've got to respect their chutzpah!"

His self-assurance irritated me. "So how do you get all this inside information, Zack?" I said.

"Through the eyes and ears, big brother. The world is made out of glass. Only the dead can't see through it."

TWENTY-FOUR

Zack checked into a two-room suite on the top floor of the downtown Westin hotel. We had a couple of margaritas each in the bar, then drove to Providence.

Sam was in ICU, still in an anesthetic twilight. His head was wrapped in bandages. The IV drip was now plugged into a heplock high on his thin chest. He looked a hundred years old. Machines beeped on the wall behind his bed. "I'm going to puke," he said.

Maggie left the privacy-screened bed to find a nurse. Two nurses came back with her. Sam had pushed himself up to a sitting position. The nurses looked for something Sam could puke in. They couldn't find anything. Sam's mouth yawned open and blood the color of burgundy spilled out of it. He filled the blanket in the depression between his knees.

"No problem," one of the nurses said. "They all puke. It's the anesthetic. We've got plenty of clean blankets." She wiped his dark lips with a wash cloth. "Don't worry about the blood. It's just drainage."

Sam sank back into his pillow. "Where is he?" he said.

"Where is who, dear?" Maggie said. "Zacharias? Zacharias is here, Sam. He flew all the way from Belgium to see you."

Sam's eyes raked his surroundings desperately, lingering on none of us, not even Zack. We were all there, around his bed, but he was expecting someone else. He slid his hands out of the covers. He touched the bandages on his head gingerly. The skin of his hands looked like wet paper. The veins and the action of the bones were visible under the papery skin.

"He's gone back," he said.

This time Maggie didn't ask who he meant.

"You took him from me," he said to all of us, his eyes full of accusation.

He turned his head to one side. He closed his eyes, shutting us out. His pulse beeped electronically, providing a rhythm for our uneasy vigil.

Maggie started to cry and Isaiah took her in his arms.

"You're going to be okay, daddy," Zipporah said.

Doctor Bill Sandy, the surgeon who had operated on Sam, pushed the curtain aside and came in. He was humming a Buddy Holly tune in a tone-deaf way. "How's grandpa doing?" he said. Bill Sandy was a tall, white-haired man with bad teeth and gin blossoms on his wide, porous nose. Fresh from another surgery, he was still in his blood-spotted OR apron. He studied the electronic displays as he hummed.

A drain had been implanted in the side of Sam's head to take away the excess intracranial fluids that collect after an operation where half the skull is temporarily removed. Doctor Sandy wiggled the clear plastic tube to make sure the drain was working properly.

"Everything looks A-okay," he said. "Grandpa should be up and around in a couple of days. We've got the biopsy back from the lab. It was the nasty thing we thought it was, all right. The good news is we got just about all of it. It was a big son of a gun, but we think we got ninety-nine point nine percent. We'll start radiation ASAP."

Maggie wiped her eyes with a Kleenex. "Doctor," she said,

"could a brain tumor that big cause someone to see the hereafter?"

"Come again?" Doctor Sandy said, smiling a little, checking the rest of us to see if we were in on the joke.

"Sam was hallucinating," Zipporah said. "Thought he saw Jesus."

"The brain's still a mystery," Doctor Sandy said. "It's like a very complex musical instrument. Mess with it, you sometimes get sounds no one ever heard." He smiled at his makeshift analogy. His long teeth were edged with black. He checked his watch, started his off-key humming again.

Sam turned to face the doctor. "You took him away from me," he said.

Bill Sandy smiled darkly. "Anything's possible, grandpa," he said.

TWENTY-FIVE

I drove Zack back to his hotel. We had another drink in the bar. Then the rest of the Walkinghorse family showed up. Zack had made reservations earlier for five in the Westin's dining room. It was a reunion, after all, the first time we'd all been together in ten years. A reunion minus Moses and Sam.

At the dinner table, Zack raised his glass of wine. "Here's to our little rainbow family," he said, and we all managed to laugh. Even Maggie smiled. There weren't going to be many more occasions to smile in what remained of her life. Zack, realizing that her smile had taken heroic effort, put his arm around her. "Everything's going to work out, Ma," he said.

I raised my glass. "Here's to things working out," I said, "and to the generosity of those who help make things work out." I was a little drunk. Isaiah glanced at me sharply. Zipporah kicked my ankle.

"*What?* What did I say?" I said. I downed the rest of my wine, poured another glass.

"This isn't the time for you to vent your bitterness," Zipporah said.

"Bitterness? I'm not bitter. I'm fine. My life is fine. I'm changing my ways, didn't I tell you that?"

"Shut up," Isaiah said.

Our food came. Flaming steak Diane for all, on Zack's hotel tab. Isaiah said grace the way Sam had said it all the years we lived together in the house on East San Pablo Street. We all

170

held hands and Isaiah in his deep sonorous voice said, "Lord make us worthy of this bounty." Then he added, "And thank you, Lord, for the safe return of our beloved brother, Zacharias."

Middle-aged yuppies seated close by looked at us as if we were dinosaurs. No one said grace anymore, especially not in a loud, unselfconscious voice in a restaurant that catered to the elite of our city. Some of the yuppies frowned, as if Isaiah had committed an unacceptable social offense.

As we ate, Zack regaled us with stories of his adventures abroad, deflecting attention from me. For which I was grateful. I wasn't looking for sympathy, but the margaritas and now the wine had made me careless. I wanted my brothers and sister to know what I'd been through, and knew I couldn't tell them. I was alone with my troubles and would stay alone with them.

And now a cheap emotion twisted my guts. Zack was the man of the hour, a bigger-than-life Walkinghorse who cut deals that affected the economies of nations, and this dinner celebrated the return of the hero. The others were mesmerized by his exotic tales. I was merely jealous. Zack was in his mid-thirties and could probably retire at forty. All I had at forty-two were a failing physique, jail threats from my ex-wife, and death threats from people who thought I was one of the expendables. In a way, it was a reverse prodigal son story: Zack left home and prospered; I stayed, and ran my life into the ground.

I excused myself from the table and headed toward the men's room. But I didn't go in. Around the corner from the men's room were the elevators. I took one to the underground parking garage, found my old Ford, and drove back into my expendable life.

Jillian Renseller's Mercedes was parked in The Baron Arms parking lot, next to my slot. I took Lenny Trebeaux's Beretta out of the glove compartment and got out. I touched the hood of the Mercedes. It was cold. The car had been parked here for some time. I went up to the fourth floor. Jillian was leaning against my door, smoking a cigarette. "Where the Christ have you been?" she said, crushing the cigarette under her shoe. She was dressed in solid black: ankle-length skirt with a wide patent leather belt, long-sleeved silk blouse, three-inch heels. No make-up. No jewelry. Nothing in her black eyes but fear and anger. She looked like a nun on the run from berserk monks.

It was dusk. The west sky could have been a first-rate motel painting—stars flickering red through grainy air, the horizon a deep magenta streaked with blood orange, the black plateau of the Malpais country—but the painter's misguided after-thought made the painting perverse: the moon's early crescent floated like a malevolent yellow smile against the vast higher dark.

"I've been standing here for a goddamned hour," she said, grim as a stood-up wife.

"Nice seeing you again," I said. "I bet you thought something unpleasant happened to me."

"Please, don't be a smart ass. I know what happened to you. I did my best to stop them."

"So I've been told."

We went inside. "What do you have to drink?" she said.

"Just tequila."

She made a face. "Mix it with something, will you? Any kind of juice."

I poured half a glass of Viuda de Sanchez, filled it the rest of the way with grapefruit juice. She took it from me and swallowed some. She shuddered. "Christ, how can anyone drink this shit?" she said.

"You didn't come here for free drinks," I suggested.

She took another swallow, set the glass down. "What you did to Lenny," she said. "That was a mistake. I thought you had some sense."

I poured myself a shot of the Viuda, then set it aside. I'd had more than my quota for the day. Then I knocked it back anyway. Sense? Why would anyone think I had sense?

"Why do you care?" I said.

She sat on the bed, swallowed more of her drink, made a face. She looked like a sick child forced to take foul medicine. I sat next to her, took the drink from her hand. I kissed her cold lips. She kissed back, heat momentarily flaring, then she broke away.

"No," she said. "We've got to get out of here."

"I've been sleeping in a different apartment. We could go there."

"No. I mean we need to get out of town for a while."

She held her arms against her breasts as if trying to contain something explosive within her body. It looked like she was having a panic attack. I put my arm around her to help contain it.

"What happened, Jillian?" I said.

She shrugged away from my arm. "I tried to save your life again. It may cost me mine."

TWENTY-SIX

It wasn't until we were in Deming, New Mexico, that she told me what she'd done. The break-in at the Farnsworth home wasn't ordered by Solís. It was Jillian's idea. She conned Forbes—who was on Solís' payroll, not hers—to break in and get the tapes of Clive and Mona acting out their obedience and punishment games in the dungeon. She convinced Forbes that it was the best thing to do for his *jefe*, the reputation of her husband, and for Cibola Savings and Loan itself. Forbes didn't check it out with Solís. He took it for granted that she spoke for *el jefe* since he and Jillian lived in the same rarefied air of the super rich. No one would ever mistake Forbes for a rocket scientist, she said.

It was an easy break-in. Forbes waited for a day when the kids were in school and Mona and Jerry were off on a shopping trip. The tapes were under lock and key, but Jillian knew where they were. The cabinet where the tapes were kept was easily pried open. There were six tapes, and they all were dated and labeled. Forbes brought them to Jillian and she told him that her intention was to destroy them.

"But I didn't," she said. "I played a few of them in my VCR, then took Polaroids of some choice scenes."

We were in the car, in downtown Deming. The town was dark and empty. An occasional eighteen-wheeler roared by on the Interstate that paralleled the main drag. Jillian leaned against me. "I did it for you," she said.

174

"Did *what?*" So far she wasn't making a lot of sense. There wasn't any reason to have Forbes steal the tapes. The Farnsworths had nothing to gain and everything to lose by making the tapes public. They were safe where they were.

"I sent the Polaroids to *Know It All!* The tabloid. I sent them anonymously."

I pushed her away from me. "Are you out of your mind? How in the hell is that going to help me?"

"The secret is out, don't you see? You're not a threat to them anymore."

It still didn't make sense. "A threat to them? You're one of *them,* Jillian. Where does this leave you?"

"I've never been one of them. Neither was Clive. Maybe you know that by now. Clive was all image. He fronted for Fernie and his backers in Mexico. They hired him because he looked like *el supergringo.* They wanted to make sure the bank had a one-hundred percent American look to it. They wouldn't even hire Mexican tellers."

"The bank is a laundromat," I said.

She laughed. "Of course it is. Most banks on the border *are,* to some degree. Drug money finds its way into them, one way or another. Cibola is a little different in that it's owned by a major *traficante.* The drug money doesn't have to be smuggled out of the country or deposited in U.S. banks in amounts small enough to not send up red flags. It can be dumped directly into Cibola by the truckload. Fernie also brokers for other *traficantes.* He buys their dollars at a healthy discount and gives them pesos, euros, English pounds, Yen, or whatever, by making wire transfers to their accounts in foreign banks. Fernie probably makes more money brokering than he does trafficking."

She started the car and idled down Deming's main drag. "Let's find a motel," she said.

She drove slowly, scanning side streets at every intersection. She turned down one of them and headed toward a blue neon Vacancy sign. She pulled into the driveway of *The Oasis,* an ancient roadhouse with no affiliations to the big motel chains. "I like these old stucco relics," she said.

I studied her. *No you don't,* I thought. *The beds are swayback and crusty with old trysts, and the art, if there is any, is palm trees on black velvet.* She'd put her life in jeopardy by giving the Polaroids to the tabloid, and now she wanted to spend the night in a rustic Deming motel, as if we were lovers on a spree. I decided that she was lying, but had no inkling why.

She checked in, and we took a room at the back of the U-shaped court. As soon as we were inside, she said, "Get naked." I did. Then she did.

We acted out the ritual of lovers in love. It was sweet and tender and false and tainted with deceit. At the height of our passion I had a realization: I wasn't capable of loving anyone. I didn't know what love was. I didn't understand how two people could come to believe that they were joined forever at the hip. The fear of loneliness seemed to me the binding force that people misidentified as love. Love didn't exist. Love was a word people used to cover the black hole that lives in the center of personality. The black hole was death and all the little deaths-in-life, such as loneliness and failure and self-hatred.

I chuckled a bit and Jillian looked up at me, scolding me with her eyes. I was thinking of Gert, how she must have sensed my secret, and how she had found the end of loneliness in the arms of a stock car racer.

But Jillian was as incapable of love as I was. Which made her story of self-sacrifice all the more puzzling. If she had actually given the Polaroids to the tabloid, then she'd done it for some other reason. A reason she wasn't willing to admit.

In the shower afterwards, she said, "Why were you laughing? You made me lose my concentration. I almost didn't get off. Were you being deliberately mean?"

I didn't want to tell her my discovery. It shamed me. No one can make that kind of confession. It would be like confessing a lust to murder children.

"Come on, *tell* me," she laughed. She put her hand on my balls. "Tell me now, or I'll squeeze the little suckers blue, I swear."

I took her by the wrist and forced her hand away. I pushed her against the cracked and mildewed tiles. I gripped her thighs and lifted, then entered her again, without finesse. Just to shut her up.

TWENTY-SEVEN

She wanted to eat. We got dressed and drove through Deming looking for something that was still open. We found a tiny, eight-table Mexican place on a street next to the railroad tracks. We both ordered *salpicón*.

"You're getting fat," she said.

I was pushing two-forty and felt it. My pants were tight, my shirts barely closed. "Thanks for reminding me," I said.

"Don't be so vain. You're still beautiful, hon."

Our food came. She attacked hers as if she hadn't eaten for a week. She didn't eat with upper class refinement. Her table manners were pure blue collar. She held her fork in her fist and she stabbed the meat with the fury of a hungry field hand. She mopped up the salsa with a folded tortilla and she chewed it fiercely, with her mouth partly open. I felt I was seeing the real Jillian Renseller for the first time. I liked what I saw.

"What are you smiling at now?" she said.

"You. The way you eat. I don't think you were raised in a mansion by nannies."

She laughed. "You're right. My daddy was a fisherman. I grew up in a shanty in Coos Bay, Oregon. We lived in a four room shack, all five of us."

Her eyes darkened with the memory of her childhood. "You grew up poor," I said.

"Poor? I guess so. There was always food on the table.

Salmon, if nothing else. But, sure. There were no amenities. How about you? You weren't born with a silver spoon in your mouth, right?"

I told her how I was born. I told her about Sam and Maggie and their five racially mixed adoptees. I told her about Sam's religious obsessions, Maggie's saintly passiveness. I bragged about Zipporah, Isaiah, and Zack, but didn't mention Moses.

"Complicated," she said. "But you turned out all right, didn't you. Or am I missing something?"

"I'm all right enough, I guess."

She finished her brisket, then ate half of mine. We lingered over a couple of beers. The owner of the restaurant, who was also cook and waiter, came by our table tapping his wrist-watch. It was late and he wanted to close up and go home. We took the unfinished beers out to the Mercedes. A long freight train passed through town, not more than twenty feet from the car. When the last car clattered by, the silence rang in my ears. I put my arm around her and drew her close, but she shrugged me off. She didn't want to get comfortable; she wanted to talk.

"I was raped when I was twelve," she said.

I started to respond but she put a finger on my lips. "He was a fisherman–Caleb Brisbane, a friend of the family. He saw me walking home from school and stopped to give me a ride. But he didn't take me home. He drove me to a little cabin back in the hills. He said it was a game. I wasn't scared because I knew him and knew he was a friend of daddy's."

"Jesus Christ," I said.

"But you know what? It wasn't really rape, not in the usual way you think of rape. He was nice looking and he was gentle. He made a game of it, and I became a willing player. I was born hot, I guess. He didn't use force. He even got me to invent new twists."

179

"But you were twelve."

"It changed my life—being made into a woman at that age, but at the time, I liked it. My family found out though. I came home late that night and there was blood on my legs. My mother had a screaming fit and my daddy loaded his shotgun. He and my brothers went to Caleb's cabin and beat him half to death. They kicked out his teeth, blinded him in one eye, and broke his back. I think I was more traumatized by what they did to him than by what he did to me. I mean, this family friend was crippled for life because of what he'd done to me, but I had been a willing participant. No charges were brought against daddy or my brothers, after it became known what Caleb did."

I said the two lamest words in the language: "I'm sorry."

"That's not the half of it," she said. "After that, my brothers began to treat me differently. One was sixteen, the other eighteen. I'd become a mystery to them. I was 'damaged goods'—a *woman,* and they were still boys.

"I slept in a lean-to addition to our little shanty. It was tiny, but it was the only really private room in the house. My older brother began to visit me late at night when everyone else was asleep. I let him. I didn't care. I didn't enjoy him the way I had enjoyed Caleb, but I wasn't revolted, either. Then my younger brother got into the act. They began to trade late-night visits to my lean-to." She took a long sip of her beer. "Lovely family, huh?"

"I'm surprised you didn't get pregnant," I said.

"Oh, I got pregnant all right. I went to a church-sponsored retreat that took care of pregnant teens. The baby—a healthy boy—was put up for adoption. I never saw him, never wanted to. It blew my family apart. The boys were kicked out. Shortly after that my daddy had a massive stroke. He lived totally paralyzed for a couple of years before he died. My mom died of cancer a few years later. My brothers found homes in the army. I've never heard from them."

"But you turned out all right," I said, "or am I missing something."

She gave me a hard look, then laughed. "We're all missing something, aren't we? It didn't hit me until years later, what had been done to me."

"You had a breakdown?"

"No. I'm too much of a determined survivor for that. I was treating men very badly. I had two early marriages that ended in weeks. I tried counseling, but the counselors pissed me off. They were textbook types without real-world experience. They pretended to know what I'd been through, as if they could get inside my experience. But everything they said rang false, even though it made good sense. The only thing I did that helped was to look back at all these things as life-shaping catastrophes that make you what you are. You either accept them as you accept the weather or fight a losing battle until you go down in flames. I'm promiscuous, I'm a bitch, and maybe it's because of what happened to me, but I might have been promiscuous and a bitch had I grown up completely protected from the craziness of others. It's a fucking mystery, all of it, don't you think? Or do you have another working version of life's little disasters?"

"Shit happens."

"To put it in a nutshell."

I swallowed some beer. She started the car and drove us back to the Oasis motel.

TWENTY-EIGHT

It was almost dawn. Neither one of us had slept. We'd talked the night away. At one point I asked, "How did Solís come to pick Clive as his supergringo?"

"Clive was manager of a small bank in Oak Grove, a Portland suburb," she said. "We went to Mexico on vacation and wound up in Puerta Vallarta. One night Clive got a little drunk and was holding forth in the hotel bar about the wonders of the banking business. He could be impressive. Solís happened to be there. He'd just bought the Cibola building to create a new bank so he could do his own laundry and get into brokering. Clive looked like the gringo face he wanted to put on it. He made Clive an offer he couldn't refuse. It was pure synchronicity. We were in the right place at the right time. It's almost funny now, but that's the way it seemed. Of course we didn't have the first clue what the real purpose of the bank was. Clive thought of himself as sophisticated, but he was a babe in the woods."

"But you eventually figured it out."

"It wasn't too hard. They did a major PR thing when the bank opened. Lots of press coverage. There were celebrity dinners, tea parties for the bigwigs' ladies. Politicians were asked to make speeches at the Cibola ribbon cutting ceremony, their palms pre-greased with campaign contributions. No bank launches itself like that. Fernando bought into the town's political power grid with Clive doing all the hand-shaking and ass-kissing. It took Clive about a year to figure out what the real business of the bank was. The monster year-end cash surplus was a clue. Solís, on the other hand, didn't find out about Clive's twisted sex life until last year."

"Who took the lid off that?"

"I'd taken up with Lenny Trebeaux, Clive's vice president. I told him about Clive's sexual problem to justify my affair with him. I didn't need to justify anything—Clive sure as hell didn't care. In fact, he got off on it. He liked me to tell him the details of what Lenny and I did together. It was part of a punishment scenario that turned him on. Lenny is ambitious. He passed the good news to Fernando."

"Solís must have been worried about this getting out to the public."

"You better believe he was worried. He made it clear that if anything came out about all this, he'd have us 'removed.' I don't think he meant removed back to Portland."

"He couldn't have liked the idea of you being involved with Trebeaux."

"He didn't know about that. He didn't know about Clara and me, either. I can almost feel sorry for Fernando. He's kind of naive for an overlord, a real straight arrow with strong Catholic values. But my fling with Clara was just an experiment. Clara is quite a bull. I played femme to her butch. It didn't mean anything. Not to me, anyway."

I wondered what, if anything, meant something to Jillian Renseller.

"You're lying," I said.

She sat up in bed. "Lying? The hell I am. Nothing I've said is a lie."

"The lie is what you haven't said."

"And what haven't I said, smart ass?"

"You haven't told me the real reason you sent the Polaroids

to *Know It All!* It doesn't make sense that you'd risk your life to save mine. You don't love me. Even if you did, you're a determined survivor. You said so yourself."

She got out of bed. "I wish I still smoked," she said. She paced back and forth in the small room. Gray light wormed through the cheese cloth curtains making everything in the room look stained. The melancholy horn of a freight train moaned in the distance.

"You don't know anything about me," she said. "I *could* love you, damn you. Couldn't I?"

I said it gently: "I don't think so, Jillian."

"I'm going to visit a friend in California," she said. "Why don't you come with me? We'd have a marvelous time."

"I've got an apartment building to manage," I said.

I got out of bed and dressed. I kissed her. A goodbye kiss with no heat. "I'll catch a Greyhound back to the city," I said.

"I want you to come to California with me," she said. "Love isn't an obsolete idea, is it? It still can happen if two people want it to happen badly enough, can't it? You want it to happen, don't you, Uri?"

She looked almost desperate but she was too proud and too tough to allow herself more than a momentary admission of loneliness and fear.

TWENTY-NINE

I slept all the way back to the city, a two hour ride through the northern reaches of the Chihuahuan desert. The Greyhound pulled into the downtown El Paso depot which was packed with veteran travelers. Most of them looked like they were on their way to attend an execution, or had just come back from witnessing one. The weather had turned hot and muggy. It was too early for the monsoon season but the wet south Pacific air had been coming earlier and earlier the past few years. The weather pundits were blaming *el niño,* global warming, and volcano eruptions along the Pacific rim. They obviously didn't have a clue but covered their guesswork with techno-babble that gave every explanation weight. They might as well have blamed Tlaloc, the Aztec rain god.

I went into the depot cafe for coffee. Copies of *Know It All!* and its Spanish language version, *¡Sabelotodo!* were stacked on a shelf next to the cash register. I picked up one of each and carried them to a booth.

Jillian's Polaroids of her husband had made the front page. Mercifully, the picture was blurred and identification would be a matter of informed guessing. A Polaroid taken of a video and reproduced on newsprint didn't have a chance at being Pulitzer quality, but it was clear enough to those in the know. Renseller on his knees, his pathetic white ass up, his big florid face down—down on Mona's feet, sucking a toe. A shadowy figure threatened to part his skull with an ax. Clive's erection

185

had been airbrushed out. The masked-face of the ax-wielder was not in the picture. The caption read:

> Could this be a prominent member
> of the local business community?

The tabloid was covering its scandal-mongering ass by not naming names. The article on the next page, though, came close to identifying the aroused toe-sucker:

> A prominent local banker recently deceased, is now known to have been a habitué of the obedience-punishment salons of our fair city. Regarded by many as a man of great integrity, this pillar of the community led a secret sex life that would have seriously compromised his standing in the many civic and religious organizations he was closely affiliated with. The banker was on friendly terms with the governor and once played a round of golf with the president.

The photo in *¡Sabelotodo!* was the same, but the printing process had worked better and the images were sharper. Sharp enough to show muscle-definition in the arm of the headless ax-man.

My vanity was piqued. I looked passably good. I looked competitive, though I'd put on some tallow since then. The picture was motivational—I had to get back into the gym. I had to get back to low-fat high-protein eating.

I took a cab back to The Baron Arms. I went up to my new room on the third floor, wondering if Jillian was suicidal.

186

What else explained what she'd done? But she wasn't suicidal. She was a survivor. The world might burn down around her, but Jillian would find high green ground. She had another motive, I was sure of that. You don't throw your life away for no reason. Something had happened. Something she'd held back from me. Whatever it was, there were going to be repercussions. Solís was not going to let this go by. Unless there was something I did not know, Jillian had signed her death certificate. As for getting me off the hook, that was about as promising as Lenny Trebeaux's job offer.

My message machine was full of complaints. I didn't want to deal with them. I went to bed and slept for an hour, an ominous sleep packed with paranoid dreams. I got up, showered and dressed, then drove across town to Yarborough Street and the Maximum Firepower Gun Shop, one of the biggest firearms outlets in the city. I wanted a shotgun.

"For *quail* season?" the clerk said, smirking a bit. He had a narrow head, big, close-set eyes, and a beaky nose. He looked like a bird. He seemed to know this, and to combat the image he kept his arms folded on his chest so no one would mistake them for wings.

"No. I want a home-defense weapon."

The clerk's smirky grin grew wider. He opened a glass case behind him and took out a short-barrel 12 gauge. "Mossberg jungle gun," he said. "Semi-automatic. Eighteen inch barrel. Nice and light—only seven pounds. Very easy to use in close quarters. You could hold off an army of thieves with this sweetheart."

It was more than I wanted to spend, but it was exactly what I wanted to have. I showed the clerk my driver's license. He pecked my name and social security number into his computer. It only took a few seconds. "You check out fine with NCIC," he said. "No criminal record. No institutional

187

commitments. Seems you're a reasonably sane law-abiding citizen, for whatever that's worth these days."

I had the urge to take his turkey neck in my hand, but instead picked out a few boxes of shells, double-oughts. I wrote a check, then drove home. I loaded the Mossberg and stashed it under my bed. Then I went across the street to the DMZ. I bought a newspaper out front, and took my usual seat at the bar. Güero wasn't in. Nor was Mando Ojara. The bartender was a woman, apparently a new hire. She was about forty, a bottle-blond, her wide frame upholstered with thick, durable flesh pink as bubblegum.

"What's your poison?" she said.

I looked at her to see if she was kidding. She wasn't. "What's my *poison?* I think barkeeps stopped saying that around 1939."

"What are you, a history buff? You want to let me in on what you want to drink?"

"Margarita, on the rocks, no salt."

"First one's on the house, Tarzan."

She brought the margarita after messing with the makings far too long. It was weak. Too many rocks, too much Triple Sec, not nearly enough tequila. Four lime wedges floated in it like green crescent moons. The rim was crusty with salt.

"Normally," she said, "that would be two-fifty, and I'm talking dollars not pesos." She slapped the flat of her chubby red hand on the bar. "But for opening week, we're treating the customers to their first drink."

My bewildered expression made her smile. I scraped the rock salt off the rim, took a sip. "What do you mean, 'opening week'?"

"Just what I said."

"This drink is weak," I said. Weak and sour and *wrong*.

"New policy. One shot per drink, no generous overspills, none of the good-old-boy doubling up. That's history."

"What do you mean new policy?"

"New policy is new policy. Self-explanatory, I think."

I thought: *Jesus, Güero, what mental facility did you rescue her from? What were you thinking, man? We can't have this! A barkeep who brings your drinks C.O.D. and is either deaf or contrary and who takes five minutes to put it together then fucks it up in every way possible and calls it new policy and blabs nonsense about 'opening week.'* I'd have to have a serious talk with him.

I picked the limes out of the glass, stacked them on a paper napkin, and buried myself in the newspaper so I could shield myself from this new policy barkeep.

Fernando Solís Davila peered out of page two. It was a group photo: the mayor, three city councilmen, Solís in the middle, smiling. His smile was the modest smile of a man who has been asked to take over the leadership of the free world. A construction company he owned, Inter-America Builders, Inc., had been given a contract by the city to build a minimum security high-rise detention center for non-violent drug offenders.

I almost sprayed my drink across the bar.

The old city jail, the article said, was overflowing with occasional users, small-time pushers, and Rio-wading mules who typically carried no more than a few baggies of *mota* grown in Tarahumara country in the Chihuahuan highlands. They were sometimes packed six to a cell in unsanitary conditions. Some prisoners contracted diseases in the lock-up—from relatively minor afflictions such as conjunctivitis and scabies, to pneumonia, galloping strep, and the various strains of hepatitis. A few cases of drug-resistant tuberculosis had been recorded. The conditions in the city jail had been the subject of criticism from human rights organizations for years. Now the city was going to do something about it. The facility would be built on a mesa north of town and would

189

employ up to a hundred people when complete. An architect's sketch of the new jail made it look like a Holiday Inn with wire fences.

I started laughing. There was an element of hysteria in it. The barmaid came over to me. "What? You reading the comic section?" she said. "Share the joke."

"The whole paper is the comic section," I said.

El jefe, narcotraficante kingpin and drug money broker, was building a jail for users, pushers, and mules. I roared. In a way, it made beautiful economic sense: Drug money coming home. What could be more civic minded?

"What?" the barmaid insisted. "Tell me about it, hon. I could use a good laugh." She'd been explaining new policy to an old timer who was stubbornly not getting it.

I headed for the door, still laughing.

"Ya'll come back to Picadilly on the Rio and share that wonderful sense of humor with us, okay?" the barkeep said.

I stopped laughing. "Picadilly on the *what?"*

"It's the new name. When I bought the place, I decided it needed a new name along with a new policy. It's classier than the old one, don't you think?"

"You bought *what?"*

"This bar. For twice what it was worth. But I really wanted a bar of my own."

I looked around the bar for the first time. Güero's collection of dangling modifiers was gone. There was a Union Jack tacked to a wall, along with pictures of Buckingham Palace and other London landmarks.

There was an actual dart board next to the john. Two men in gray suits and salon-cut hair were lofting darts at it. Darts in one hand, gibsons in the other. The regulars never drank gibsons in the DMZ. Give them darts and they'd put their eyes out.

"Güero wouldn't sell the DMZ," I said.

"I made the gentleman an offer he couldn't refuse."

Rule Britannia boomed out over a new speaker system. The dart throwing gibson drinkers raised their glasses.

I stepped out into old policy sunlight, shaken.

THIRTY

L ife is structured by routine. Remove one piece of a routine and your life finds a new tangent and is never the same. The DMZ was a major part of my daily routine. It was *my place*. How could Güero do this to me?

Something must have happened, some family catastrophe. I went back to my apartment and looked for his number in the phone book.

No Odonaju. He'd never told me where he lived. I'd assumed it was here, in town, close to the bar.

I checked the far more numerous Mexican listings. He was there: G. Odonaju, the only Odonaju in the book. The street address was across the Rio in the Juárez: *Calle Vicente Zamora*. I called the number listed.

"¿Bueno?" he said.

"Güero? This is Uri. What have you fucking *done*, man?"

"What are you talking about?"

"You know what I'm talking about. The *bar*, man. There's some dipshit barkeep in there claiming she owns it."

"Beatrice Westfall. She met my outrageous price. What can I say?"

"You can say it isn't so. You can say it's a fixable mistake. I can't *go* there, Güero. She's ruined it. Picadilly on the fucking Rio! How can you let her call the DMZ a dumbass thing like that? Jesus Christ, she's even hung a dart board up next to the john."

"Sorry, man. I needed the money. I'm opening a place over here, on the east side of Juárez. A classy sea food restaurant. *La Paloma.* There's going to be a very nice bar. Come here for your margaritas."

"How can I do that, Güero? I need to cross the *street* to get to my bar, not the fucking Rio Grande. You never said the place was up for sale. How can you fucking *do* this to me, man? I thought we were *compas?*"

"It's business, Uri. Don't take it personally."

"How can I not take it personally? This *is* personal, man. And don't tell me it's business—like business is a righteous excuse for every shitty thing that happens in the world. You might as well say it's God's will."

"Everything that happens *is* God's will."

"Then God must be out of his fucking mind. You could get a dart in your eye coming out of the john!"

"Easy, man. It's monsoon season. You might get hit by lightning."

"It was a good bar, Güero. It was profitable, and don't tell me it wasn't. You had paying customers. I was one of them, damn it."

"I had to sell it," he said. "You remember the *pendejo* I smacked at the University? His lawsuit is picking up steam. He wants five million from me. I thought I'd better put my assets in Mexico where they'd be harder, if not impossible, to get at. I have dual citizenship, you know. I don't want to give that pedantic motherfucker a red *centavo.* You can understand that, *ése.* Right?"

"She's got a new policy, man. Pisswater drinks for more money. She says shit like, 'What's your poison, sir.' Christ, Güero, if you had to sell why didn't you sell it to someone who knows how to run a bar?"

"Beatrice was the only one who met my price. She comes

from oil money. Her daddy is one of the Permian Basin jillionaires. Take a dart in the eye, *vato*, then sue. You'll be rich."

"Jesus, I didn't feel this bad after Gert left me, Güero."

"You exaggerate, Uri."

"Do I? Maybe, but not by much."

I pissed and moaned some more before we hung up, promising to have a drink together soon. Without listening to my messages, I went up to the Hildebrand's apartment with my tool box.

Bill Hildebrand, in his tattered bathrobe, answered the door. He looked a hundred years old, but his ragged toenails had been trimmed. "How's the tureen, Bill?" I said. He opened the door wide and limped to a chair.

"Rosie's in the hospital," he said.

The fish were back. Neon tetras and fantails zipped about in the clear water. The cats lay on the carpet like growths in the shag.

"Sorry to hear that, Bill," I said.

"She had a stroke," he said. "She's got a bad temper. Something on the TV got her goat and she started yelling at it. Next thing, she was on the floor. I called 911."

"I'll send her some flowers," I said.

"Won't do any good. She can't see or hear. She's paralyzed on both sides. They don't think she's going to make it."

The old man looked at me, an apologetic look I recognized. It was the look he gave me when I pulled the fish out of the toilet.

"Hell of a note," I said, avoiding his eyes.

I went into the bathroom and flushed the toilet. It was working okay. I flushed it again to make sure. A long breathy sigh came from the bedroom. The door was ajar. I pushed it open. A woman was in the bed. She pulled the sheet up to her chin. "Who is this?" I said.

"That's Dorsey," Bill said.

"Dorsey," I said.

"Dorsey Jim," he said.

Dorsey Jim smiled at me. Three of her front teeth were gone. She looked about sixty, her hair a wild tangle of gray and black wires. "I'm Bill's cousin," she said. "From Flagstaff. That's in Arizona. Lots of Dineh in Flagstaff, though you'd never know it passing through."

I looked at Bill. He looked shyly away.

"Dorsey is Dineh–Navajo," he said.

"You've got Navajo relatives," I said.

Dorsey kept smiling. "We're all cousins," she said. "Or don't you believe that. Maybe you think some people were created on the moon." She swung her legs out of the bed, holding the sheet to her neck. She had a tattoo the size of a dinner plate high on her back. It looked like a hematoma.

"Rosie wouldn't mind," Bill said. "She worries about me being alone."

"Don't say her name," Dorsey said. "Not when I'm around."

"She doesn't mean that," Bill said. "Not in a jealous way."

"You speak the names of the dead," Dorsey said, "you bring *chindi.*"

"*Chindi* is the evil the dead leave behind," Bill said. "You could get contaminated."

"Bill," I said. "Rosie isn't dead."

"Good as," Dorsey said. "She could be dead right now, and you saying her name opens the door for *chindi.*"

I went back to the front room. What evil did Rosie have to leave behind besides her bad temper? Maybe that was evil enough. But I didn't feel up to giving Bill a hard time about it. The power of loneliness is very great.

As I started to leave Bill caught my sleeve. "They came by, looking for you," he said.

"Who?" I said.

"Nervous boys. One was a big fella with a funny looking haircut. The other a little Mexican. I figured they were looking to rent, but they said they just wanted to talk to you."

"What did you tell them?"

"I said you were gone off with a lady. I saw you drive off with that little gal in her car. I couldn't tell them where you went 'cause I didn't know."

I thanked him for telling me this, then went back to my apartment and listened to the messages on my answering machine. One was from Zack: "I decided to stick around a couple of days, to see if Sam's going to make it. Come on up for a drink. We'll have dinner, just you and me."

There were three tenant complaints, two plumbing problems, one noisy neighbor problem.

The last message was no message at all. A breather who kept the machine recording for a full minute before he hung up. I pulled the shotgun out from under the bed and worked the safety until my thumb memorized the on and off positions.

THIRTY-ONE

The Y is six blocks from the Westin. I went there first. Ray Fuentes was working his lats on the universal gym. He quit when he saw me. *"¿Qué pasó?"* he said. "You look like the big white whale, man. Where you been, anyway?"

"Everywhere but here," I said.

"Got yourself mixed up with a married woman, right?" He grinned. The grin of a *sabelotodo,* a know-it-all. An irritating grin.

"What are you, a psychic?" I said.

"You got the *look,* man. Husband coming after your ass with a .38, but the pussy's way too sweet to give up. I've seen that look before. Wore it myself a few times. Sometimes there's no way you can keep your *tronco* behind your zipper."

"It's a little more complicated than that," I said.

"Nothing's more complicated than that, *ése.* "

I went to the free weights and loaded a bar with three-hundred and eighty pounds. Fuentes spotted for me at the bench but once I lowered the bar I couldn't press it off my chest.

"She give you a haircut, too, Samson?" Ray said, grinning again. He peeled a twenty pound disk off each side, but I was only able to do six reps with the lighter bar. I had a long way to go to get back into form.

"Too much pussy and you lose your edge," Ray said. "Take

Samson for instance. He couldn't bench press shit after Delilah took his juice. Her cutting off his hair had nothing to do with it. Man could knock over stone synagogues once he laid off the muff."

"Do me a favor, Ray. No Bible stories. Okay?"

"Bible's got a lot to say about jamming yourself up with split-tail."

"I didn't know you were religious, Ray."

"My uncle Lino is a fucking priest, man," he said, grinning.

I gave it up, headed for the showers. Then I walked to the Westin. The door to Zack's top-floor suite was wide open. I went in.

He was in sweats, doing Tai Chi. "Be with you in a minute, Uri," he said. "Got to get my chi moving."

He was graceful as a ballet dancer. Each move segued perfectly from the one before it. It was like visible music. Slow music, driven by the rhythm of the lungs. It was hypnotic.

I quit watching. His Tai Chi routine was like a victory dance. Zack had money, and was well-balanced and positive. I was poor, unsteady, and blundered through life without a compass. My dance, if I had one, had no music, no theme, no purpose. I was a stone free-falling through time. Zack on the other hand was buoyant and focused. He was the perfect world citizen, a man for the new century, comfortable anywhere on the planet. He didn't have a woman as far as I knew, but he was not lonely and never would be. The global community embraced him like a prince.

I went to the window that overlooked the city. Cibola Savings and Loan rose like a green finger raised to the world. A defiant up-yours finger or a welcoming beacon. Maybe both.

Then Zack was beside me. "Money," he said, as if he were

seeing and thinking the same thing I was. "The heart blood of the world. It's out there and it isn't all that hard to get."

"Thanks," I said. "I need these little reminders. Sometimes I forget that if it wasn't for Mose, I'd be considered the black sheep of the family. Maybe I shouldn't get him cleaned up."

"I've been thinking about you and Mose," he said.

"And thanks for lumping us together."

"Your plan stinks, Uri. But I've decided to give you the money anyway."

"Why the change of heart?"

"You're the big brother I looked up to when I was a kid. It doesn't make me feel good turning you down, no matter how fucked your ideas are. I'm going to give you five grand. Do whatever you want with it, I don't care. You want to waste it on Mose, fine, I won't second guess you. I'd rather you put a down payment on a decent car for yourself, but that's up to you, Uri. You get him to stick out de-tox for a month, I'll write another check."

He wrote the check and gave it to me. "Now, let's go get that drink," he said.

THIRTY-TWO

The evening sky was gray with an overcast made of steam. It was nearly a hundred degrees and the heavy wet air pasted my clothes to my skin. Sheet lightning flared behind the Mulero mountains south of Juárez like distant artillery bursts. This was the local version of hell and it would stay here for the next two months.

The hot drizzle mixed with the oily asphalt making the streets dangerously slick. I drove as if I were on black ice. Most drivers didn't. A car hydroplaned past me doing sixty, the driver not realizing he was out of control even though his car was moving in a straight line. Another rode my bumper, honking. I honked back and we exchanged middle fingers as he roared past me, his rear wheels fishtailing.

It wasn't a good time to be out on Mesa, but I was driving slowly for another reason. I was checking out possible substitutes for the DMZ. There weren't any. All I saw were sports bars, stripper bars, lap dancing bars, people-meeting-people bars, biker bars, wino bars, and eateries with bars. No bar bars.

I pulled into the parking lot of the little credit union next to the university and dropped Zack's check into the night deposit slot. I liked this credit union. It was tiny and the tellers were friendly. It didn't have the sanctimonious atmosphere of the big stately banks. It didn't give you the feeling that you were

200

a non-swimmer on the shores of the money ocean. The great green god Dollar presided here, but he presided in a one-story stucco temple, humble as a *taquería*. If Cibola Savings and Loan was a cathedral, this credit union was a poor man's chapel.

I went back to the apartment and called Isaiah. "I want to take Mose up to the re-hab clinic tomorrow," I said. "When can you break free?"

"After work. I'll meet you in Junktown at six-thirty."

"You can't get off early?"

"Sure. I'll dump a hundred overnight express packages in the Rio and see you at noon."

"Okay, six-thirty it is. We may have to tie him up. Bring some duct tape."

One of his kids started screaming. He covered the phone and yelled something. His wife yelled something back. The sounds of domestic chaos echoed in my ear for a few more seconds, then he was back. "It's a waste of time, not to mention money," he said.

"Maybe we ought to just shoot the brain-dead bastard. Save the family a lot of trouble."

"Who'd you con the money from?—as if I didn't know."

"No con. Zack came through from the goodness of his heart. I just hope it's enough."

"Never be enough for a die-hard junk punk. This is a mistake, Uriah."

"It'll be my mistake, Isaiah."

"So be it."

"Amen."

A pair of old testament Hebrews on the line, discussing family matters. It made me smile. I wondered if Isaiah was also smiling as I recradled the phone.

I made myself a yogurt shake with raw egg and desiccated

liver thrown in. Then I called New Mexico information to get La Xanadu's phone number.

I asked the woman who took my call at La Xanadu for directions to the clinic. She asked why I wanted to know. I told her I was bringing my brother in for treatment. "Your brother has a substance abuse problem?" she said. I squeezed the phone as if it were her neck. *No,* I wanted to say, *my brother is so straight he makes the rest of the family feel depraved. We need to fuck him up a little first.*

"Yes he does," I said. "He uses heroin and probably crank to boost his energy. My mother is worrying herself into the grave over it."

This made her sigh. "Oh yes, if they only knew what they were doing to their families." She went on in this vein for a while, abandoning her initial caution to gush a bit about the tragedy of addiction. "Unfortunately," she said, "we have full occupancy right now."

"Shit," I said.

There was a moment of chilly silence. "However, sir, we are expecting a vacancy in a week. If you'd like, we can accept your brother for evaluation. That normally takes five to seven days. We hold the client in a secure evaluation room during that period. When the evaluation is complete, we should have a vacancy."

Then she told me how to find the place.

I went to bed, but sleep wasn't a given. When I finally dropped off it was into the technicolor dreams of half-waking. Jillian in one of the dreams offered me a plate of poached salmon. She was a little girl. A man in red rubber boots took her by the hand and led her away crying. I was crying too because I knew I'd never see her again.

Sometime during the night the phone rang.

"You were thinking about me," Jillian said.

"Not thinking—dreaming. I could be dreaming now."

"You're not. I'm still in Deming. I don't know what to do."

"You're going to California."

"I don't know. Do you love me, even a little. . . ?"

Though my air conditioner was turned up high the sheets were sticky with sweat. I grabbed the clock radio on my night stand and looked at the numbers. "Jesus, it's three A.M.," I said.

". . .because I think I love you, Uri," she said. Her voice broke a little. "There's no air in this little room. I'm lying in twisted, sweat-soaked sheets thinking of you, and the way you move with me."

It sounded too poetic, too worked out. "Why did you call?" I said.

"You didn't answer my question," she said.

I got up, carried the phone to the table, sat down on the vinyl-cushioned chair. I looked out on the parking lot. A man and a woman were smoking cigarettes next to a car. The woman was leaning against a fender. The man was facing her. They looked drunk. Music from the car radio thumped against my window. *Norteña* music from one of the powerful AM stations of northern Mexico.

"I like being with you," I said. "I want you. I want you right now."

"But you aren't in love with me. You think I'm too messed up to love or be loved. You don't trust me."

"Why did you call?" I said.

"You're sick, you know that? You don't know a good thing when you see it. You always need a reason for things. Well maybe sometimes there isn't a reason. Maybe sometimes things just are what they are."

She hung up. I sat at my table looking at the couple in the parking lot. They were kissing. He was holding his right arm out to avoid burning her with his cigarette. She had both hands clasped at the back of his neck. Fists of music pounded against my window.

He broke off the kiss. He turned and looked up at my window. My lights were off and I knew he couldn't see me looking down at him, but he raised his middle finger just in case. Then he went back to kissing the woman.

I looked out across the Rio Grande at the lights of Juárez. They were blue and spread out to the southern horizon. Two million people lived under those blue lights, most of them so poor they made most Americans look like software tycoons. The thought should have put my life in perspective. It didn't.

THIRTY-THREE

saiah's VW was parked in front of the Regency when I got there. "You're late," he said.

"It's six-thirty five, Isaiah."

"Like I said, you're late."

He didn't want any part of this, and now he was pissed because I was five minutes late. He pulled himself out of the bug. He looked like a bear climbing out of a barrel. He was still in his UPS uniform. "Bad day?" I said.

"Soon will be, I'm guessing."

"We're going for a nice drive in the country, man. This will be good for you, a break from the old routine."

He glared at me. "I should be thanking you, is that it?"

I slapped him on the shoulder. It was like slapping a side of beef. "Now you've got the right attitude. Be grateful for life's little perks."

He gave me a sour look but said nothing.

We went up to Mose's flat. He didn't answer my knock.

"Go away," a squeaky female voice said.

"Open up," I said. "We've got something for Mose."

After another long silence the door opened a crack. It wasn't Rusty Odegard but another anorexic junky. Frizzy yellow hair with orange streaks and black roots. She had protruding hyperthyroid eyes, the vague blue of a scratched marble. A developing goiter lumped the lower part of her throat.

205

"What've you got for him?" she said.

I pointed to Isaiah. "UPS. A big package but he, or someone at this address, will have to sign for it."

She looked at Isaiah, then around him for the big package. Her view wasn't adequate. She unlatched the chain and opened the door wide and tried to step into the hallway for a better look. I pushed her gently aside and went in.

"Where is he?" I said.

"So where's the package?" she asked, looking up and down the dark hall.

The fires of genius did not burn in her bulging white eyes. Her skin was old, but she was probably still in her teens. Her withered track-marked arms hung out of her sleeveless blouse like mottled rags.

"What happened to Maria Guadalupe?" I said.

"Who?"

"Rusty Odegard."

"Oh her. She kicked it the hard way. She died."

"You're the new Maria Guadalupe, then. Where's your off-ramp 'help my starving niños' sign."

"I don't speak Spanish," she said. "What do you guys want, anyway?"

"Moses. Where is he?"

"You going to kill him? I hope so. He's such a prick. Won't give me a nickel hit unless I do shit like wash the fucking dishes or clean the fucking bathroom."

"Maybe he wants you to experience the pride in having earned your way. Maybe he wants you out on the street working the tourists, like Rusty."

She rolled her eyes in mock exasperation. It made her look like a death-head in a horror movie. "I'm *sure,*" she said. "I'll go out there and play tag with the traffic. No thank you, *sir.* My mama didn't raise no street beggar. I've got my pride."

She lit a cigarette and started pacing back and forth in herky-jerky little steps. She walked from the knees down; from the knees up she was immobile as a stick. Her thin arms were folded severely across her non-existent breasts. It was mesmerizing. It was like watching a skeletal corpse magically re-animated and learning how to walk again.

"Come on," Isaiah said, slapping my shoulder. "Cut the chit chat. We going to do this or not?"

"I'll blow both you guys for ten bucks," she said. "Maybe one of you guys likes to watch. I'll blow the big black dude while the big white dude watches, okay? I'll do you any way you want but first let me see the ten. I'll fuck you both too, straight or non-traditional—in case one of you likes to pack fudge, but *that's* going to be ten *each.*"

"Where's Moses," Isaiah said.

"I don't care where he is," she said. She stepped toward Isaiah and hooked her hand in his belt. He grabbed her arm and for a second I thought he was going to tear it off. But he only moved her gently to a chair and sat her down.

"My brother here will give you five dollars when you tell us where he is," Isaiah said.

She looked at him, then looked at me, the wheels in her head visibly turning. "Uh huh," she said, the quizzical look fading. "Hey, listen. That stuff about killing him? I was only kidding. He's a prick, sure, but he's all I got right now. You understand?"

"We're not going to kill him," Isaiah said. "He's our brother."

The quizzical look reappeared then faded again. She'd learned, somewhere, that curiosity led you nowhere, or somewhere you didn't want to go. "He's on the bridge, supposedly scoring China white," she said. "Which I don't believe. All we get here is your basic black tar. Gee, I wish I lived in some neat place like Los Angeles. I bet you can get most anything you want there."

"What bridge?" I said.

"I don't know what it's called. The one downtown."

"The Santa Fe," Isaiah said. "Let's get it over with."

I gave her the five and we headed for the door.

"You sure you guys don't want some head?" she said. "I'll job you both for five more bucks. You going to tell me you can buy head cheaper than that? Don't make me laugh." She smiled derisively. The smile made her head look like an amused skull.

"Thanks anyway," I said.

"Hey," she said, miffed at the rejection. "I'm going to community college next year. I'm going to be a beauty consultant. Moses and I are going to buy a house. We're saving for a car. So fuck you. Okay? Just fuck you."

When we were back in the street, Isaiah said, "I'd pray for that girl but I think it's too late."

These were the first words of despair I'd ever heard coming from Isaiah. "Hey, there's some hope for you yet, big guy," I said.

He gave me a hard glancing look that made me want to duck.

"Shut your mouth, Uriah," he said. "Some things aren't funny. Some things can't ever be funny."

THIRTY-FOUR

I wanted to take my car since it had more space in it than Isaiah's, but he wasn't about to leave his bug in Junktown. It was my gig so I couldn't argue. The doors of the VW barely shut on our combined bulk and there was practically no room for Isaiah to work the gearshift around our knees. He kept it in third or neutral most of the way to the bridge, which was only two or three miles from Junktown, all of it downhill.

We parked in the pay lot on the U.S. end of the Santa Fe bridge. I slipped two dollars in the money box and we headed into the crowd of American tourists and Mexican day-workers that moved in slow procession toward the Mexican side of the Rio. The Mexicans, who held either local passports or work visas, were going home after working in the homes of the Americans—cleaning, cooking, mowing lawns, trimming hedges, tending the elderly, or looking after children. For the most part it was a good arrangement for people on both sides.

"He won't be on the Mexican side of the bridge," I said. "The *judiciales* catch him buying skag, they'll thump his ass then give him ten years in prison, which in his case would be the same as life."

"Might do him more good than re-hab," Isaiah said. "Be a lot cheaper. Then you could put Zack's money to better use."

We moved through the crowd to the crest of the bridge and

the invisible line that separated the two countries. A hundred feet below us, sloping concrete walls channeled the slow brown flow of the Rio Grande. On the Mexican side, painted in ten-foot letters on the concrete embankment, was the plaintive graffito, *Todos somos ilegales:* We are all illegals. In smaller letters farther down the concrete and harder to read was an older complaint: *Pobre Mejico, tan lejos de dios, tan cerca de los estados unidos.* Poor Mexico, so far from God, so close to the United States.

"He's not here," Isaiah said.

We pushed our way back through the slow-moving crowd to the USA side of the bridge. No Moses.

"Maybe she was lying to us," I said.

"To protect him from his brothers?"

"I don't think she bought the brothers bit. She probably thought we meant to bust him up for non-payment of dues."

"It doesn't work that way, Uriah. Junk dealers don't offer lines of credit. Cash up front only. You don't give time-pay coupons to a strung out pinhead."

I looked at him. "What do you know about it, deacon?"

"My church has a counseling program. Sometimes junked-up souls who want to get clean come to us. We're not all that successful. Jones is a jealous emperor."

A motley crew had gathered in a vacant lot between two abandoned buildings a block away from the Santa Fe bridge. Pint bottles, as they were passed back and forth among the merry-makers, glinted red and gold in the late-day sun. Someone raised his face out of a brown paper bag and yelled *"¡Qué fucking loco man!"* He passed the bag to the huffer next to him. The stink of the toluene-bearing solvents was strong. We shouldered through the mob of human wreckage.

Isaiah, who was four inches taller than me, saw him first. Mose was surrounded by a group of the walking dead–fellow

210

junkies, a few winos, and one female huffer—an unlikely cross-section of bottom-feeders. It looked like they were trying to organize a social club for the terminally useless. Mose was dancing—a slow motion junkie jitterbug—and mumbling an old Nat Cole tune, "Straighten Up and Fly Right."

"I guess he means that ironically," Isaiah said.

"You think?" I said.

Isaiah looked at me as if to say, You want my help or you just want to piss me off?

Mose quit his Nat Cole impression, as if siezed by an inspiring thought. He opened his arms like wings that could gather and save the failing sunlight. "China white Tuesday, my people!" he said. His tone was prophetic, as if he'd received a celestial directive. "I fucken declare to *day* as China white Tuesday!"

Someone in the crowd yelled, "Yo *vato*, what about Wednesday? What do you *chiva*-heads call fucken *miercoles?*"

Moses scratched the side of his neck and petitioned the sky. "Rest of the week's black tar," he said. "But today is China white's day, the unstepped-upon virgin queen. I saw her in a dream I had just a minute ago, like she was cut from a block of pure angel shit."

"Speedball dreams, more'n likely!" someone suggested.

"Hey, dope fiend!" the female huffer yelled. "You're full of last week's shit! You better find Jesus 'fore it's too late. Satan's got you by the short hairs."

"Fucken brain-dead baghead," Mose said to her. "Anybody ever told you Jesus don't live in a bag of airplane glue?"

"Benzene!" the female huffer yelled, ignoring Mose. "Benzene for Jesus!" She was tall and looked pregnant. Her stiff white hair looked like it had been cut with a chainsaw and styled in a blender. Her expression was righteous but her eyes were dead. She wore a crucifix on her neck big as a

211

hammer. "Don't you pinheads forget Jesus!" she said. "I'm carrying the second coming of the holy child! I speak to him, and he speaks to me. Don't got to stick pins in my arm or suck tourist cock for him, either, like you dope fiends."

"You fucking meltdown," Mose snapped back. "Clean yourself up, make a pact with doctor smack. Straighten up and fly right. Junk *rules,* glue is for fools. That spray paint got you all ate up. But then, who gives a flying fuck."

"Junkies can't shit proper," she said. "They die jammed up with shit hard as pavement."

"Fuck this," Mose said, fed up with the game, his enthusiasm for this temporary doper ecumenism gone. And then he looked bewildered, as if he suddenly couldn't account for his reasons for being here.

"Let's take him," Isaiah said. His glistening neck bulged with outrage, his eyes wide with adrenaline. Ordinary family life was the best thing that ever happened to Isaiah. Without its checks and balances and he would have ripped a hole in the world and filled it with the blood and bones of everything he found offensive.

"We'd better let the crowd break up first," I said. "They might take exception to us canceling the freak show." I didn't want Isaiah to have an excuse to crack skulls. It would mess up his life, and I would have been responsible.

In fact, I was having second thoughts about the whole project. Maybe I had it wrong. This was Mose's world and he was comfortable in it. It was a self-contained world. It understood itself. It knew what it needed and how to get it. It was complete and self-satisfied. The people who lived in it were probably no more unhappy, neurotic, or suicidal than anyone else. They were self-deluded and speeding toward oblivion. But then who in his own way wasn't?

It occurred to me that taking Mose to La Xanadu was a

product of *my* delusion. I told myself that I was doing it for Maggie, but I also knew I was doing it for myself: It would make me look good, even heroic, in the eyes of my family. Uriah, savior of the unsavable—the moral alchemist who transforms dirtbags into scrubbed, well-adjusted Republicans. We took Sam's delusion away by forcing brain surgery on him. Now we were going to strip Mose of his. I knew my thinking was wrong, out of synch with common sense, but I was never on good terms with common sense.

"I'm not going to stand here and listen to their crap another minute, Uriah," Isaiah said. "Let's take him now."

Isaiah waded through the ragged crowd and threw his arms around Moses. It looked like a re-union of long lost friends. The crowd mumbled approval at first. But when Isaiah picked up Moses and trucked him off like a bag of groceries, a growl of protest rose up. "It's the fucking thought police!" someone yelled. "Storm troopers!

Isaiah took long, powerful strides. People moved out of the way or risked getting walked on. Then bottles and rocks began to fly, bouncing off Isaiah's broad back. I took an empty spraypaint can to the neck, a rock to the knee.

Mose was passive, stunned and bewildered by this turn of events. I kept pace with Isaiah, and as I did I went through Mose's coat pockets. I found his prize, a small heavily-taped package of heroin. I threw it at the crowd. "China white Tuesday!" I yelled. The junkies lost interest in Mose and broke ranks to get at the dope. The huffers went back to their fume-filled bags and soda cans, the winos to their fortified muscatel.

"Son of a bitch!" Mose screamed. "That shit cost me twelve and a half bills! What are you assholes *do*ing?"

"Ask him," Isaiah said. "Uriah's got a plan for you."

Mose bucked and kicked, but Isaiah moved forward

unimpeded. "Uri you prick! Stay the fuck out of my fucking life!"

"It isn't just your life, moron," I said.

"Since fucking when?"

"Since Sam and Maggie took your worthless ass in."

"What are you, a goddamned priest? Where do you get off, you fucking steroid freak? What gives you the right to judge my life?"

I thought about that. I didn't have to think long. "Maggie's pain," I said.

THIRTY-FIVE

We transferred Mose to my car when we got back to Junktown. I said goodbye to Isaiah, then drove to the Baron Arms. I went up to my apartment and got the Mossberg. I put it in the Ford's trunk. There was a chance I'd be gone overnight and I didn't want to leave the shotgun behind, thinking the nightcrawlers that frequented the apartment complex might find it. An imaginative huffer might pour paint thinner into the barrel to suck up the fumes and accidentally behead himself.

When I got behind the wheel, Mose was gnawing at the duct tape that held his wrists together. His teeth were too dull and his jaws too weak to break the sticky fabric. He kept at it for a few minutes but didn't have the mental resolve to stick with the job, which didn't surprise me. A moan of self pity escaped his lungs.

I said, "You see this as a disaster, Mose. But you know what the *I Ching* says about disaster, right? The flipside ideogram means *opportunity*. In other words, every cloud has a silver lining."

"Your *puta* mother should have chopped you up for dog food before she dropped you on some poor fuck's doorstep," he said.

"I've never thought much of you, Mose, but Maggie thinks there's this little spark of decency left. We're going to see if we can fan that little spark into a nice little campfire. Who

215

knows what the possibilities are? Heck, you might be a solid tax-paying citizen in a year."

"Fuck you," he said.

"Personally, I think you're as valuable to society as a baggie full of snail shit, but I admit to bias. Objectivity is for people more noble than me."

He quit responding to me. We rode in silence for a couple of hours. I'd left the freeway and had turned west into the foothills of the Black Range of the Mimbres Mountains. It was dark and my headlights were reflected in the eyes of small animals on the sides of the road. The road was narrow and winding. Mose, at one point, sucked in air and coughed.

"I'm going to puke," he said.

"Whoa. Not in my car. Hold on to it for a couple of seconds."

He started retching. I pulled the car onto the shoulder of the skinny road. We were somewhere in the high country, west of Hillsboro, New Mexico. I got out and opened his door. I pulled him out of the car. His ankles were taped so there was no danger of his running off. He knelt in the gravel. A silver thread fell from his yawn. I strapped him back into his seat and we resumed the trek to La Xanadu.

I'd hoped Isaiah would stick with the project all the way, but he wanted no more of it. He did his part, he said, and there was no way he was going to worry his family by being gone all night in the New Mexico wilderness with his two deadbeat brothers. His wife Rosette had begged him to not go anywhere near Junktown and the derelicts Mose associated with. She wasn't all that fond of Isaiah hanging with me, either. According to Rosette, there was something un-Christian about someone whose sole occupation in life was the pagan glorification of the body. She saw me as sculpted meat destined for the charnel house. When Isaiah told me this I protested, but couldn't offer a convincing counter-

216

argument since I'd apparently given up loftier pursuits, namely my master's degree. It was the one thing that would prove I had a goal in life. "I'm going to get that degree, Isaiah," I'd said. "Sure you are," he replied. "And I'm going to play defense for the Cowboys." The inescapable truth about family members, whether they're Rockefellers or Walkinghorses is this: they are unsparing judges of each other.

The last leg of the trip was a stretch of switchbacks on a six-percent uphill grade. I kept the Ford in second gear all the way, one eye on the rising temperature gauge. Just as it touched the redline area, the grade leveled out on a moonlit plateau. I drove for five minutes before the wild land showed signs of human interference. Mile-markers with reflectors on them were set at even intervals along the road. I counted seven of these before I came to a stone arch that marked the entrance to La Xanadu. A hand-painted sign hanging from the apex of the arch said

Rejoice In Hope
Be Patient In Tribulation

At the far end of the plateau the buildings sat unfenced against a dense thicket of ponderosa. There was a post-modern administration building with rows of two-story barracks on either side. The curved spine and the scalloped red-tile roof of the administration building made it look like a headless armadillo. Sodium vapor lamps mounted on tall steel poles lit up the park-like surroundings. The lamps turned everything peach-yellow. Trees not native to this alpine plateau—mimosa, gingko, and Russian olive—rose up from the meticulous landscaping like pale feather dusters.

I got out of the car and stretched, then cut Mose free of the duct tape. I pulled him out of the car and got him on his feet.

217

I didn't worry about him trying to run away. There was no-where to run.

"Your new home," I said.

He didn't have anything to say. His skin glowed toxic orange under the sodium lamps. He stared dismally at the buildings as if he were facing the gallows.

"They're going to take good care of you, Mose," I said. "You're not going to have to go cold turkey. They'll clean you up gradually, in steps." I tried to sound convincing, but in fact I didn't have any idea how they treated junkies here. I just knew their success rate was the best in the west.

The woman I'd talked to said La Xanadu took admissions twenty-four hours a day. We hadn't talked money. La Xanadu was the sort of place that if you had to ask how much it cost you couldn't afford it. I felt comfortable with Zack's five thousand in my checking account.

I led Mose up the walkway to the glass doors of the administration building. The insides looked like a hunting lodge—exposed beams, wood paneling, furniture made of varnished lodgepole logs and upholstered in red leather tacked to the pine frames with brass studs. The glass-eyed heads of elk, mountain goats, and pumas stared at me from their mounts high up on the walls. A stuffed owl, wings spread for the predatory swoop, perched on one of the beams.

A tall angular woman behind a mahogany desk stood up and extended her hand. I took it. She had big hands with prominent knuckles. Her grip was warm and solid, meant to reassure. "Mr. Walkinghorse?" she said. I nodded. She fixed me in her unfaltering gaze. "We expected you earlier."

"There were some complications," I said.

"There are always complications," she said. "These family situations are never as simple as one would like."

We shared knowing smiles. She had a long narrow face.

218

Her nose was thin, the nostrils meager slits. She had shiny blue-black hair, and her large gray eyes were flecked with yellow.

"I refuse to be admitted," Mose said, mustering up some remembered dignity. "I want that on *record*. I have been abducted illegally, my rights as a citizen have been violated. I want to go home right now. If I am not allowed to leave, then I will sue. I'll sue for ten million—a hundred million! I'll own this fucking gulag!"

"Try to control yourself, Mr. Walkinghorse," the woman said, freezing Mose's outburst with her steady gray eyes. Then, turning to me, she said, "I'm Margo Combs, admissions officer. I know your brother's stay here will be rewarding, not only for him but for his family." She offered her hand again. I took it. She held my hand a beat longer than I held hers.

Mose made a noise, a groan tailing off to a sob.

"We'll need you to sign a durable POA—power of attorney," Margo Combs said. "You will need to attest to your brother's incapacity to handle his own affairs. I am a notary and I will affix my seal to the form." She touched an intercom button on her desk and said, "Edgar, Harold, please come to the front desk."

Two hulks in hospital whites came in through double-doors that led to a long green corridor. One was carrying a straight jacket. "Edgar and Harold will be witnesses," Margo Combs said. She found the forms and put them on the desk for our signatures. I signed, then Edgar and Harold signed, and Margo Combs fixed her notary public seal to the document.

"There," she said, looking at Mose again, "all very proper."

"I'm not incapacitated, bitch," Mose said.

"Your brother believes you are," Margo Combs replied, unperturbed. "He is acting in your best interests. We consider

219

long-term addicts to be not responsible for themselves, in the same way people suffering from various forms of dementia are not. Most courts and appellate courts agree."

Mose began to panic. He looked at Edgar and Harold, at the straight jacket in Harold's huge paw, then at me. "Jesus Christ!" he said. "Don't let them do this, Uri!" He staggered sideways, recovered, then broke for the door. Harold caught him and brought him back.

"Please, Mr. Walkinghorse," Margo Combs said. "You don't want to be put into restraints, do you?" Something in her eyes made me think she'd be more than pleased to see Mose put into restraints.

She turned to me. "We will require a check for the first month of treatment, Mr. Walkinghorse. Seven-thousand five-hundred dollars. The first month covers one-time items that won't be included in the bill for succeeding months. The rate then drops to six-thousand."

"Seventy-five hundred?" I said.

"You've accomplished the first stage of recovery—interdiction," she said. "We will follow with assessment and treatment. It might take only a month. Considering your brother's resistance, I would say we'll need ninety days, minimum."

"But seventy-five hundred," I said. "I'm sure it's very reasonable, considering. . . ."

Mose picked up on my tone. He barked out a triumphant laugh. "He hasn't got seventy-five hundred! He's fucking broke! He's a goddamned bum, like me! Ask him what he does for a living!"

Margo Combs raised her eyebrows and studied me. I took out my checkbook and wrote the check. I'd have to transfer the rest from my stash. "I can cover it," I said.

"*Bull*shit he can," Mose said.

Edgar and Harold took Mose by the arms and led him away.

"Hang in, Mose," I said.

"Climb up your donkey-fucked mother's dead maggoty cunt, you fucking Judas!" he yelled.

The double doors closed behind Mose and the orderlies. Margo Combs and I found ourselves alone in the awkward silence.

"That was odd," Margo Combs said, unruffled by Mose's foul curse. "Does he hate his own mother?"

"We were adopted and had different mothers. He thinks our birth-mothers were whores. There's no way of knowing for sure. I apologize for my brother's language, Mrs. Combs," I said.

"It's Miss Combs," she said. "I'm not married."

"I'm sorry."

"Don't be," she said.

I looked at her and saw what she meant. She'd seen enough of family-generated hell and saw no need to join the parade of fools. Single and self-sufficient, answerable only to herself– it was Margo Combs' way of lasting out the madhouse world.

THIRTY-SIX

I sat in the parking lot of La Xanadu studying my road atlas under the Ford's dome light. Deming was directly south of La Xanadu, a seventy mile trek through the south range of the Mimbres mountains. The realization that I'd been planning unconsciously to drive back to Deming hit me with a mild shock wave. The mind is a wily trickster. It knows what you need even if you don't. You never quite catch up to it. It leads, you follow—even if you drag your feet. And when you set a course it makes you think the choice of direction was yours in the first place. The mild shock wave made me chuckle. I chuckled until tears leaked from my eyes.

I drove to the Oasis motel. Her Mercedes wasn't there. I asked the night clerk if the room we shared was occupied. It wasn't. The woman, he said, checked out a few hours ago. He was an old biker. Elaborate tattoos serpentined up his arms to his shoulders and neck. He looked like he belonged to a race of blue-skinned people. I asked him if he noticed what freeway access she took. She went east, he said. He wouldn't normally pay any attention to the direction a car took when it left the motel lot, but Jillian seemed so bent out of shape when she checked out that he couldn't help taking an interest. Her tires smoked as she left the Oasis and turned up the frontage road to the eastbound on-ramp of the Interstate. She was crying at the check-out desk, the old biker said, and too nervous to sign the credit card receipt legibly. He showed me the receipt. Her signature looked like a line traced by a seismograph during a major quake. The receipt was dimpled with dried tears.

"She was one sweet piece," he said, "Table pussy, we'd call her back in my road days. One hot little mama." He grinned, displayed his tongue. It was mossy and fissured. He made a dirty noise in his throat. Half purr, half growl. He looked at me, then looked again. "Hey, no offense, man. I just pictured her makin' a run with me—you know, this primo snatch humpin' the fuckslave pad of my chopped hog, knees clamped on my skinny ass, as me and the brothers wheeled into San Jose or Oakland. I'm talkin' the uptight early sixties when it meant somethin' to be an outlaw." In his own way he was paying Jillian a high compliment.

"Thanks for your help," I said.

"No problem. She's choice muff, Jack. A keeper."

"I know."

He pulled at his gray beard and slipped into a nostalgic reverie. I turned to leave.

"I think that big asshole with the weird hair and bad suit scared her off," he said.

I was already through the door when he said that. I stepped back inside. "Tell me about him," I said.

"He had a badge—Texas Rangers. I figured it was fake, but I can't take a chance, you know? I'm a parolee, did a sixpack in Huntsville on a dime B and E rap. So I didn't want to fuck with this fat-ass Lone Ranger, even though I was sure he was a lying cocksucker."

"Wait a minute," I said. "This guy came to see *her?*"

"Claimed she didn't own the Benz. Said she stole it from her boss. He said 'boss' like a priest would say 'Jesus Christ.' I guess he wanted to impress me. I don't impress anymore."

"So you gave him her room number."

"Like I said. There was this slim chance he might've been what he said he was. The cops hire all kinds of dildos these days, so you never know for sure. I watched him. If he'd a got rough with her, I'd a peppered his ass with rock salt."

He reached under the counter and pulled out a sawed-off double barrel 12 gauge. "I keep rock salt shells along with the double oughts. Left barrel rock salt, right barrel double oughts. They don't straighten up with the rock salt, I got serious back-up." He gave me a broad yellow grin. His eyes dimmed. He looked fried enough to forget left from right in a pinch.

"Did you hear him say anything to her?"

"No. She came out and talked to him for a minute. He seemed respectful enough, keeping his distance and bowing his head a lot. It didn't seem like anything serious. Then he took off. She left a few minutes later, all fucked up, like I said."

I thanked him again, then went out to my car. My heart had picked up a few beats. I got the Mossberg out of the trunk and put it in the front seat next to me.

THIRTY-SEVEN

At least Forbes hadn't taken her by force. That thought kept me sane on the Interstate. Even so, I kept the speedometer on ninety. The old Ford protested. A thin vibration buzzed in the dashboard and the steering wheel shimmied. The temperature gauge red-lined. Ten miles west of Las Cruces, steam began to spill out from under the hood.

I pulled into the rest stop that overlooked the Mesilla Valley. It was an hour before sun-up. The sky above the black silhouette of the Organ Mountains was a starless blue-gray. The lights of Las Cruces twinkled under the false dawn.

The Mercedes was parked next to the restrooms. There were no other cars in the parking area, so I figured Forbes had gone back to the city. Even so, I approached the Mercedes with the Mossberg in my hands.

Jillian was in the car, asleep, or dead, in the back seat. The doors were locked. I tapped the window with the stock of the shotgun. She sat up, her eyes wide with fright. She'd been sleeping hard and was caught in the twilight between dream and waking. She unlocked the door. I climbed in next to her, set the gun down on the floor, and took her in my arms and kissed her eyes and face and lips.

"Christ, you're shaking," she said.

"You scare me." *In more ways than one,* I could have added.

Her smile was pleased. She liked me being scared for her. She kissed me. "I almost went off the road," she said. "I had to sleep. I hadn't slept since we slept together. You work wonders for me, big fella." She smoothed back her hair. She'd used her purse for a pillow and the grain of its tooled leather had imprinted her face. "Why the gun?" she said.

"Why do you think? People want me dead."

"No, not anymore. I told you. They have no reason to kill you now."

"I don't think they need much reason."

"Then why are you here? If you believe what you say, you should stay the hell away from me, shouldn't you?"

"I never claimed to be a genius," I said. I pulled her close. "I want to be with you, Jillian. I think we can make it."

"It?"

"It. Whatever you want to call it. Love. Call it love."

She touched my face with her fingertips and smiled. It was a sad, fatalistic smile. I didn't like it. "You were right, you know," she said. "I lied to you. I didn't make the pictures public to get you off the hook–though that would be a given. I did it for revenge."

My mouth was on her neck. Her quickened exhalations blew warm and moist in my ear. I didn't want to hear anything but that soft rush of breath.

"That goddamned Fernie," she said, pulling away from me. "He took it all back. The house, the bank accounts, the annuity. I wanted to mess him up a little. I wanted to hurt him."

"How could he take your house?"

"Clive and I didn't own a thing, not even the furniture. It was all bank property. Clive was a prop, a piece of stage art. We didn't even have our own account at the bank. Fernie let us draw what we needed out of special accounts, up to a million a year–but the money belonged to the bank. We had an annuity, a good one, but I wasn't listed as a beneficiary in case of Clive's death. We played our parts well. We could have made a lot of money eventually if Clive hadn't screwed himself into the ground." She was losing it. She stopped herself for a moment to regain composure. "The bastards took everything from me, Uri," she said. "They took it all."

"Clive and Fernie."

"I'll give you the full list if you want it. Got a couple of hours?" I thought about that. Her list had to begin in Coos Bay with the fisherman Caleb Brisbane and her brothers. Then there were her ex-husbands, and others I didn't want to know about.

"So you gave the tabloids the pictures," I said.

She smiled and her eyes narrowed. "You've got to watch out for me, tiger. I always get even."

"So why are you going back? What did Forbes tell you?"

"Fernie wants to make nice. I'm not sure why. Maybe it's because I haven't gone to the bank regulators with what I know about the Cibola laundromat. I don't know. He's offered to make me sole beneficiary of Clive's annuity on the condition that I go back to Oregon. The annuity is worth half a million. That's why I'm going back. I don't want to be poor again. I can't afford it."

"You were crying when you left the motel," I said.

"The lech behind the desk told you that, did he? They were tears of joy, Uri. One minute I'd been broke with nowhere to go, and the next minute I had half a million. They were tears of *relief,* for God's sake. I broke down a little. Do you blame me?"

She was reaching, but I didn't push it. We got out of the car and stretched in the cool morning air.

"Why doesn't Solis just mail you the annuity?" I said.

"For one thing, I don't have a mailing address. I'm officially homeless. And Fernie doesn't like the impersonal approach. He's an old-style face-to-face kind of guy. He would have been at home in the nineteenth century. Plus, he's going to give me time to re-locate. He'll let me stay in the house through the weekend. It could have been a lot worse. He could have made me one of the concubines for his troops. He's got a standing army over in Juárez of over a hundred men. He won't let them go to whorehouses. They've got to be combat ready, and he doesn't want them laid up with any STD. So he equips them with clean women. The women are treated decently, but they have no choice in the matter."

It was an ugly thought. I shook free of it. "How did Forbes find you?" I asked.

"Forbes used to be a cop with the city. He's still got a couple of connections in the department. They traced the credit card for him. The motel clerk ran the numbers through when I checked in. A phone call and a five minute wait is probably all it took Forbes to track me down."

I took her in my arms again. "Don't go back there, Jillian."

She held my face in her hands and kissed me. "Thank you," she said. "No one's ever worried about me before you. It's okay, sweets. I know Fernie. He's a man of his word."

I followed her into Las Cruces and we stopped at a cafe for breakfast. A chorizo omelet and black coffee fueled her optimism. I had oatmeal with skim milk, no sugar.

"Half a million isn't exactly a fortune these days," she said, "but I've got a good head for money. We'll invest some of it, and maybe start a small business."

"We," I said.

"Partners. If you can't call it love, Uri, call it partners."

It sounded too good. Too easy. But whatever she was offering, I wanted it. More than I had ever wanted anything.

Outside the café she said, "I'm going to stop in Mesilla. I've always liked that little town. It's somehow insulated from all the crap in the world, like time was stopped dead in its tracks there two hundred years ago."

I followed her the few miles to the old Spanish settlement just outside of Las Cruces. She parked at the edge of the plaza. I pulled in behind her. A mariachi band occupied the pavilion, tuning up for an afternoon concert. The tourist shops on all four sides of the plaza were not yet open and the streets were empty. The splendid old San Albino church sat at the north end of the plaza, a presiding entity.

"If we ever get married," she said. "I want it to happen in this church. I want some kind of sanction next time around, even if I can't buy into the mumbo jumbo behind it."

"Let's wake up the priest and do it now," I said.

She squeezed my hand. "We'll do it on our way to Oregon," she said.

What was I thinking? I wasn't thinking. Thinking was done by people who had a dependable view of reality.

She climbed the steps of the church and pulled open the door, but she didn't enter. "This is where he lives," she said, looking inside.

I didn't ask her what she meant. The wind had come up strong and the morning sky was suddenly dark with sand. I could taste grit lifted from the desert floor. I thought of the *narcotraficante* graveyard, the sand that filled the yawning mouths of the dead.

"The god of self-sacrifice," she said. "This is his house. The sacred assassin lurks in the basilica. I could ask him for mercy, but he doesn't deal in mercy. He deals in blood. God's only mercy is death. He's right at home here in Aztec country."

"Love doesn't count?" I said.

"What do you mean?"

"As a mercy."

"Sure, but it doesn't come from God. Love is human—poor fucking doomed humanity hanging onto itself for dear life."

She turned to me. Her smile was the sad complacent smile of a fatalist. She had me scared again.

THIRTY-EIGHT

As soon as we got back on the Interstate she was gone. I didn't try to keep up. I nursed the Ford home by staying ten miles an hour below the speed limit. Maybe I should have taken Zack's advice and bought myself a newer car and left Mose to his fate. Now I'd have to dip into my own stash to make good on the check I wrote to La Xanadu. If I couldn't raise enough to keep Mose in the clinic for another two months, it was wasted money.

Money. What did Zack call it? Heartblood of the world. "It's out there," he said, "and not all that hard to get." Easy for him to say. He had the knack. He understood money— where it was, what you gave up to get it, how to manage it when you got it. He understood its green language. I only understood the red language of need.

Jillian. I had let myself need her. And this scared me. How could we have a future? I wanted to believe we could. Maybe her annuity would make it happen. Five-hundred thousand and a clean slate. Money was the genie out of the bottle, granting all your pipe dreams. Maybe we *could* go to Oregon, some small town in the empty central part of the state. I could finish my degree and get a teaching job; she could run a little grocery or deli, or some kind of specialty shop. Life was pure possibility. Pick something you can live with, stick with it, see what happens.

Güero mocked this kind of thinking; to me it still had appeal—the gringo belief in imaginary upbeat futures. I wanted it, and want is the engine that makes things happen.

I stopped at The Healing Witch and picked up some hi-protein powder, vitamins, and herbs. There was a new edition of *Know It All!* on the rack just inside the store. The front page featured another picture of Clive Renseller in Mona Farnsworth's dungeon. It was captioned, and this time he was named:

Clive Renseller Playing Horsy

Mona Farnsworth playing June Cleaver. Riding Clive's spine. Her panties dangling from his thrilled jaws. One hand fisted in his hair. The other pulling back hard on the leash attached to the dog collar around his neck. Her expression theatrical: the murderous joy of a housewife gone over the edge. Her crazed eyes believable. Clive's twisted face believable. The entire thing unbelievable. I felt a twinge of nausea thinking about the sacrifices you make when you have to make money.

The article writer knew how to have fun. He played with the horsy idea all the way through. *(Clive Renseller, local banker, was actually a horse of another color, folks . . . Old Clive was rode hard and put away wet on a regular schedule . . . Makes you wonder who's playing the trifecta with your life's savings . . . Ah, but there's no use in beating a dead horse, is there?)*

Mona's business, *Mind Me!* was not mentioned.

I played my archived messages until I found Mona's. Her offer now seemed like the opportunity I needed. Not my kind of work, but I imagined Zack had done things that made him a little queasy—sacrifices to Almighty Buck. Almighty Buck ruled the world. Our jealous greenback god with hard vindictive ways.

Since the tabloid article didn't mention *Mind Me!* Mona's business shouldn't have been affected by the photos. I showered, put on a clean pair of tan slacks and a light blue

231

chambray shirt, swallowed a handful of vitamins and herbs, and drove up to Heaven's Gates Estates. Money was on my mind. If Mose was going to stay in La Xanadu for ninety days, I had to make a lot of it, fast. I could ask Jillian to pay it. But the annuity, if there was one, was escape money—seed money for a possible future.

The Farnsworth's Lexus was parked in the circular drive. A Chevy Malibu sedan was parked at the curb. I parked behind the Chevy and got out. The door of the Malibu opened simultaneously and a man in Bermuda shorts, two-hundred dollar "Maui Jim" sunglasses, running shoes, and mesh tank top, got out. He stood in front of me, jogging in place. He looked like he was ready to go out for his afternoon jog.

"Hi there," he said, smiling. He took off his sunglasses and extended his hand. "Corey Butterfield," he said. "I'm a reporter for the local independent weekly, *Know It All!* You a client here, big guy?" He had jaded, smirking eyes, eyes that loved corruption. He'd sought out and found humanity's darker impulses long enough to believe they ruled.

He was in my face, shifting his weight from one foot to the other, letting me know I wasn't going to get past him until I answered.

"No," I said, but he didn't move.

"Come on, you can level with me, sport. I won't name names. I just want an insider's point of view. You know— what you do in there, or rather, what she does to you. It's the *news,* man. The people have a right to know. So, tell me. What's the thrill of getting whipped by Big Mean Momma? What's it feel like—on the emotional level I mean?" I tried to move past him again but he stayed in front of me.

"What's your special twist, man?" he said. "You like to taste *la mierda?* She take her dumps on your shit-eating grin? She hang you up in a closet like a side of beef?"

232

I grabbed the waistband of his shorts in one hand, his tank top in the other. I picked him up, carried him to his car. I threw him through the open front window. He got hung up half way through. I helped him. I kicked his ass half a dozen times before he managed to crawl all the way into the front seat. Where he stayed, fetal, his very wide eyes no longer smirking.

"That's how it feels," I said.

"That was beautiful," Jerry Farnsworth said.

He let me in. "That demento son of a bitch's been out there since nine this morning." Jerry was wearing his banker's suit. His red Mohawk needed some hairspray. It was too long to stand up on its own. It lay flat, like a midget wig, the ponytail braided into red rope.

Mona was sitting on the sofa, as white and severe as her Danish modern furniture. "I'm ruined," she said.

"She's depressed," Jerry said. "She'll snap out of it. We're far from ruined."

"I'm finished," she said. "They're all terrified now. No one's shown up since the first picture came out."

"But it will pass," Jerry said. "This is just a temporary thing. Heck, it gives us the opportunity to take a nice vacation. We'll go to the Amalfi coast, or to Corfu. We'll stay six months. When we get back, all this will be ancient history, believe me. Things will go back to normal completely."

She regarded her husband as if she saw a new defect in him. Her gaze could freeze water. She lit a cigarette and held the burning match in her fingers. Then she dropped it, still burning, on the glass-top coffee table in front of her. "Things will *not* go back to normal. You remember that restaurant on the north side that served homemade preserves tainted with botulism? *They* never came back. You don't realize how chicken-hearted these masochists are. Oh, some might come around again. But not for a year or two. A lot of them will go out of town for their thrills and spills."

She looked at me. "What are *you* doing here?" she said.

"You said you had steady work for me. Looks like the offer is off the table."

"Everything is off the table," she said.

"We've still got the web site and the 900 line," Jerry said.

"Which pays the electric and water bills," Mona said.

"How did they find you?" I said.

"How do you *think?*" she said. "I advertise in their rotten little rag. They probably sent their geeks to all the dominatrix services in town. There are only about six or seven of us. The bastards are camped out in front of my colleagues' houses all over the city, hoping to strike gold. My poor chicken-livered clientele are suffering at home, begging their wives to whack them, and the wives won't cooperate, or if they do they do it without enthusiasm and with absolutely no sense of invention."

"Bad things happen to good people," I said.

She turned that cold gaze on me but didn't respond. She lit another cigarette even though the first one was still burning in the ash tray. "Maybe I'll open a boutique," she said. "Nice silk things for menopausal but still horny hausfraus." She got up and left the room. Jerry went after her.

I got up to leave. Babs came down the hallway wearing a thong bikini. "Oh hi there," she said. "Want to go for a swim . . . *Strobe,* isn't it? Daddy uncovered the pool this morning. You could wear one of his old suits, when he wasn't so chubby. Or you could wear nothing at all if you've got the chutzpah. I can deal with it. Daddy goes swimming in the buff all the time. We have advanced attitudes toward the body."

"No thanks," I said, wondering if there was anything her advanced attitudes couldn't deal with. "I've got to be going."

She plopped down on the sofa. "What's the big rush?" she said.

"I came for a job. There isn't any. So I'm going."

A thought puckered her lips. She frowned. "Wait up," she said. "I need some advice—from a man. And you're a man."

"That's my understanding."

She looked at me for a blank second, then smiled. "A *funny* man, too. I like that. A good sense of humor indicates intelligence. I admire intelligence more than anything. I don't hang with kids at my school because I can't deal with their juvenile issues."

"You're a snob, then," I said.

She didn't take offense. She thought about it. "Yes," she said. "I guess you could call me a snob. I don't think being a snob is a bad thing when all you're doing is recognizing idiocy for what it is."

She had filled out a bit since I saw her last. Her tea cup breasts had become round, the nipples visibly dark behind the pale fabric of the bikini. Her thin legs had taken on muscle. Her lips were fuller, her cheekbones more prominent.

"Tell me," she said, "since you're a *man,* and possibly a man who *knows* something. . . ."

"Shoot."

"I'm thinking of having my pubic hair waxed. Good idea, or bad?"

My advanced attitudes had some trouble with this. A mischievous grin lifted the corners of her small mouth. She enjoyed shocking grown-ups. She was good at it.

"Why do that?" I said.

"Why? To claim innocence, of course. To hold on to it. Innocent as a baby. You see, I never intend to marry or have sex."

"But you *are* innocent. I mean, at least you're still a virgin."

"No, dummy. I mean innocent with a capital I. I mean, you know—*pure*. Like Joan of Arc. Oh sure, I jobbed some boys on the playground in middle school, but that was just a stupid status thing. My God, I was only twelve and *so* clueless. I wanted to be job queen of Cabeza de Vaca middle school. So I got a reputation for being a swallower. Most girls are decent enough *hummers* but hardly any swallow. But I did. I was *so* competitive. You don't get to be the BJ queen of Cabeza de Vaca unless you *swallow*, not just hum. I hummed like a bee-hive—you know, to prove you relish the act—but I also swallowed. I have to laugh just thinking about it."

"I don't think removing your pubic hair would symbolize innocence," I said, feeling a bit depressed.

She thought about this. "Maybe you're right," she said. "Maybe I should just give it shape, like topiary. A heart, or a diamond, or maybe the wings of a dove. A lot of kids are doing it."

"You're on the wrong track, Babs," I said. Almost everyone I knew was on the wrong track. The country was on the wrong track. The world.

Her eyes flared with playful anger. *"Hairy* then? You think wild and hairy is preferable? The matron's rank unkempt bush *appeals* to you? You think embracing one's own bestiality reflects *innocence?* How totally dis*gust*ing."

She opened her thighs and looked down at her barely covered crotch. I did not let my eyes follow her gaze. She looked up quickly to see if they had.

"Maybe there's no way out," I said.

She smirked at me. "Thanks big loads for all the help."

"Sorry," I said.

She vaulted off the couch. "Okay Strobe. How about that swim? I'll race you to the pool."

"I'll pass," I said.

"Fussy old man," she said, rolling her eyes.

"That's me," I said.

236

THIRTY-NINE

Corey Butterfield was still out in his Malibu holding vigil. When he saw me he leaned across the seat and rolled down the passenger-side window half-way. "Show me a contusion, man," he said. "At least show me a blue bruise." I stepped toward him. He rolled up the window. I put my hands on the car and rocked it until the wheels came off the pavement, Butterfield held onto the steering wheel, eyes wide. I stopped short of rolling the car over.

I got into my car, relieved and disappointed. I didn't want to be a stage-prop goon for Mona Farnsworth while her clients worked through a punishment scenario that had its roots in some godawful childhood trauma. But who else would give me a thousand dollars a week to wave an ax at a rich pervert?

The money overrode my misgivings. You could carve that on the gravestones of most dead American men and not be far off the mark.

I would not have chosen the Life Insurance
business but the money overrode my misgivings

I still had to raise twelve thousand dollars more to keep Mose in La Xanadu for the additional two months the clinic needed to put him straight. I had around half that much left in my stash but nothing more was coming in.

Which made me think again about Jillian and her half-million annuity. I couldn't ask her for money until I'd committed myself to our life together. I assumed that by then she'd realize our fates were linked. I assumed that by then she would think enough of me to be a willing contributor to my family-healing crusade.

I assumed a lot of things. I assumed, for instance, that she was no longer fucking Lenny Trebeaux. I assumed she was no longer experimenting with Clara Howler, playing the femme to Howler's butch. I assumed that she had quit lying.

I assumed her private god, the one who believed in irony, not happiness, would give us a break, I assumed Fernando Solís Davila really was going to make her the beneficiary of the five-hundred thousand dollar annuity he'd given to Clive. I even assumed there *was* a five-hundred thousand dollar annuity.

It was possible I was assuming too much.

When I got back to my apartment the light on my answering machine was blinking. It was Zipporah. "Uriah—I'm calling from Providence. Get your butt over here ASAP. Sam is sinking fast. Zack is in a plane on his way to somewhere and can't be reached. Isaiah and Maggie are here. Sam's not comatose, but close to it. Make him happy, Uri. Kiss the old man goodbye."

I drove to the hospital. Sam was still in ICU. I stopped short of the privacy screens. Isaiah was praying aloud. I peeked through the gap between screens. They were all kneeling before the bed, Isaiah, Maggie, and Zipporah. Isaiah's basso intonations rumbled through the ward. I didn't want to interrupt. I stayed outside the screen.

Sam was propped up but unconscious. He was getting oxygen through plastic tubes in his nose. He looked dead, but his rising and falling chest made it unofficial. When Sam ended his prayer, the silence was filled by the beeps and wheezes of the various ICU machines. I stepped in. My cell phone chirped. I switched it off before it chirped again.

Sam opened his eyes as if my cellphone had been an alarm clock he'd set. He looked at me. "You're here," he said. He almost smiled. The papery flesh around his mouth twitched. I stepped around to the other side of the bed and held his hand. I bent down to his face and kissed him. "Hi, daddy," I said. I hadn't called him daddy in twenty-five years.

He tried to grip my hand but his fingers didn't have the strength to dent a marshmallow. "I was afraid you wouldn't come," he whispered. I knew, then, that he didn't mean me. His eyes had the wide lateral gaze of distant focus. He was looking through me, at something far beyond me. Isaiah cleared his throat. I glanced at him. He nodded, as if to say, *Play along.*

"I wouldn't let you down," I said.

His smile faded gradually and his eyes closed. His chest continued to rise and fall, but at a slower rate. My face was wet, and this surprised me. Zipporah came around the bed and put her arm around me. "Tough guy," she whispered in my ear. She kissed my wet cheek.

I was crying, but not just for Sam. The emotion pulling my face in six directions was for all of us, but it was mainly for Maggie. There would be no end to her suffering. In my heart I knew Mose was not going to stick with whatever program La Xanadu imposed on him. He was a junkie. Dyed in the wool. He'd come back to Junktown, load up, eventually OD, die of AIDS, or get his head caved in for his stash.

I was crying for me, too. I imagined myself in thirty or forty years, my sculpted body gone to cracked leather and brittle bone, my spotty mind drifting through half-remembered scenarios of a solitary and useless life.

"Jesus Christ," I said, a soft curse.

Sam opened his eyes again, but now it was a reflex. They were blind eyes, blind even to the landscapes of hallucination.

I kissed Zipporah, hugged Maggie, hugged Isaiah, then got the hell out of there.

FORTY

I wanted a margarita, even a bad one. The Picadilly on the Rio was empty. No dart throwers. No gibson drinkers. The bartender was a young Anglo guy full of energy and cautious good will. He made me a piss-poor "new policy" margarita. I had to stop him from riming the glass with rock salt.

"Where's Beatrice?" I said.

"You *know* Miss Westfall?"

"I've met her."

He looked nervous. "She's in Belize. On vacation."

"Vacation? She just started."

"She's the boss. She does what she wants."

"I hope she finds God in Belize," I said.

He relaxed. "She's totally mental," he said. "When she's here she measures the level in the bottles with a fucking ruler then counts the money in the register. She's got this formula that compares inches of booze and cash, and there's never enough cash in the register to account for the level of booze in the bottles. She thinks all her bartenders are thieves and that we give free drinks to our friends, relatives, and undercover cops."

"And business is thriving."

He laughed. "You're the first customer this afternoon. Probably the last, too."

I thanked him, left a good tip, then crossed the street to The Baron Arms.

I'd neglected the business side of my job too long. I had half a dozen tenants who owed back-rent to threaten. I taped "Quit Premises" notices on their doors. They'd have three

240

days to pay up or get out. This was the nasty part of managing. Some of the delinquents hadn't drunk up or gambled away their rent checks. Some had been laid off their jobs, some were sick, some were crazy, some had been robbed; all were down on their luck. Bad things happen to the good, the bad, and the indifferent. But I was in no position to suspend the rules of the capitalist regime. Money talks, charity walks.

I did some janitorial work. Trash had accumulated everywhere. It was overcast and hot. The brick factories across the Rio, their kilns fueled with old tires, sent fingers of black smoke into our shared canopy of air. A copper smelter on this side of the border turned the sky under the overcast hazy orange. It was the kind of day that made you believe breathing was dangerous.

The dirty damp air congealed on my skin like a living membrane. By the time I'd hauled the last twenty-gallon garbage bag of trash to the dumpster my shirt was pitted out and my sinuses ached with pollution.

When I got back to my place I turned the AC down to sixty-five and made myself a yogurt and fat-burner shake. I picked up a book on Number Theory, but couldn't concentrate on it. I put the text aside and turned on the TV. I watched Jeopardy, the news, the weather channel. From the God's eye perspective of a satellite, I watched masses of clouds slide north from the Baja coast. The wind ahead of this front had kicked up a sandstorm.

I called Jillian but only heard her impersonal answering machine voice, which made me inexplicably sad. "Call me," I told the machine.

I felt oppressed by weather, by delinquent renters, by answering machines. I felt boxed in by a wall of vague but unyielding barriers.

Thunder, like a great stone bell, tolled in the south.

Lightning webbed the orange sky above the Mulero Mountains. Juárez looked under siege. Weather mimicking history.

I ejected the shells from the Mossberg then reloaded it.

My phone rang. I didn't let it ring twice. It wasn't Jillian.

"How do you want to die?" a voice I recognized said.

"Who is this?"

"You know who it is, dumbfuck."

"Forbes?"

"Here's what you do. You come sniffing around for the quim. The nympho's always in heat, so you shouldn't have any trouble picking up the scent. I'm smelling some residue right now. There's this nice sweet and sour quality, like fish marinated in vinegar and honey."

"You son of a bitch."

"But clue me in—what's her favorite way to take hose? I just ask out of curiosity, man to man. I mean, so far so good, but us bush pilots got to hang together, you know? We need to trade notes. I'm not one to disappoint a lady, so any pointers you can share will be appreciated."

"What do you want, moron? Or did you call just to prove your brain is clogged with shit?"

"Thanks for reminding me. I got sidetracked. Pussy distracts me. The subject is you. How about this—we take you in a chopper and drop you from a couple thousand feet. Or we coat you with pancake syrup and stake you to a hill of fire ants. Sound good? No way you take a bullet in the head. Too easy. Besides, that would be charity, putting a dumbfuck out of his misery. Like they say, I gave at the office. Anyways, blowing holes in dumbfuck heads gets to be boring. There's a lot more entertaining ways. I've thought real hard about how I'll do you."

"Don't give yourself a stroke, Forbes."

"Thanks for your concern. But here's what I came up with—I heat this two-foot long piece of rebar with a torch until it glows—got the picture? Then I personally shove it up your hole. You like that idea? It's pretty good, right? You got any pre-cancerous polyps hiding up there, this will burn them out. Think of it as preventive medicine. I believe in rectal health. So does Mrs. Renseller—who incidentally has lost some standing with the boss. She squeals nicely. It just came to me a little while ago, the idea I mean, while I was hosing her rectally. You know, like I had this beautiful inspiration. They'll hear your screams in Albuquerque. She screamed too but I don't think I hurt her much. I figure it was a scream of pleasure mostly, the rebar in this case being my personal wood. We even gave Victor a shot at her. These cholos got a thing for white pussy."

I didn't believe him. I wouldn't let myself believe him. "You've got a knack for picturesque language, Forbes. You should write poetry."

"Thanks very much. I take that as a compliment. I like to be appreciated. Especially by the ladies. I'd like the nympho to whisper compliments in my ear during the old in and out while you sing like a soprano when the rebar burns off your pre-cancerous polyps. All that excitement should make her come like a train, don't you think?"

"God damn you, Forbes. I'll tear your head off."

"Oh, *good!* Let me write that one down. Tear-your-head-off. Wonderful! I'll add that to my collection of picturesque words and phrases. Where do you come up with this stuff, dumbfuck?"

I hung up. I grabbed the Mossberg and Trebeaux's Beretta. My hands were shaking.

The fine drizzle mixed with sand had leopard-spotted my car. It looked like brown sweat was oozing through the enamel finish. I got in, almost broke the key off in the ignition.

FORTY-ONE

By the time I got to the Renseller mansion the drizzle had become a pelting rain. The wrought iron gates at the foot of the driveway were open as if guests were expected.

It looked like a gathering, but I didn't think Jillian was having a party. The Suburban that took me to Samalayuca was parked ahead of Jillian's Mercedes. The big Lincoln with the *Distrito Federal* plates sat behind it, blocking it in. Lenny Trebeaux's 300SL Gullwing coupe was also there. It was parked at an acute angle, as if it had made a panic stop. The driver's side gullwing was raised. With one door up, the car looked hobbled, like a one-winged bird doomed to live in the world of earthbound creatures.

I slipped the Beretta in my pocket, but there was no place to hide the shotgun. I went up the porch steps to the front doors of the house. I rang the bell half a dozen times then walked around to the port-cochere and tried the side door entrance. It was locked. A giant in sweats answered my knock. He had a big square hairless head; his jaws looked like they could crush paving stones. He wore a shoulder holster harness with a large caliber automatic in it over a tee shirt that said

Carnivores Eat
Vegan Women

I didn't give him time to find his gun. I drove the barrel of the Mossberg into his gut then swung the stock against his

244

head. He reeled sideways but didn't go down. I kicked his knee and whacked his head again with the stock. Something cracked. I hoped it wasn't the shotgun. But he was down, and he was going to stay down. I took his gun and went back outside. I threw the gun into some oleander bushes. The heavy tropical rain roared against the slate roof of the port-cochere, drowning out all sound.

I walked to the rear of the house, back through a maze of hedgerow landscaping to the flagstone apron of Clive Renseller's Oregon trout pond. Two naked women were frolicking in the soupy, algae-thick water. One stood tall in the chest-deep pool, the other splashed wildly in a slapstick pantomime of a swimmer in trouble. The tall one was a white-haired blonde. She was muscular and had coppery outdoor skin. The swimmer was small and white as porcelain and comical in her poor mimicry of a swamped swimmer. They were having immense fun in the rain-dimpled water. They weren't children but they looked as if they were remembering how it was when they were. I saw it that way because I did not want to see it the way it really was. But then I did: Clara Howler had Jillian by the hair and was holding her under.

"No!" I yelled, but Clara pushed Jillian down so that only her legs below the knees broke the surface, and now the legs were no longer kicking.

Forbes came out from behind a clutch of mountain ash trees. He was wearing jockey style swimming trunks. His hairy gut hung over them. He had an AK. Before he could get the barrel up I fired the Mossberg from the hip. The recoil almost tore it out of my hands. The load of double-oughts caught Forbes above the knees. The impact knocked his legs out from under him and he went down, face-first, his thighs ripped open, the white bone showing. The AK clattered on the flagstones. He pushed himself up, his face slack with disbelief and shock. He tried to gather in the AK. I fired again, this time from the shoulder. The first shot tore open his gut. The second made pulp of his head.

I dropped the shotgun and ran along the flagstones toward Jillian and Clara Howler and jumped in. I leaned into the water and tried to run toward them but it was with the legs-in-cement pace of nightmares.

When I reached them, Clara released Jillian and pushed the face-down body away from her. I threw a punch at her but she slipped it and I didn't take the time to try again. I grabbed Jillian by the hair and dragged her to the side of the pool. Her eyes were open and unblinking against the driving rain. They had the same look of long-distance focus Sam's had. She was calm and invulnerable and I hated her looking that way because it left me far behind.

I climbed out and pulled her onto the flagstones. I started working over her small white body, pressing the water out of her lungs, trying to remember the life-saving technique I learned in the army. "Don't go, please don't go," I said to her as if she could hear me and change her mind about dying and water came out of her mouth in a surge that sounded like a cough and I was elated. "I love you, Jillian," I said, and even now it rang false. I cursed myself but said it again and again and each time I said it it became truer. Someone tapped my shoulder. I looked back at Victor Mellado. He was smiling. I tried to duck the leather sap he swung at me but it caught me behind the ear.

It didn't knock me out but it took away my equilibrium. The world went sideways when I tried to stand, and I fell and stayed down in the sideways world. Victor kicked me in the ribs. When he kicked again I grabbed his leg and twisted and he flopped into the pool on his back throwing a wave onto the flagstones and Clara Howler laughed. I took the Beretta out of my pocket and found her in the front sight. She was coming out of the water downhill then uphill and I was feeling sick because the world dipped to one side then to the other but I held the sight on her unmoving middle and put pressure on the trigger.

"Go ahead, shoot," she said. "I'm not feeling real good about this. I loved the little bitch, too. We had one last fling. It was more than nice. But like they say, orders are orders."

I pulled the trigger but the wet gun didn't fire. Victor climbed out of the water. He wasn't smiling. He came at me, cursing, walking on a flagstone ceiling, the downpour rising from the subterranean sky. The Beretta misfired again and he took it from my hand as I started to black out. He kicked my head and neck, then rolled Jillian back into the water and now she did not float. She slipped dreamily under the green algae and the silver flash of cutthroat trout.

I screamed something, or thought I did, but the scream may have been locked in my head.

FORTY-TWO

The knife blade in my side was more likely a broken rib. Even short breaths hurt. I came to tied to a chair in a room with concrete walls and no windows, a basement room. I wasn't alone. Lenny Trebeaux sat opposite me, his arm in a cast, a sick smile on his face. He wasn't tied to the chair but his posture suggested restraint, even if self-imposed.

"You didn't know what you were getting into," Clara Howler said to me. "Our little *bruja* Jillian put a spell on you."

"You didn't have to kill her," I said. My voice came out as a hoarse whisper. I cleared my throat, tasted blood.

"Creo que si," Fernando Solís Davila said, stepping out of the shadows. "Jillian's death was necessary. Yours is not, but *mi empleado,* Forbes, acted foolishly. He should not have lured you here. He was not acting under my authority. *Pero,* he was hoping for revenge. Of course, he came to regret his disobedience."

"Jillian didn't deserve to die," I said.

He shrugged. "I would have given her the annuity. I would have allowed her to leave this city. But she did a very foolish and treacherous thing."

He looked at Trebeaux. It was a difficult moment for Trebeaux. He turned away from his *jefe's* calm gaze.

"I learned of her treachery only days ago," Solís said.

"The photos? You killed her for that?"

Clara Howler stepped behind Trebeaux and put her hands on his shoulders. She began to massage the thin flesh between his neck and shoulders. His face whitened under his careful tan.

"Oh no," Solís said. "Señora Renseller was very . . . *como se dice . . . vengativa . . .* vindictive. Foolish as well, but I do not find such behavior worthy of mortal revenge. No, Mr. Walkinghorse, she was killed because she killed. She killed her husband. In my *organización* only I authorize who shall die and who shall be spared. You see?"

"Renseller died of a heart attack," I said. "I was there, for Christsakes. No one touched him, except Mona Farnsworth."

Clara stopped massaging Lenny. She put her hand in his hair and pulled his head back severely so that he was looking straight up at her. Cords of veins in his tanned neck stood out. "Tell him, Lenny," she said. "Tell him what you told me." She let him go and he lowered his head gingerly as if some damage had been done to his neck.

"It was Jilly's idea," he said. "She thought his perversions would come out eventually and ruin everything for her."

"Listen to this weasel," Clara said. "He wanted to be bank president, and now he blames Jillian for hatching the scheme." She slapped the side of Trebeaux's head. He reacted as if he'd been hit with a flatiron. He brought his free hand up to his face, choked back a sob.

"What the hell are you talking about?" I said.

"You're the chump in this little fiasco, Walkinghorse," Clara said. "And you *still* don't get it. She worked you like a nickel slot, *vato*. You fell for a murdering piece of white trash. You thought you had a future with her, right? When you tongued her cute little *panochita* she said, 'Oh yes do me there, that keeps me true, darling,' didn't she? That was one of her stock phrases. I've heard it dozens of times. But she was totally cold, an ice queen, anesthetized by sexual trauma. She told you the I-was-raped-at-twelve story, right? One of the few things she didn't lie about, I think."

"You're wrong about her," I said. I was sullen in my grief. I knew Jillian, the real Jillian, not the banker's wife, not the sexual experimenter. Not the piece of white trash. I knew the woman who loved me.

Clara pulled Trebeaux's head back again so that he faced her. "Tell our friend here about the sleazy plan you two dreamed up."

"It was Jilly's idea," he said again. "Clive had this heart condition. He took blood pressure meds, and nitroglycerin for his angina. Jesus, he was already taking a big physical risk messing with that Farnsworth bitch. All we did was make the inevitable happen sooner. I don't think you can honestly call that murder. He always took his meds just before he went to the Farnsworth's. So we—Jilly, actually—crushed a sildenifil citrate tab—you know, la viagra—and put it in one of the beta blocker caps he took for his blood pressure. Viagra mixed with the angina meds opened his arteries enough to drop his blood pressure to nothing. For Christsakes it was going to happen sooner or later anyway! All we did was put the miserable bastard out of his misery!"

"It is my responsibility to decide who is miserable and who shall be put out of his misery," Solís said. "It is unacceptable to me that one of *mi empleados* should take this responsibility as his own. This is how control becomes . . . *como se dice* . . . eroded."

"I'm really sorry, sir," Trebeaux said. "Please believe me, I was thinking only of the bank. Renseller would have ruined everything. I did it for you, *señor,* please believe that."

Solís studied his fingernails. "You insult me further with these transparent lies," he said softly. "And you insult yourself by such . . . *cobardia.* This is not the time for cowardice, *señor* Trebeaux. To die *como un hombre* is to redeem yourself."

Trebeaux stood up. He touched the cast on his broken arm as if to suggest to Solís that he had suffered enough. Clara pressed him back down. "Die?" he said. "What are you talking about? You mean in the philosophical sense? Death as the final adieu—so that it must be faced with composure? Yes, I believe that, too. In time I hope to have achieved that kind of basic, uh, spiritual solvency. I have debts to pay, I understand that, *señor,* but I have the resources to do just that . . . my accounts will be in order, I assure you, my futures will be fundable again, my stock. . . ."

"Ahora," Solís said to Clara. He turned his back on Trebeaux, then left the room.

Clara took Trebeaux's head in the crook of her muscular arm and applied sudden and explosive torque. The cervical vertebra that failed made a sound no louder than a finger snap. The banker's legs kicked out wildly for a few seconds. She held him until they stopped, then let him drop to the floor.

"I guess I should have let him take the thirty-story dive into the street," Clara said. "By the way, that was very inventive of you, Walkinghorse. He crapped himself while hanging by his ankles. Hard to do upside down, but he managed it." She checked Lenny's carotids for a pulse. "The hotshot bragged about what he did to Renseller, thinking I'd be impressed. He wanted so badly to be a hard guy. He didn't think for a minute that what he did would piss off the *jefe.* He actually believed he'd get more respect. He came here like a shot when Fernando asked to meet with him. He was only interim bank president, you know, while Fernie conducted a search for a new supergringo. He thought Fernie was going to make the promotion permanent. All he managed to do was shorten his life. No great loss."

She came to me and pinched my cheek gently. "See you in hell, Walkinghorse."

I looked into her eyes. She was serious.

FORTY-THREE

The Aztecs," Solís said, "gave their sacrificial victims *toloatzin* to make them oblivious to their fate. It was a narcotic, given in kindness. They were religious people, not cruel, as is so often believed. The drugs I transport do the same kindness for the gringos. It is hard to live in the United States without the use of some species of narcotic. The pressure to be successful and to secure the approval of others is overwhelming to some, and so they choose *olvido*... oblivion. My business is insignificant next to the producers of alcohol products—*el narcótico mayor en el norte. Los yanquis necesitan sus juiski.*"

"My major narcotic isn't whiskey," I said. "But I wouldn't turn down a margarita right now."

Solís laughed pleasantly. His matador's pigtail trembled as he chuckled. He was in an expansive, good-humored frame of mind. The image of his bank had been sullied badly, and that would translate into an economic loss, but Solís was upbeat, even cheerful. Life, for him, was very good. He would recover his losses ten-fold and more through his brokering business.

"Did you know that the American tobacco companies smuggle their product into countries such as Canada to avoid the high taxes imposed upon them?" he said. "They earn hundreds of millions in this illegal manner."

"Everyone is corrupt, is that what you're saying?" I said.

"Corruption is the rule, *señor* Walkinghorse. Or have you, a man of some experience, failed to understand this?"

"I'm not corrupt."

"You merely have not had the proper opportunity or incentive. And now you will never have it. *Pero* do not go to your grave self-deceived. Anyone can be corrupted."

We were in his big Lincoln, heading south, toward Samalayuca. After Victor had his fun, I'd be buried in the graveyard of the *narcotraficantes* where I'd never be found.

The desert around Samalayuca was a major dumping area for the *maquilas* that dealt with highly toxic materials—mainly radioactive iron and cobalt. No one was going to dig around in a poisonous landfill to look for bodies.

Victor was driving. Solís was seated next to him. I was in the back seat, my ankles and wrists taped. Trebeaux and Forbes were packed together in the Lincoln's big trunk. The bagged and sealed bodies thumped every time we hit a pothole. Clara was back at the house, dealing with Jillian's body.

I tuned Solís out, closed my eyes. I was with Jillian, in the Oasis motel, in the sweat-damp bed.

It keeps me true, darling, she said.

True to what?

Love, the idea of love. I can't live without it.

Love, as in Love conquers all?

Don't be mean, darling. Not now. I'm serious.

I'm not being mean. I want to be true, as in truthful.

There's more than one kind of truth, she said.

You killed your husband.

You were there, you helped. Your hands are not clean.

Your lies multiply even in death, Jillian.

I could almost smell her; her taste was on my tongue. My skin remembered the feel of her body; my eyes remembered her eyes, the deep waters behind them. In those depths was her truth, the only one I cared about. Something erupted from my lungs. I strangled it back. Some of it escaped. It came out–something between a growl and a whimper.

The rain hadn't let up. Victor had the windshield wipers going as fast as they could and still the driving water made visibility a guessing game. We were in the desert, south of the Juárez, and the desert was flooding.

"...money laundering," Solís was saying. "It is done worldwide by respected men. Even your political parties receive laundered money from secret donors–such as myself. Money always finds a way."

"Green blood," I said, thinking of Zack. Was Zack corrupt? Or did he just work within a corrupt system. Can an uncorrupted man work in a corrupt system and not be tainted? It didn't seem likely.

"Green blood," Solís said. *"Sangre verde.* And Cibola is a blood bank." He chuckled again. He was a happy man who was not shackled by an abstract morality. Jillian said he was religious. But when did religion ever restrain the behavior of its advocates?

Water ran in the ditches alongside the highway. The hardpan desert could not absorb it. In the distance temporary lakes mirrored the sky. Victor slowed as the road dipped into a runnel of brown water. He entered it tentatively, water swirling about the hubs, then he stomped the throttle and powered through it, and we resumed highway speed. For a moment, I felt the big sedan float.

"Do you comprehend, señor Walkinghorse, that a bullfight is an emblem of life?" Solís said.

I understood something about him then. By speaking casually to me he was honoring my ability to separate myself from my circumstances. He was giving me credit for staying cool–I was a man who knew how to die *como un hombre,* a man who could chat amiably with the hangman on the steps of the gallows. He was giving me too much credit.

I didn't answer him, but I figured he was going to offer the traditional apology for the ritualized slaughter–the bullfight demonstrates man's dominion over nature; it is the dance of life and death in which the bull is the sacrificial victim.

I was wrong.

"The *corrida* celebrates corruption over integrity," he said. It seemed like blasphemy coming from an old matador. He looked at me to see if I had been surprised. He smiled when he saw that I had.

"The matador is corrupt," he said, "*pero,* the bull is not. Human beings succeed through deception and courage. The bull has only courage; he is pure. He desires one thing, to kill his tormentors. But his searching horns cannot find the matador. The matador behind the *muleta* is here and he is not here, and the bull cannot conquer this deception. He never sees the sword hiding in the cape. *¿Comprende?* To deceive for your own gain–is this not a definition of corrup-tion? Is not the *corrida,* then, a true *alegoría* of how men of ambition have always dealt with the world?"

"Then it's okay to lie, cheat, and steal," I said.

"It depends upon the *integridad* . . . integrity . . . of the liar, the cheat, and the thief." He laughed at this little paradox.

And then Solís was through talking. He reclined his seat and seemed to nap. My thoughts went back to Jillian. If she had really plotted to kill Clive, she had done it for Trebeaux. So it was Trebeaux she loved, not me. I could not believe this. My vanity wouldn't allow it. But it wouldn't have had to be love. She and Trebeaux, as partners, could have grown rich together. It was the security of wealth she loved. And yet she'd been willing to run away with me. But by that time

Trebeaux's star had fallen. Even before he'd stupidly bragged to Clara that he had killed Renseller, Solís had no doubt made it clear to him that he would not inherit the presidency of Cibola. He just did not have the supergringo look. He didn't have the weight. He was cheap looking, his venality visible in his eyes. And Jillian took the next best thing—the annuity. And me.

Why me? Because she loved me. Goddammit, she loved me. She did.

I can't live without it, she said. I'll wind up a middle-aged woman, sitting alone in a bar listening to old love ballads, responding with a shiver of hope every time some insurance peddler in a bad suit hits on me. I can't help it. I'm one of the last romantics, Uri.

Love conquers all, I said.

Don't be mean, darling. I just want you to know who I am.

I didn't know who she was. And now I'd never know.

FORTY-FOUR

Lightning veined the blue-black sky. It was late afternoon and all daylight was gone. Victor was having a hard time of it behind the wheel. He had the headlights on but they only lit up the rain. He leaned into the steering wheel, as if getting close to the windshield would open paths of visibility.

"I will stay in Samalayuca tonight," Solís said. "I had planned to drive on to Mexico City, but that would be unwise in this weather."

I saw this as a straw of optimism. I reached for it. Solís liked talking to me. Maybe we'd get drunk together in Samalayuca. Maybe he'd decide against leaving me there with Victor, in spite of Victor's need for revenge.

"If you die well, I will see to it that the local priest blesses your grave," he said, ending my fantasy.

Victor took his eyes off the road long enough to look at me in the rear view mirror. His smile said there would be no chance that I'd die well. I could tell he wanted to say something to me, but he was inhibited in the presence of his *jefe*. He was on a short leash, as all of Solís' employees were. Solís' manners were always impeccable and he expected the same of the people who worked for him. Clara Howler seemed to have a longer leash than the others. And Jillian turned out to be a loose cannon.

"To die is not a punishment," Solís said, as if reading my mind. "Life is the punishment, death is the release."

"Life is not punishing you very badly," I said.

He shrugged. The fatalistic Mexican shrug. *"Sí.* This is true. But I have suffered through difficult times, and, *quién sabe,* I may suffer those times again."

I said, "You cause suffering." I was thinking of Maggie, not Mose.

"Please, Mr. Walkinghorse, do not moralize. It does not suit you." He turned around in his seat to face me directly. "The gringos took much of our country away from us. You think this did not cause suffering? *Tejás, Nuevo Méjico, Arizona, California* were stolen by your government. And now Mexico provides *los locos* in those occupied territories and elsewhere with *la cocaina* and *la heroina.* You are a people of unquenchable appetites. You take everything from the rest of the world. It is these appetites that cause suffering, not our willingness to satisfy them."

This man was going to kill me. That should have been the only thing on my mind. But something else seemed at stake. I said, "If it makes your life easier, *señor,* then go ahead and believe what you need to believe. People believe what they have to, to justify their lives."

"I have no need to justify myself," he said. "The drug problem is your problem, it is not my problem. My only problem is the . . . *logísticsas* . . . of transporting the product, and to re-allocate—*launder,* as the gringos say—the profits. The product is like any other, and no more destructive in most cases. *Por ejemplo,* the vulgar and stupid movies the gringos export all over the world corrupt taste and manners everywhere they are exhibited. They are perhaps the most dangerous drug of all. And since we are discussing morality, consider this: The gringo capitalists use cheap labor from Mexico, Guatemala, Bangladesh, China—to name but a few poor countries—to make your stereos and television sets and clothing. Without this *barata* labor, you would have double-digit inflation and your economy would fail. Your prosperity rests on the shoulders of slave labor. But then, this was the way your nation began, did it not? This is how it first prospered. You moralize about freedom on the one hand, and you enslave on the other. So please, Mr. Walkinghorse, do not presume to give me moral instruction."

Victor stopped the car. *"Boss, look there!"* he said in Spanish. *"The road is gone. It is a river now."* He got out of the car and disappeared into the darkness. When he came back he looked frightened.

Solís got out of the car and both he and Victor went to inspect the washout. I took the opportunity to gnaw at the strapping tape on my wrists. I'd broken through a couple of strands by the time they returned to the car.

The right lane of the road was under a foot or so of water, but the left lane was gone. From where the center line should have been, white water boiled down into a ravine. It looked like a mini Niagara. The road crossed a dry river bed, as many desert roads do, and the river had returned with a vengeance. It was probably five feet deep left of the center line, and farther to the left the water moved with the slow, unperturbed current of an established river. Solís came back to the car, thinking over the options.

"Take the flashlight," he told Victor. He spoke Spanish with Castilian perfection, but without the lisp. *"I will drive the car through the shallow water. You will guide me with the light. Stand at the point where the road has failed. I will keep the car to the right of that point".*

"You will have to drive very fast, boss," Victor said. *"But you need to steer carefully. The section of road remaining is only as wide as the car itself, perhaps half a meter more, and the current will*

push the car toward the deep water—you will have to correct for that."

"I know how to drive an automobile," Solís said, reverting to English.

Victor looked sheepish. *"Seguro,"* he said. "I know that, *jefe."*

Solís slid behind the wheel. Victor walked into the surging water. It was only half-way to his knees but he had trouble keeping his balance against the rapid flow. He waved the flashlight at Solís.

Solís backed the car up a few hundred feet. He looked back at me and smiled. It was a matador's smile—the carefree smile of a man who put his life on the line routinely and enjoyed it.

He gunned the engine, then slipped the gear lever into Drive. The car fishtailed on the wet pavement, then lurched forward.

Samalayuca was only a few miles on the other side of the washout. This would be my only opportunity. Die here, or die at the hands of Victor. Here, where Solís was making one of the few mistakes of his life, seemed better.

I was sitting directly behind him. I guess he felt I had resigned myself to die *como un hombre* and was docile with philosophy. I wasn't. I reached over the seat and caught his neck between my taped wrists and yanked back. He took his hands off the wheel to fight me off. His hands clawed at mine. To give himself leverage he jammed his feet against the floorboards. One foot rammed the accelerator. The big V-8 roared.

By the time we hit the water we were doing fifty but no one was steering the car. I caught a glimpse of Victor waving the flashlight desperately. Then he was on the hood of the car, face against the cracked windshield, eyes wide at the aspect of his own death, and then he was gone.

We hit the deep end, the side of the road that had given

way. We hit it at an angle, and the car pitched over on its side. I got my wrists free of Solís and tried to roll down my window but the engine had quit and the power windows were stuck.

There was no light. The car rotated lazily in the swirling waters. It scraped along the bottom of the temporary river and the interior was beginning to flood. My back was flat against a door, and then the car rolled again, and I was on the ceiling, under water.

I surfaced, choking. There was about a foot of breathing space, but that was shrinking. I took enough breaths to hyperventilate then went under the water, on my back.

Ray Fuentes said, *be explosive, man.* He was encouraging me to squat with six-fifty. *Move like you were going to launch the fucking barbell through the roof.* I remembered his advice now as I rammed my feet into the Lincoln's side window.

Not enough of the window collapsed. I came up again for air, but now there was only about three inches of it left. I hyperventilated again, then went back to work. It took two more kicks to clear away all the glass.

I came up for another breath, but now the breathing space was gone. I snaked out of the window on my belly, my jaws clamped shut against the suicidal demands of my lungs, then managed to get my feet down in the mud of the washout, and I launched myself upward into the black air.

I floated, face up, into shallow water. I dug my heels into the mud and beached myself in a soggy field. It took me an hour to bite through the tape on my wrists, and then only a minute to unwind the tape from my ankles.

There was no sign of Victor. Solís was still in the car, I was sure of that, but I think I crushed his windpipe before he had a chance to drown. There was no sign of the car. There was the river, the desert, the rain.

I rested another few minutes, then started walking north.

261

FORTY-FIVE

More coffee?" Güero said. He was in pajamas and robe.
It was past midnight.

I nodded. He poured. His wife, Xochi, heated chicken *mole*
for me in her microwave, along with black beans and corn
tortillas—left-overs from their supper. Xochi—short for
Xochimilco—was pure indian, an immigrant from Chiapas.
I'd never met her. In fact, I hadn't known that Güero was
married. Xochi spoke no English, and her Spanish wasn't all
that good. She spoke a dialect of Nahuatl, the indigenous
language of southern Mexico. She was dark and lovely, her
skin the color of lightly creamed coffee, her fine Mayan nose
prominent. She was not shy and retiring. She looked at me
frankly, judging my character as well as my relationship to
Güero. And she was an unapologetic smoker. She tapped an
unfiltered Faro out of a pack lying on the table and lit up
while Güero and I talked. Pale, red-haired Güero was clearly
proud of her.

I'd made my way back to Juárez, first by walking north
along the rain-swept highway, then by catching a ride with a
melon farmer who was heading into the city for a night of
hell-raising. He was driving an old Studebaker pick-up with
a quarter-million miles and decades of rust on it, top speed
45. One windshield wiper worked, the one on the passenger
side. The truck had an AM radio, and it was tuned to a *norteña*
station. The low notes of the *guitarón* rattled the old loud-

speaker, and the highest accordian notes frayed into screeches. Now and then the melon farmer, a happy man, challenged the stormy night with a shrill *ai-yai-yuh!*

The rain had let up a bit, but the temperature had dropped. I was wet and dirty and shivering. The melon farmer didn't ask what happened to me, for which I was grateful. I didn't feel inventive enough to fabricate a believable story.

I remembered Güero's street address from the telephone directory but I couldn't let the melon farmer take me there. Later, he might be asked by interested parties where he dropped the big gringo off. No need to get Güero involved in my problems.

I got out of the truck at a long stoplight. There was a restaurant on the corner. I pointed to it. I want something to eat, I said. *"Me estoy muriendo de hambre."* I sounded sincere, a hungry man in need. He scratched his head, gave me a squint-eyed once over. They won't let you in looking like that, dying of hunger or not, he said. I told him not to worry, I'd go in by the back door. I had a friend who was a waiter there. Lying in Spanish was somehow easier than lying in English. Maybe because Spanish inflections were so sincere. My waiter-friend could lend me a jacket, I said. The melon farmer shrugged. I gave him a wet ten dollar bill, which he refused indignantly. *"No pedí su dinero,"* he said, shaking his head sternly. I said I would be humiliated if he refused to accept this token of my gratitude. He took the ten reluctantly, and we shook hands, completing our small but necessary ritual. He rolled down his window and leaned out of the truck. The rain had quit. He pointed skyward. I looked up into the star-dense night. *"Ya todo está limpio,"* he said. The rain had made everything clean. *"Sí,"* I said. Until the next bad wind kicks up, anyway.

The farmer drove off in a cloud of black hydrocarbons,

norteña polkas sawing away. I waited until he was out of sight, then started walking.

I knew where I was, only a couple of miles from Güero's street. It was past midnight when I got there. His house was not big but it was in the *rincones de San Marcos* neighborhood, one of the nicer residential areas of Juárez. His house was a bungalow-style stucco, surrounded by a chain-link fence. I woke Güero and Xochi up by rattling the locked gate and yelling Güero's name for minutes. The neighborhood dogs sent up a chorus of howls. Güero came out with a .44 in his hand. "Jesus Christ," he said. "You could get your head blown off banging on locked gates in the middle of the night."

I'd made pretty good time from the washout to Juárez. I'd wanted to put as much geography between me and the washout as quickly as possible. To be connected to the death of a major *traficante* and money launderer would make me interesting to the wrong kind of people. That would do nothing for my peace of mind. And peace of mind was high on my list of priorities. When the bodies of Solís and Victor turned up, their deaths might be seen—with any luck—as accidental: they tried to cross dangerous waters and didn't make it. The *judiciales* would have to come up with another explanation for the two dead gringos in the Lincoln's trunk. And of course they would. And of course, whatever the official version of their deaths turned out to be, the death of a kingpin would never be seen as accidental. There would be people looking into it, people from both sides of the law.

After I ate, Güero brought out a bottle of *Viuda de Sanchez*. Xochi chopped up a lime, and we drank straight shots of the good *agave azul*. She brought out a pair of salt shakers. I politely refused. It was not easy to refuse anything from the hand of this lovely woman.

264

Güero wanted me to tell him everything. I looked like I'd been dragged through a culvert, he said. For his own safety, I made up a story: I'd been at a party. Some of us wound up in Juárez. I wandered away from the group and got lost, too much *mota,* and, as someone once told me, the back streets of Juárez are as confusing as the back streets of Madras, India. I wound up in Boy's Town, the red light district, got rolled by a pimp. At one point, I fell into the Rio. How I got from the interior maze of the city back to the Rio was anyone's guess. "Damned lucky I didn't drown," I said.

Güero wasn't buying. "You don't like parties," he said. "And you don't smoke reefer. Remember?"

"And now you see why. I get out of hand too easily."

Xochi whispered something into Güero's ear. "She says you're lying. She can pick a lie out of the air like a bird snatches a bug."

"I thought she didn't have any English," I said.

"She doesn't. It's not the words, it's the shape of your face when you say them, the look in your *yanqui* eyes."

"Okay. There was no party. But I can't tell you a goddamn thing—for your own safety. Look in *El Diario* in the next few days. The newspapers are going to get real excited about a certain event. Then use your imagination. That's all I'm going to say about it."

He looked at Xochi. She was lighting up another Faro. He said something to her in Nahuatl. She replied in Spanish, a Spanish I hadn't heard before and could not decipher.

"She says your face is telling the truth now."

I filled my shot glass again and raised it to her in tribute. To Güero I said, "You're either the luckiest man alive or the most endangered."

Xochi said something. Güero replied, again in Nahuatl.

"She says your face is telling the truth again," Güero said.

I looked at her, astonished. My face must have shown it. She smiled a wide, beautifully open smile, then laughed. Güero joined in, and then I laughed, too.

All the social barriers were down. There was nothing to stop us now. We got drunk, Güero and I, while Xochi cut limes, smoked Faros, and made small comments in pigeon Spanish. At one point she poured herself a neat shot of Johnny Walker Red.

I got drunk enough to loosen the lock on my heart. Something in me opened up and released a tidal wave. In the middle of a funny story Güero was telling about life at the DMZ, I started sobbing. I couldn't stop. The renegade emotion pulled at my face. I tried to control it by attempting to smile, pretending it was an act of sorts, but I knew I was only making myself more grotesque.

Then I gave in to it. I rolled out of my chair and fell to the floor fetal with grief and making awful noises. Jillian's name wrenched itself out of my throat, but I was sure they could not understand me.

Xochimilco knelt beside me and touched my wet face. Her tobacco-scented hand was cool. She sipped her Scotch and said something in Nahuatl that sounded like *oh stuck love.*

FORTY-SIX

The turf wars began a week later. Solís had been found, his death officially declared accidental and blamed on the washout. There was no mention of Forbes and Trebeaux sealed in their plastic bags, or of Victor, no mention of foul play of any kind. But now there was a lot of foul play as competing gangs fought for control of the *plaza*—the territory once ruled by the ex-matador. Men with machine guns sprayed a bar in Juárez, killing six. Several professional men—lawyers, doctors, business executives—were killed in an identical way, by decapitation. Every level of society was involved in the corruption Solís so confidently believed in.

Even tourists were caught in the crossfire. The bodies of the Americans were shipped back to Wisconsin or New Jersey or Missouri with condolences from both governments. The turf war wouldn't last long. Eventually, through attrition, one gang would dominate and a new narco king would be crowned. Life on the border would go back to normal, and the temporary interruption of the drug supply would end. I kept up with the war by reading newspaper accounts from both sides of the Rio Grande. After a few weeks the outbreaks of violence became fewer, and the papers became less interested.

Jillian's body had been found by the Renseller's gardener on his weekly rounds. He found her in the trout pond, a drowning victim. One paper speculated that she might have become despondent after the death of her husband and committed suicide. But there was no suicide note or other evidence that might suggest suicide, and so the coroner's office declared her death accidental. No one explained why she was swimming nude in her deceased husband's trout pond.

My car had been returned to the parking lot of The Baron Arms. Clara Howler, thinking that I'd been killed, did not want me linked to the Renseller estate, something that might open up a new line of investigation. There was no mention of Clara in any of the news reports. I figured she was distributing her résumé among the probable *jefes* of the new order, a résumé that would make the most cynical heart fibrillate.

Cibola Savings and Loan stayed open for business, as if it had no ties at all with the upheavals. A former member of the city council assumed the presidency of the bank. Who was behind this appointment was not made public. At this point in my education I would not have been surprised if it had been the mayor, the governor, or the president of the United States. "Corruption is the rule," Solís, my teacher, said, but I promised myself to stay alert for the exceptions.

My mini-breakdown in Güero's kitchen had been triggered by that scene of domestic happiness. I'd understood something, seeing him and Xochi together. They had something I would never have. Jillian and I may have had a chance at it, but that doubtful chance was gone.

My dreams were nightmares: Jillian in my arms, cold and lifeless. I carried her out of the raging waters of a washout. In this dream I was the one responsible for her death. I'd wake up shouting *No! it wasn't me!* but the dream had an undercurrent that drowned my claim of innocence.

The dream lost intensity. It became diluted. Sometimes she was alive in my arms. We were in a motel swimming pool, and we made love again. I would wake from these dreams, reaching for her across my empty bed. These were the cruelest dreams.

In a month, I stopped dreaming of her altogether, though I did not stop thinking about her. I admitted to myself, finally, that we could not have had the kind of domestic bliss Güero and Xochi had. We weren't cut out for it. We both wanted something more, even though neither one of us could have said what that thing was.

Sam's funeral service had been held at Isaiah's church, a black Baptist church. Maggie and I and a scattering of Sam's old army friends were the only white faces in the small crowd. The minister hadn't known Sam, but his eulogy celebrated the life of a war hero who raised a mixed-race family, all of whom became useful citizens. The minister spoke glowingly about all of us except Mose, who he didn't mention at all. Zacharias, the globe-trotting corporate lawyer, Zipporah the school principal, Isaiah the hard-working family man, and me, the apartment manager and one-time champion athlete. He didn't call me a one-time champion body-builder—a narcissistic activity that perhaps wouldn't play well in church.

Mose was still in La Xanadu. I'd raided my stash for another month's treatment, and now I was broke. Isaiah said he might be able to get me on as a relief driver for UPS. I said I'd consider it. I was also considering an offer Güero had made. He wanted me to tend bar at his new place, *La Paloma Libre,* in Juárez. I'd have to improve my Spanish, but the pay would be decent and living in Mexico would be cheaper and probably less depressing than dealing with the sad rags of humanity who haunted The Baron Arms.

My neglected mailbox was stuffed, mostly junk. I packed
the load up to my apartment and dumped it on my table. I
went through it, tossing most of it in the trash. Among the
heaps of junk mail was a letter from Gert. It had weight, the
weight of a legal document. But it was a letter, several pages
long, written in a school-girl hand.

Her stock-car driver, Trey Stovekiss, had been killed. "They
were four wide in the north turn," she wrote, "and Trey hit
the wall then came back down and a Thunderbird went on
top of him and then a damn rookie in a Trans Am hit them
both broadside. Trey's Camaro came apart in pieces. He
didn't have a chance."

Gert was alone and pregnant and broke somewhere in
Georgia. She was in desperate straits, and couldn't afford the
lawyers she'd hired to threaten me. She wanted to come home.
"I know what's wrong with you now," the letter went on,
"and maybe it's what's wrong with me, too. I've been seeing
a therapist in Atlanta. She says people like you—you know,
people who think about themselves a lot, how they look and
so on, and I guess that's me also—have this thing called
"attachment disorder." It's hard for them—you, I mean, and
maybe me, to connect to others. It starts in childhood. You
were thrown away by the person who gave birth to you, so
it's understandable in your case. My childhood was sort of
okay, I guess, but even so I also have marginal AD, says the
therapist, doctor Loftus. Mildred. She wants me to call her
Mildred. Half the cure is in being able to say in words what's
wrong with you, she says. I'm thinking that maybe, just
maybe, we can work things out between us? What do you
think, Uri? I treated you bad, but I never forgot you. Do you
still love me a little? I wouldn't blame you if you said no, me
being pregnant and all with Trey's child, but the baby can

hardly be blamed for the faults of the grown-ups, and he deserves to have a family to raise him loved and cherished. Mildred said Trey probably had AD, too. It's a fairly common problem. It would be a tragedy if the baby grew up with AD like us. I know it would be hard, but don't you think people need to be bigger than themselves at times? Being with child, the world looks a lot different."

I didn't throw the letter out.

There were solicitations from credit card companies. One was from Cibola Savings and Loan. "Dear Mr. Walkinghorse: If you don't already have a platinum card from Cibola," the letter began, "then consider these unusual benefits. . . ." I laughed, but laughing didn't seem adequate. I stepped out onto the balcony and howled like a drunk dog. Some of my tenants came out to see the source of the howling. They knew better than to press for explanations.

The air was still washed from the storm. It smelled alive. I went across the street to the former DMZ and had a margarita. The "new policy" owner of Picadilly on the Rio was still in Belize. To celebrate her absence, I had two more pisswater margaritas.

I asked the bartender for a piece of paper and a pen. He rummaged around and came up with a sheet torn out of an old receipt book. I wrote

Being with child
the world looks a lot different

I finally understood what a dangling modifier was. I congratulated the world for being with child.

I'd take this one across the Rio to Güero when I went to work for him. I knew he'd appreciate it.